# FIRE SEASON

## STEPHEN BLACKMOORE

**DAW BOOKS, INC.**

DONALD A. WOLLHEIM, FOUNDER

1745 Broadway, New York, NY 10019

**ELIZABETH R. WOLLHEIM**

**SHEILA E. GILBERT**

**PUBLISHERS**

www.dawbooks.com

## ACKNOWLEDGMENTS

I set out to write a jaunty little list humorously talking about and thanking all the wonderful people who helped me get this book into your hands.

And then California burned.

In and of itself that's not new. California burns every year. The whole U.S. West burns every year. But this year. Jesus. This year.

As I'm writing this California is recovering from the Camp Fire, the deadliest wildfire it has ever seen. Not one of the deadliest. Not in the top 10. THE DEADLIEST. It's the worst the entire nation has seen since 1918. Eighty-six people dead. Almost 19,000 structures destroyed, more than half of them single family homes. Over 150,000 blackened acres. The entire town of Paradise wiped from the face of the planet.

The previous California record holder was here in Los Angeles in 1933 in Griffith Park. Only 29 people dead. Only. As if any number could be acceptable.

Every year we lose people, pets, homes, money. The sky fills with smoke, the flames race down the hills, and it always, ALWAYS, comes closer than you think it will. Even in this cement jungle surrounded by bonfire material it's disconcerting. I'm always thankful that concrete doesn't burn. Usually.

But you drive out a couple days later and you wonder. The sidewalks are black. The hills are naked of anything that isn't stone. Abandoned cars are nothing but fire-mottled steel and molten lead. Glass has liquefied, run over the sides, pooled on the ground. There are no tires. They exploded in the heat and the treads burnt to nothing. You can see the places the fire jumped the freeway.

People ask me where I get my ideas. Well, now you know.

So first and foremost, I'd like to thank all of the men and women who risk their lives in the face of these wildfires. The first responders, the paramedics, doctors and nurses, dispatchers, pilots, ambulance drivers, search and rescue teams, animal rescue, evacuation coordinators. Hell, even the guys who mix the Phos-Check that gets dumped onto the flames and turns everything bright pink.

Thank you.

As to the book, well, there aren't maybe quite so many who've helped make this a reality, but it feels like it sometimes.

My wife, Kari, who might be the only person on the planet willing to put up with ~~all most~~ some of my bullshit. My agent Al Guthrie. My editor Betsy Wollheim, Josh Starr, and the outstanding staff at DAW. The incredible cover artist Chris McGrath who brings Eric alive to me more than any of my words could. Thanks for helping make this the best book it could be.

And then there are friends whose support I cherish, like Chuck Wendig, Richard Kadrey, K.C. Alexander, Jaye Wells, Jaclyn Taylor, Delilah Dawson, Lilith Saintcrow, Kat Richardson, Brian McClellan, Kristin Sullivan, Jeff Macfee, Brian White, Lela Gwen,

Cassandra Khaw, Madeline Ashby, Margaret Dunlap, Jaime Lee Moyer, Andrea Phillips, Robert Brockway and holy fucknuggets so, so many more.

Not to mention all of the wonderfully sick people who talk to me on Twitter. Especially the Russian porn bots.

And finally, to my wonderful friend Kevin Hearne, he of the Iron Druid Chronicles (which you should totally read if you haven't), beard aficionado extraordinaire, imbiber of impossibly large beverages. Because you see, Kevin killed me in one of his stories. Tore me apart piece by piece. Painfully. Horribly. On a whim!

Ball's in your court, motherfucker.

# Chapter 1

**Necromancy 101: You're too late.**

Whether it's watching empty Echoes playing their last moments over and over again, or talking to Haunts and Wanderers with their fading memories and draining personalities, they have one glaring thing in common; they're all dead.

See, necromancers are like really bad ambulance drivers. We don't get there until way after the body's cooling in the middle of the road.

Ghosts aren't really people. They're tattered bits of soul left over from the dying. Shreds of memory, personality, will. Whether it was yesterday, last month, twenty minutes, two hundred years ago. Doesn't matter.

You're. Too. Late.

Because ghosts? They don't just happen. You're not getting a ghost if Grandma strokes out taking a shit on the toilet. No, it takes trauma. Mental, physical, spiritual. It can be sudden, or take a lifetime to build.

Suicides, homicides, accidents, gunshot wounds, stabbings, beatings, poisonings, car crashes, hangings, Colombian neckties, hacked to pieces by crazed cannibal killers. You get the idea.

We necromancers get to experience it all in night-mare color and THX sound whether we want to or not. Sure, any schmuck with some talent can talk to the dead, but we're born to it.

There is no such thing as a pretty death. It doesn't exactly paint a rosy picture of the human experience.

Some of us don't care. They're the scary ones. You get some serious Patrick Bateman shit with them.

Some of us care way too much. They're the tragic ones. By thirty they've dug themselves into a hole, too afraid to keep living and terrified of dying because they know that's not the end of things. There aren't many nec-romancer suicides, is what I'm saying.

Like doctors or morticians, most of us land some-where in the middle. Dying's tragic, but shit happens. Death is something that needs to be accepted. It's not good, it's not bad. It just is.

But some deaths are a little harder to take than others.

Burn victims, for example. The ones who go from smoke inhalation or carbon monoxide don't usually leave a ghost behind, but if they burn to death? Jesus fuck, it's rough. It's not just agonizing, messy, and loud, it can last anywhere from five minutes to an hour or more.

First time I saw the Echo of a burn victim was a car accident on a back road that had happened three or four years before. Middle of nowhere. Guy inside slow roasted for almost an hour before he finally died. He was con-scious for way too much of it.

That's what makes this particular Echo I've been watching for the past couple hours, a woman set on fire in a burned-out shell of a three-bedroom bungalow in the West Adams neighborhood of Los Angeles, so unusual.

She starts at the door to the kitchen, becoming visible

as she enters the living room. There's panic on her face. Someone I can't see shoots her in the back. Her legs go out from under her. She hits the ground screaming, but keeps dragging herself away.

Then the flames kick in. I see flickers of their light shining across her skin, though I can't see them, yet. They won't be a part of this scene until they're eating her alive.

Doesn't take long. They erupt around her in seconds, crawl up her legs as though she's been dipped in liquid oxygen, bright blue flames dancing up her body, relentless, unforgiving.

She catches fast when the flames touch her. Her skin already blackening and cracking. The fire sweeps over her like piranha devouring a cow. Bits and pieces shred away as ash and char. Conscious and screaming until there's nothing left but a blackened corpse that's more skeleton than person lying among the ruins. Ash drops in clumps from her body as pieces of her disintegrate.

The scene disappears like a soap bubble, there one second, gone the next. I can still smell the stink of charred pork, hear the screams and the crackle of searing skin.

Then it starts all over again. It's the fourth time I've watched it. I crouch down to look at it from another angle, time it with my pocket watch. The moment the flames hit her she goes up like flash paper. From ignition to ash can be measured in seconds.

Nobody burns that fast. Even knowing it's obviously magic, it's surprising how fast she goes from burning to ash.

At least, it would be if I hadn't seen it before.

I take my phone out, dial a number. Hear a sleepy grunt when it picks up. "Hey," I say, "it's Eric. It's happening."

"Can we all die in a horrible rain of fire after I've had coffee?" Gabriela says. Most people know her as the

Bruja, and she's at least as powerful a mage as I am. Maybe more so. We fought once. Called it a draw. To say we're friends would be stretching things. A lot.

"I think you got time for a cup."

"Oh, good. I'd hate to meet the apocalypse uncaffeinated."

"We should all be so lucky."

"All right. Spill. What's going on?"

"Xiuhtecuhtli's fire." I describe the scene to her. The man, the gunshot, the flames—particularly the flames.

"Fuck me. You're sure about the fire?" she says.

"Well, I am standing in the burned-out shell of a house, so . . ."

"I meant about what kind of fire. Are you sure it's Xiuhtecuhtli's fire? You're the only one who's seen it in action."

"Yeah," I say, watching the flames consume the Echo in front of me one more time. The preternaturally blue flames turn it to char and ash in moments. "I'm sure. And I'm sure it's Quetzalcoatl doing it."

"You can't know that for sure," she says.

"He pretty much told me that this is exactly what he was going to do. Anyway, it gets better."

"How so?"

"Last I saw him Q was a fifteen-foot-tall trash fire in the shape of a winged serpent. Not exactly in a position to hold a gun."

"He's got a friend," she says. "You see the shooter?"

"No. Too far away. Didn't get captured in the Echo." Not that it probably would have, anyway. The shooter isn't the one who died.

"You piss off the best people," she says.

"What can I say? I'm a high achiever."

About five hundred years ago, give or take, a Spanish dickhead by the name of Hernán Cortés de Monroy y Pizarro Altamirano, Marquis of the Valley of Oaxaca (a title he gets a little later), shows up on the Aztecs' doorstep and proceeds to kick seven shades of shit out of them. It's touch and go for a while. His attention's split. He's not the most popular guy with the Spanish government at the time. When they send troops after him he pretty much turns them into reinforcements.

That out of the way, he turns his attention to not only conquering the Aztecs, but their gods, too. Cortés puts a lieutenant, guy named Juan Rodríguez Cabrillo, in charge of the invasion of the Aztecs' thirteen heavens. The ace up Cabrillo's sleeve is an eight-thousand-year-old Djinn named Darius that Cortés loans him, and an alliance with the Aztecs' own wind god, the feathered serpent Quetzalcoatl, who's turned traitor for fuck knows what reason. Gods fall like dominos; Tlaloc, Ixcuina, Citlalicue, Tezcatlipoca, Huitzilopochtli, Xiuhtecuhtli, Ometeotl, and on and on.

Then they reach Mictlan, the Aztec land of the dead, where its two rulers, Mictlantecuhtli and his wife, Mictecacihuatl, set a trap. Cue Epic God Battle. Doesn't end well for anybody. The Conquistadores die, Quetzalcoatl is seriously wounded, Darius is trapped in his bottle, Mictlantecuhtli is turned to jade and trapped in a hole deep below Mictlan.

The only survivor is Cabrillo, who limps back to the mortal world with Darius in his backpack. Quetzalcoatl does a runner to licks his wounds, and Mictecacihuatl tries to hold what's left of Mictlan together. The thing with

Mictecacihuatl is that she's a survivor. Flexible, changes with the times. By the time I ran into her she'd restyled herself as a folk saint in Mexico by the name of Santa Muerte.

She's got other names. La Flaca. La Señora de Las Sombras. Saint Death. She's a saint for the outsiders, the narcos, the disconnected. She's not evil. She's not good. She is death and blood, lust and love, vengeance and redemption and all the visceral things that make us human. She's messy as life, inevitable as death. She is the Saint of Last Resort.

And I had to go and marry her. I didn't know that's what was happening at the time. I pledged myself to her for help in finding my sister's murderer. Should have read the fine print. That bond turned me into her husband.

But as it turns out, the cosmos doesn't like paradoxes. Mictlantecuhtli is the King of Mictlan. The King of Mictlan is married to Mictecacihuatl. I'm married to Mictecacihuatl. So, I'm the King of Mictlan. Except Mictlantecuhtli is the King of Mictlan . . .

The universe's solution is to swap Mictlantecuhtli and me. That little detail about Mictlantecuhtli being turned to jade is kind of important, because I find out real fast that green is so not my color. I'm turning to stone. Mictlantecuhtli is turning to flesh.

Enter the wind. The spirit of the Santa Ana winds, actually. While I'm trying to figure out how to get a speedy divorce before I turn into a lawn ornament, I find myself needing some help, and they're the best shot I have. They help me find a guy I'm looking for, and I give them . . . something weird. They want me to burn my home down. I was squatting in a rancid, little rat trap at the time, so what do I care? Sure. No problem.

Except they don't mean my home. They mean the King

of the Dead's home. They mean Mictlan. Whole goddamn place. And why is that? Because all the wind spirits are connected. The spirit of the Santa Anas connects to the Chinook in Alaska to the Abrolhos in Brazil to the Zonda in Argentina and on and on, and eventually to a half-dead Aztec wind god, named—surprise!—Quetzalcoatl.

He gives me this spiffy Zippo that holds the fire of the god Xiuhtecuhtli. It could burn anything in the mortal world in no time flat and all of Mictlan with one flick of the wheel. I tried it out on a creepy little island outside Mexico City filled with the trapped ghosts of murdered children.

Since I'm heading down to Mictlan to divorce my death goddess wife and take out her jade statue ex-husband with extreme prejudice, it sounds like a win-win to me. Only it isn't. Because burning Mictlan, I find out, means destroying the thousands of souls calling it their afterlife. I'm a bastard, but I'm not that big a bastard. Mictlan stays unburned. In the kerfuffle between me, Santa Muerte and her husband, I lose the lighter.

After seeing what happened to the house in West Adams I know for sure the lighter is back in play, and I can only think of one guy who'd try using it.

I've been waiting for Quetzalcoatl to show his face and burn shit down ever since I got back from Mictlan. He couldn't have come at a better time for it. Triple digit temps, high winds, everything dry as kindling.

As the man says, the hills of Los Angeles are burning. The palm trees haven't turned into candles in the murder wind, yet, but it's just a matter of time. Brushfires spread through the green spaces like syphilis through a Victorian dockside. Laurel Canyon, Calabasas, Verdugo Mountains, La Crescenta, Griffith Park. No matter how many firefighters and tanker planes they throw at them, they can barely contain the fires.

Outside it's well on its way to a hundred. I've rolled up my shirtsleeves, left my suit coat in the car. Some places it would feel weird with so many of my tats showing, but in L.A. they just figure I'm some white hipster from Silver Lake with too much money. All I need now is a fancy mustache and artisanal toast.

I stop on the sidewalk to look back at the house, streaks of soot radiating out onto the cement from the house's blackened lawn, crawling up the trunk of a palm tree. There isn't much left of the house to tear down. Exposed framing, disintegrated drywall.

Xiuhtecuhtli's fire really did a number on it. Surprisingly, it didn't catch the houses on either side. Was that on purpose? And if it was, why this house in particular? Why this woman? It can't be random. Q's batshit crazy, even by god standards, but I don't think he's stupid. He's got a reason even if I don't know what it is.

I'm so preoccupied trying to puzzle out what's going on that I almost don't feel the flare of magic on my skin from the protection spells in my tattoos. Less than a second later I hear the gunshot behind me. The magic pushes the bullet away, but not enough. It rips my sleeve and runs a gouge across my left bicep.

I wonder who I've pissed off this time.

# Chapter 2

**I bolt for cover,** the closest being my Cadillac Eldorado parked next to me. I get it between me and the shooter as three more rounds go off.

They're too high and punch into the side of a scorched palm tree in front of the house. The last time somebody shot me I was partly jade and I couldn't feel it. Bullets just ricocheted off me. But now, Jesus. I'd forgotten how much this shit hurts.

I pull my own gun, a Browning Hi-Power covered in Nazi Waffen marks. It's an ugly piece of hardware and I always feel like I'm shoving my hand into a barrel of cockroaches when I pick it up. It's filled with all the hatred and nastiness from the war and I can tap into that with my own magic, making a .357 look like a popgun.

I look under the car and see the shooter's feet as he starts running toward me. More gunshots, more misses. One of them punches through the driver's side door of the Caddy and dents the steel on the passenger side.

Sonofabitch. Shoot at me all you like. I'm used to it. Shoot my car? Fuck you.

The Browning likes to shoot people, and I can feel it pulling at me to pop this guy in the head. Somebody else might listen to it, but I've had years of practice at telling it to fuck off. I decide to do something a little less final.

Magic's like improvisational cooking. But instead of spices, you're using bits and pieces of negotiated reality. Mages don't throw fireballs. They collect oxygen into a sphere, give it some spin, heat it up until it burns, tell gravity to fuck itself, and then shoot that bastard across the room.

In this case, reality and I have a conversation about loosening the binding of pavement, liquefying tar, stretching a little pocket of the world like it's taffy. This all happens in less than a second.

I shouldn't be doing this to a normal, but if it's that or putting giant holes in his head, this is probably the better way to go. I slam my hand onto the street and let the spell loose, the magic bending the world around me. Thick ropes of pavement leap out of the street and wrap around the shooter's legs. His yell of surprise turns into one of pain as everything just below the knee stops moving and everything above keeps going.

Including the gun, which is the important part. It skitters across the street, stopping at the curb. I step out from behind the Cadillac, the Browning in my hand and . . .

It's a kid.

Late teens, early twenties at most. Rumpled shirt, stained pants. He clearly hasn't slept, hasn't shaved. Everything about him is haggard and raw.

He looks an awful lot like the ghost I've been watching all morning. His eyes are filled with rage. I know that look. I wore it myself when I killed the man who murdered my parents. Dragged him screaming across the veil and fed him to ghosts. If that was his mom in there I'm not surprised.

What is surprising is that he looks like he thinks I had something to do with it.

He screams at me, tries to yank his legs out of the pavement. I'm too far away for him to be a threat, and I'm not about to get any closer. He struggles for a bit, but then exhaustion gets the better of him and he gives up, his whole body slouching in defeat. I put the Browning away. I get a strong sense that the gun feels disappointed. I've been getting that feeling a lot lately.

"Fucking murderer," the kid screams.

If the gunfire doesn't get the cops coming, his screaming like a maniac will. The street's empty, and only a couple of cars are in driveways in the next block. That should give me a few minutes to figure out what the hell is going on without worrying about police.

"Narrow that down a little for me. Who exactly do you think I've murdered?" I say, because let's be honest, it's not like he's wrong. "Her? In the house? Who was she? Your mom? Sister? Aunt?"

"So, you did do it," he says. "You fucking murderer."

"Nope. Just saw her ghost. It's kinda my thing."

"Yeah, I know all about you and your fucking army of the dead."

"I— What?"

"They told me you killed her. Showed it to me. Told me all about you."

"Whoa, hang on. Who did what to the how now?"

He gives me a smile that never reaches his eyes. That's when it occurs to me then that I have made a tactical error. Mages don't go running around with hats that say MAGIC BOY in big, neon letters. The only way we know that there's another of us nearby is if they either fire off a spell or start pulling power from the environment.

Magic collects in pools. Cities and towns have the most concentrated magic, people, events, the environment all mixing to give it a unique taste as individual as the city itself. But you'll find it in the wild, too, if you know the right places. We can tap into it, draw some off if we don't have enough of our own available for a spell.

If you drink from the pool fast enough, another mage is going to feel it. Drink it in sips over a few minutes or longer and nobody'll ever notice until you're good and ready to use it. It's an old trick. I've used it myself lots of times.

I really should have seen it coming.

Everything happens too fast. I feel the magic flare out from the kid like an explosion, warping the world around it as it spreads. The pavement I've wrapped around his legs uncoils. A thick sheet of it peels up from the street to create a six-foot-tall wall between us. Sharp, thin spears of asphalt a few inches long form out of the wall.

I have a shield spell that I've used so often it's become almost automatic. When the spears of asphalt forming in the wall shoot out at me, I'm already bringing it up. It catches most of them, but two get through. One screams so close past my head I can feel the air as it passes.

I'm not as lucky with the other one. My protection tattoos push against it to slow it down, but not enough. A half-foot-long spear of compressed gravel and tar drives itself an inch into my left shoulder right next to the bullet graze.

That little shit. The pain is blinding. I can feel the magic in my tattoos doing . . . something. I honestly can't remember what half of them are for, but whatever they're doing can't be good.

I use the shield as a battering ram, shoving it so hard against the pavement wall that it explodes in a cloud of dust and debris all over the street. Halfway down the block a car alarm goes off.

I can feel him drawing more power from the pool. That and the pavement wall tells me he's got skill but not a lot of his own power.

Since any of us can tap it, I could start pulling some in, too. Then it turns into a race to see who can pull in more the fastest. I did that in Mexico with a Cartel mage, effectively shutting him out completely.

But I haven't tried it since. I had access to Mictlante-cuhtli's power then and could draw in a fuck-ton of magic in one shot. I don't know if I can still do that, and now's the wrong time to find out. If it turns out I can't, then I'll have wasted my time and given him an edge he doesn't need.

So instead I push the shield out toward him. I have more than enough power, to the point of not having to draw on the pool to maintain it. I can't remember if I had that much before I was with Santa Muerte, but I'm pretty sure I didn't.

The shield reaches him, pulling in at the edges until I've got him in a bubble of force. Just as I finish wrapping it around he lets his spell loose.

The inside of the bubble goes bright as thousands of red and purple arcs of power shoot out from him, hit the shield and ricochet back. It looks like watching a plasma globe on acid. Within a second there's nothing but light.

When it finally stops, and the globe clears, I see the kid collapsed, twitching, smoking. He doesn't look too badly burned, but it's clear that whatever he was trying for was lethal. I can feel him die right then and there, a tiny kick in the gut whenever someone nearby kicks the bucket. Yet one more side benefit of necromancy. Yay.

I lower the shield and run to him. Anybody else I'd

probably just let go, but come on, he's just a kid. I try to remember how to do CPR. I'm not in the business of keeping people alive so it's not like I ever paid much attention.

I can feel the kid's ghost starting to separate from him, and whatever's left of his soul going wherever it needs to go. I've only felt this happen a few times before. Usually it all separates so fast it's over before I even know it's happening.

I've always wondered if I could do something about it. Now's as good a time as any to find out. I can't do anything from this side besides watch this all happen. But over on the dead side I might have a chance.

I will myself over to the other side, colors muting to midnight shades of blue and gray. There's a rushing sound, like stepping through a waterfall. The city noises fade to a low, hissing wind. The cars on the street are missing, and some of the houses look different. Places leave a psychic footprint over here. With enough belief and history tied into a place or an object it'll show up, regardless of what's on the living side. There are whole buildings over here that were demolished decades ago.

The kid's ghost hasn't pulled away from the rest of his soul much. It's more like a slow peeling than a clean break. The kid's body is visible, though if he were alive he'd just be an indistinct blob of light. But he's still in the process of shedding his soul, so it's right here.

Neither piece, the ghost nor the soul, really looks like him, or even human. It's too soon. They're just ropes of white light splitting apart.

I don't have a lot of time. This is a land of entropy. I can already feel it pulling my energy away from me. Stay too long and I'll be just as dead as anything else here. Though the ghosts will probably eat me first.

The blood seeping out of my shoulder where the pavement arrow hit me (and there is a surprising amount of it) is already getting the attention of the local ghosts. They feed on life, and there's a lot of life in blood. One of the reasons it's used in so many rituals and spells to call and control the dead.

They can see me from their side the same way I see them. Light and sound, but like a girl in a peep show booth, there's no touching. To me they mostly look like half-formed nightmares, caught in a form inherited from their final moments of death. Gunshot wounds, cracked skulls, stabbings. To them I look like a gourmet meal stuck behind glass. And now I'm on their side of the window.

This is probably a monumentally bad decision, but I've never been accused of making smart ones. I reach out with both hands, grabbing the kid's ghost in one hand, and the soul in the other.

My hands sting as if they've just been flash frozen, but I hold on tight. I pull the two pieces together. They fuse into one as soon as they come in contact with each other.

Okay. Now what? This is brand new territory for me. I go with the first thing that pops in my head. I shove his soul into his body like I'm tamping down an overfull trash can.

His body's eyes and mouth snap open in shock, or terror, or something. But it clearly worked. He's blurring and brightening, and soon all I can see is a man-sized form of shapeless light.

The sound of Wanderers is getting closer. Though they look like they're running, their feet never touch the ground. And if there's a wall over here, they can't go through it. They're constrained by their own memories of how human bodies and the world work.

Which is a good thing, because otherwise they'd probably be flying overhead and dive bombing me, instead of running at me like Labradors after I just rang the dinner bell.

That's my cue. The last thing I need is to get gnawed on by Wanderers. Just like coming in here, I have to will myself back to the other side. Used to be it took me a good twenty minutes to cast this spell. But I've done it so many times now I can do it in between heartbeats.

I pull myself over just as I see the first running Wanderers round a corner. There's that jet engine blast of sound, a searing light, and then I'm back on the living side.

The kid's gone. A silver Audi heads jerkily down the street, then straightens and picks up speed. I suppose motor control takes a minute to come back when you're raised from the dead.

I turn to run to the Cadillac, maybe I can catch him before he's gone, but the burst of pain in my shoulder reminds me that I've got a fucking arrow in my arm.

I limp over to the Cadillac, pull the pavement arrow out of my shoulder. I'm starting to get woozy. Can't be from blood loss. Haven't been bleeding enough yet.

My tattoos are still doing something. The hell did that kid do to me? I run through what I can remember of my tattoos and the only thing I can come up with is that it might be poison. That or demon brain worms. I really hope it's poison.

I slide into the driver's seat, grab my suit jacket and tie it tight around my arm. It's a shit job and I don't know if it will do anything, but direct pressure's all I've got until I can get somewhere safe. I don't have time to do any kind of first aid. I can already hear sirens.

I pull the Caddy away from the curb and round a

corner just as the first cop car pulls up. The Caddy's got some spells engraved in its frame to make the normals not pay attention to it. They'll see it as any other car on the street, but it's never going to seem out of place.

Police aren't usually more than a pain in the ass, but I need to get this arm dealt with. The wound's bleeding pretty heavily. Hospital's out. I don't have time for questions there aren't any good answers for.

There's only one place I can think of.

# Chapter 3

**I pull up to the warehouse** gate just east of the L.A. River and honk the horn. My heart started hammering in my chest about ten minutes ago and I'm having trouble seeing straight. The wound in my shoulder is still bleeding, soaking through my shirt. I look like I've rolled around on a slaughterhouse killing floor. I really hope Gabriela knows a good back-alley doctor. Or better yet, a mage who's a good back-alley doctor.

Nobody comes out, so I lean on the horn again. They know I'm here. Gabriela keeps snipers on the top floor in case somebody gets through the gate. Normally she's got three armed men in the parking lot, but today the lot's empty.

If nobody's here, I'm in trouble. Of course, if there is anybody here I might still be in trouble. Gabriela's one of the more stable mages I know, which isn't saying much—mages and pragmatism aren't something that usually go together. She might think it's easier to let me bleed out in my car than it is to let me inside.

I don't think that will happen. Unlike most mages, Gabriela actually cares about people, whether they're human or not.

She had a hotel Downtown a while back where she was taking in the supernaturals of Los Angeles: vampires, aswang, naga, ebu gogo, xana, and so on. We're very multicultural out here. There aren't many, and the ones that can pass for human mostly hide among the homeless, eke out a living on street corners, try not to grab too much attention.

Problem is, nobody was going to take a five-foot-tall sorority girl with an advanced sociology degree seriously as a mage protecting homeless vampires. She looks less Morgan le Fay, and more Manic Pixie Dream Girl. Sexism is alive and well in magic land.

So, she went all Baba Yaga on everybody and made up this ancient, withered hag called La Bruja. Carved a swath through the gangs and Mexican Mafia in her little corner of Downtown. Left calling cards, messages written in blood, skinned corpses, that sort of thing.

The whole time these guys are thinking they're dealing with a hundred-year-old monster witch. Even her own people thought so. Until a bunch of Russian thugs followed me to the hotel and burned the place to the ground. And I kinda got a bunch of her people killed. We didn't talk much after that.

Word that she was La Bruja got out fast. Things went south. Chunk of her army bailed, Mexican Mafia started sniffing around. A lot of boys who thought they were men had to be forcefully reminded that she was still very much not someone to fuck with.

Considering that I've probably brought a pissed off Aztec god to L.A. looking for revenge, letting me die would really be the best move.

I honk the horn again. Longer and louder this time. My vision swims for a second before going clear. My heart's really getting a workout.

Finally, someone comes out of the warehouse and opens the gate. I drive in, the car lurching, and park crookedly in one of the empty spaces.

I'm going downhill fast. I'm fever-hot, hotter than can be explained by this weather. I can't tell if it's from whatever I've been dosed with or my tats really doing their best to keep me alive.

I push the door open. A step turns into a stumble turns into a fall and the next thing I know I'm face-down in the parking lot as everything goes black.

———

When I bolt back into consciousness my heart's slamming in my ribcage like a monkey on a tambourine, but at least now it's got some rhythm. My breathing is fast, but not as bad as before. Most importantly, my tattoos aren't reacting. Whatever I was dosed with isn't in my system anymore.

My vision is still spotty. It takes a minute to focus on where I am. Then a woman stands over me, silhouetted by a light behind her. It takes a few seconds to realize who it is.

"Vivian?" She's grown her red hair out and there are a few more lines around her eyes than I remember.

"Eric," she says.

"What are you doing here?" I'm in a plain room that almost but not quite feels like a doctor's office, lying on a portable surgical table. The scene is far more familiar than I'm comfortable with. If this is a dream, it's a pretty shitty one.

"Saving your life," she says. "You really need to get some healing charms in that mess of tattoos, if you can find any more space for them." There's no sarcasm there, not even a resigned sigh. The last time I saw my

ex-girlfriend, she was handing me the deeds and paperwork for my sister's house and a bunch of properties and
storage units that my family kept from my sister and me
while they were alive.

It was cordial, but final. I never expected to see her
again. And sure as hell not after passing out in front of
Gabriela's warehouse.

"Thanks," I say. "I'll take it under advisement."

"You're welcome."

"You know I wasn't asking why you were *here* here,
right?"

"Yes." She pulls off a pair of purple nitrile gloves and
tosses them into a wastebasket with a biohazard sticker
on the side. There's a nicely bandaged dressing on my
shoulder covering both wounds. The arm's a little numb,
but it seems to mostly work, as long as I don't lift it very
high.

"Where's my shirt?" I say.

"You're not going to want to wear that again," she
says. She gestures over at the wastebasket with a bright
red piece of cloth sticking out of the top.

"Ah, right. I was doing a lot of bleeding in it."

She looks warily at my chest and carefully puts her
stethoscope against my heart, all the time looking like
touching me is going to shock her. She hands me a white
tablet. "Here. Put this under your tongue. Sublingual
lorazepam. Should help calm things down a little pretty
quickly." She slowly lifts the stethoscope off my chest and
quickly steps back.

"Is there something wrong I should know about?"
I say.

"One of your tattoos tried to eat my stethoscope."

That's new. "Let me guess, the birds?" One of the tattoos on my chest, right in the middle, is a circle of Celtic

ravens. When they're charged with power I can turn them into actual ravens that fly out and make somebody else's day really miserable. Until I use them they shift position within the circle, changing configuration from moment to moment. After they've been used they're just another static tattoo until I charge them again.

At least they used to be.

"They've changed," she says. "Didn't they used to be Celtic or something? Because they don't much look like it now."

When I was turning to jade all my tattoos stayed intact. But this one changed. Instead of Celtic imagery, they look more Aztec, and they're not ravens anymore. I think they're eagles.

They also seem to have acquired a mind of their own. When I was in Mictlan they saved my life by coming out without me triggering them. I haven't done anything with them since it happened. They should just be a static tattoo of birds, but they're still moving around on my chest.

"I'm really not sure what their deal is," I say. "You said they ate your stethoscope?"

"Tried to." She shows it to me. There's a small dent in the disk.

I have no idea what to do with this information, so I change the subject. I'll think about it when I'm not lying on a hospital table.

"Thanks for saving my life," I say. "Poison and blood loss really do a number on a guy, huh?"

"Double whammy. You'd been pumped full of . . . something. An anticoagulant, something like oleander and warfarin, I'm thinking. You weren't clotting. Your heart rate was cranked way up, making you bleed out faster. I'm honestly surprised you're alive."

"I lose a lot of blood?"

"Enough. But I gave you a charm that should get your blood volume back up without a problem. And the lorazepam should help with the heart rate."

I'm surprised she saved me. I got her fiancé, Alex, probably the best friend I've ever had, killed. Then I brought more trouble to her doorstep in the form of a face-shifting Russian gangster. And now this.

"I don't think my heart's slowing down," I say. Vivian starts to put her stethoscope to my chest and pauses.

"It's okay," I say. "They won't do it again." I hope. The birds stay calm as she listens to my heartbeat.

"Take a few minutes," she says. "It was a lot worse an hour ago. I got the poison out of you, but there are some effects that we just have to wait out."

"How did you—"

She shows me a disposable, plastic water bottle filled with a tarry, black liquid.

"Come on, Eric. You know I'm not a regular doctor. I see you haven't broken your nose again."

"You did such a good job with it last time, I'd hate to mess up your work."

"Doc's on retainer for us," Gabriela says, stepping into the room. I catch a glimpse behind her. She's built this surgical suite inside her warehouse. Between the infirmary and a mage doctor on her payroll, I wonder how much use she's getting out of it. She doesn't do anything without a reason, so things must be worse for her than I thought.

Now that she's not doing her Old Hag of the Woods shtick, she's gotten a lot more colorful, and clearly gives no fucks about it. Purple jeans, sparkly Doc Martens, a t-shirt for some punk band called Bad Citizen Corporation.

She dyed her hair since the last time I saw her. Red

fading into purple, with blue highlights. It's pulled back in a ponytail, and despite her My Little Punk Pony getup she gives off this sixties rebel, Che Guevara vibe.

Of course, that just might be because of the big fucking machete in a scabbard across her back.

She throws a white button-down shirt at me. "That should fit. I understand you and the doc know each other."

"Not anymore," Vivian says before I can open my mouth. The pause goes on a little longer than anybody's comfortable with.

"Okay, then," Gabriela says. "Moving on."

I pull the shirt on, wincing as I lift my arm. Even with healing magic, that's gonna suck for a few days at least. The shirt's a little too tight across the shoulders, but it'll do.

"I like the My Little Pony look," I say.

"Thanks. Since I can't scare the shit out of the Mexican Mafia as somebody's nightmare grandmother, I figured I'd go the other direction and really make them underestimate me."

"Is it working?"

"You want to see the heads I've collected?"

"Maybe later. How bad was I?"

"Almost dead," Vivian says. "A couple more minutes and you would be. Dan could have done a hell of a lot worse to you."

I slowly slide off the table. I accidentally brace myself with my left hand and pain shoots through my arm. Yeah, I'll be popping Vicodin like breath mints for the next week or so.

"Wait. Who?"

"Dan Malmon," Gabriela says. "I had one of my guys run the address you gave me. The guy who died in the fire was his mother, Kate. She was one of us."

"Dan's a real winner," Vivian says. "I'd heard Kate

had died in the fire, but I thought—hell, I'd hoped—Dan had gone up with her. If for no other reason than to get a menace off the street. I didn't hear anything about him so I figured he was either dead or bailed. When I got here Gabriela told me where you'd been and what was happening. I assumed you had a run-in with Dan."

"Let me guess," I say. "His knack is poisons?"

"Poisons, drugs, whatever. Let's call it creative chemistry," Gabriela says.

Every mage has one particular area that they're stupidly good at. Divination, protection wards, predicting the weather, whatever. I got dead things. Dan, apparently, can give Pablo Escobar a run for his money.

"A guy who can make his own ecstasy must get invited to a lot of parties."

"Not anymore," Vivian says, anger bleeding through her professionalism. "He's a serial killer. He's murdered at least thirty people, that I know of."

"Normals?" I say.

"Of course," Vivian says. "So of course nobody cared." Nobody important, at least. That's the thing with mages; we don't have any laws per se. And let's face it, when you can bend reality around your pinky, some of us don't see normals as real people. You have to draw too much attention, piss off enough of the wrong people, whatever, before someone decides you need to get stomped on for messing with normals.

"Then he killed a mage last year," Gabriela says.

"And then people cared? We kill each other all the time."

"Yes, but we usually have a reason for it," Gabriela says. "Even if it's just 'Hey, I want your stuff.' He said he wanted to see what it would be like."

"They blackballed him," Vivian says. "That's all.

He's murdered more than thirty people and people just kind of shrugged their shoulders."

"'Excitable boy, they all said,'" Gabriela says.

"Hang on. He's what, nineteen now? Twenty? How long had this been going on?"

"I think since he was, what, twelve? Thirteen?" Vivian says. "Apparently it was an open secret among the sorts of people we don't hang out with."

She's pissed off about it, and doesn't like it any more than I do. Normal, mage, inhuman, people are people. A lot of us can't see that. I've never been in the loop much, mostly because I hate people, other mages in particular. But this seems like something I'd have heard about.

"Don't look at me," Gabriela says. "I can't kill every motherfucker in this town. I got shit to do."

So do I, but if he comes for me again I will kill him. I'm really regretting not letting him die on the street back there.

"Let me see if I've got this straight. His mom gets killed, he comes after me, poisons me—"

"Yeah, about that," Gabriela says. "Did he hit you with an arrow or something?"

"The street."

"He poisoned the street and threw it at you?" Vivian says.

"Shot it at me, but yeah, pretty much. Here's what I don't understand. Why? He said I'd killed his mom. Only I didn't. I haven't killed anybody."

"Recently," Gabriela says.

"Uh huh. How's that head collection coming along? Stones and glass houses, chica. I didn't even know who the hell either of them was until just now. So why did he think I'd killed his mom?"

"Not just his mom," Vivian says, not meeting my eyes. "All the other ones, too."

# Chapter 4

"**Other ones?**" I say. "Back up. What the hell are you talking about?"

"Kate's not the first to die that way," Vivian says. "Over the last month this has happened to at least seventeen families scattered around the city. All mages. House burned down, one person in it, nothing but fragments of bone left." And too hot to find a bullet, probably. Just a little dot of slag in a pile of ash and bone.

"How did I not hear about this?" But I know how I didn't hear about it. I didn't hear about it the same way I didn't hear about a serial killer mage who was poisoning people.

We're a secretive bunch, us mages. We don't talk to each other much and what little community we have is tight-knit and paranoid. Probably nobody started putting pieces together until it hit critical mass. And even then, information wouldn't just get out there. The ones who knew would keep it close.

And let's face it, though I grew up here, I'm an outsider. My name's known, and not in a good way. I've brought some shit down on this city a couple of times. Gotten good people killed.

A lot of mages won't give me the time of day. Gabriela's an exception, but I understand why she does it. Hold your friends close, your enemies closer, and your shit-magnets close enough to use them as a shield when the shooting starts.

"People started connecting the dots about a week ago," Vivian says. "I only found out myself yesterday. Once I came over and heard about what had happened and that it was you, I told Gabriela about it."

"You didn't know about this?" I say to Gabriela. She doesn't say anything, but I can tell she's not happy.

"Great, we're all out of the loop. Now what's this about me killing all of them?"

"I don't know where it started, or how, but it seems everybody got the same message a couple days ago. Eric Carter killed your fill-in-the-blank."

"And they believed it?" Gabriela says.

"I did," Vivian says. "At first."

"Fair point," I say. "Wherever it started, it would have to have come from a trusted source. There's nobody out there all of us trust. So, it can't be just one. It has to be a lot of them."

What would I do if I wanted to find who killed a family member? I know exactly what I'd do because I've done it. I'd track down their ghost and ask them. I tried that with my sister, but like the woman in the West Adams house, she was just an Echo.

Everybody's got their own methods for finding things out that they trust. Maybe not talking to ghosts. Could be tarot cards, goat entrails, whatever. The point is that they're all only going to trust their own methods.

"Divination," I say. "They all went looking for answers their own way. Something got in the way."

"Somebody broke into a divination to point this shit

at you? Some of these people are really, really good, Eric," Vivian says.

"If you really believed that you wouldn't have pulled that poison out of me. Because they're so good is why they fell for it. They all made a phone call and the wrong guy answered."

"Somebody really has it out for you," Vivian says. "Have you narrowed it down to the thousand or so people you've pissed off in the last fifteen years?"

Gabriela and I exchange a look. "Doc," Gabriela says, "can you give us a minute?"

Vivian looks between us, not happy about being kept out of what's going on, but finally relents. She collects her plastic water bottle full of poison, drops it in her bag. "Sure. Some of your boys and girls need a checkup anyway. I'll be downstairs." She doesn't say goodbye, or even look at me as she leaves.

"Jesus," Gabriela says. "What'd you do to piss her off so much?"

"Dated her," I say.

"Oh. Yeah. That would do it."

"You know who this is," I say. "Quetzalcoatl's the only thing I can think of both strong enough to intercept divination spells without the casters noticing, and also wants my head on a stick. You heard Viv. These people are powerful."

"Were you this much of a pain in the ass before you came back to L.A.?"

"If you ask Vivian she'll probably tell you I was this much of a pain in the ass before I left."

Gabriela pulls up a plastic chair and falls into it. "Jesus fucking Christ, Carter. How did all this slip past your radar? I thought you were watching out for this crap?"

"Me? What about you? Dead people aren't as chatty

as you might think. Or as smart. What about this whole fucking criminal empire you got going on here?"

"When I was an old, scary hag people came to me. I was like Don Corleone. Now that I'm the upstart little shit who fooled everyone it's the other way around. Nobody talks to me. Everybody from La Eme to the fucking Armenians are testing me, not to mention the other mages who think they can take on a little girl." She laughs. It's a bitter, tired sound. "Thing is, they're not wrong. I'm hemorrhaging resources faster than I can replace them."

"That bad?"

"Enh, I've been here before. I'll win this fight again. Enough about me. Quetzalcoatl's helper—how do we find them?"

"I wouldn't trust any divination spells. If Q's fucking around with the victims' families, it's not a stretch to think he'd do the same with you or me. I could ask some of the Wanderers in the victims' neighborhoods if they saw anything. But if everybody thinks I did this, those might not be the smartest places to be seen."

That little shit hit me with poison today and almost killed me. He's good, but there's better and smarter out there. Who knows what the hell I might run into next time?

"How about Darius?" I say. I don't like the idea, but it's the only one I've got.

The Djinn has doors all over the city that lead to his own little pocket universe. He can't get out, but it doesn't mean others can't get in.

He saved my ass in Mictlan by sending me some conveniently well-timed information. He wanted Santa Muerte and Mictlantecuhtli out of the picture as much as I did. He could have told me sooner, or at least given me some breadcrumbs to follow. But he didn't. He wanted me to go to Mictlan. Whether revenge for getting him locked in his bottle, or something else, I don't know. Whatever it was, he wanted me there.

"Already tried," Gabriela says. "He won't even let me through the door."

"That happen often?" I thought she and Darius were besties. I've been formally banned from his place.

"A few times," she says. "But only when he's pissed off at me. It passes in a day or two, but the timing is a little interesting."

"You think he knows what's happening and he's gone to ground?"

"I think he knows more than he lets on, at least," she says. "If shit's going down that has him looking to weather out the storm, it's gonna suck for everybody else."

Could Quetzalcoatl hurt him? Who knows. An eight-thousand-year-old Djinn versus a broken-down god? But why would he try? They fought on the same side against the Aztecs, not that that proves anything. Darius probably didn't have any choice in the matter.

"Well, shit," I say.

"I got an idea," Gabriela says. "But you're really not gonna like it."

"No," I say, wondering when we were going to get around to this. "Abso-fucking-lutely not. I've already considered it, and I'm not going down that road."

"She's the only one left who actually knows him besides Darius. Probably knows him better than Darius."

Goddammit. I know she's right. I've known for months. But I've been avoiding thinking about it. Thinking about her. And it's not for her lack of trying to get hold of me, either.

I pull a couple of cards out of my pocket, slightly larger

than standard playing cards, and hand them to Gabriela. The images are used in a bingo-like game called Lotería. Each card has a title, an image, and a little nonsense rhyme associated with it. If you've got a divinatory bent, you can use them like tarot cards.

The first is El Corazón, showing a picture of an anatomically correct heart with an arrow through it sitting in the middle of a very familiar looking ring with tiny calaveras carved into its surface. Compared to the one on my ring finger the detail's not as good, but close enough.

The other is La Muerte, depicting a half-skeletal, half-flesh woman. Though the image is stylized, I know exactly who it's supposed to be.

"These first showed up a week or so after I got back from Mictlan. I was getting two, three cards a day for a while. Then they stopped. They started back up last month. This is the fifth pair I've gotten in the last two weeks."

"You sure they're from her?"

"Who else would they be from? I just don't know what they mean."

"At least she's still in one piece. That's something, right?"

"No. The plan was to cut her goddamn head off and mount it on a wall." Things didn't go as planned. I'm not sure how much of Santa Muerte is still Santa Muerte and how much is her human avatar, Tabitha Cheung. Tabitha played me like a goddamn piano to get me into Mictlan under her boss's orders.

My goal had been to kill Mictlantecuhtli and hopefully stop the progression of the jade taking over my body, and then Santa Muerte for killing my sister, though I wasn't picky on the order.

Only it turned out to be a con job and Tabitha and I were the marks. Santa Muerte as her alter-ego Micte-cacihuatl and Mictlantecuhtli wanted me close enough and mad enough that I'd stab at least one of them in the heart with a god-made obsidian knife.

If that sounds like a sacrifice, it's because it was. Once I did it, the connections between me and Mictlantecuhtli and Tabitha and Santa Muerte would be so strong they'd boot us out of our bodies, letting the two gods wander the mortal world in more than just their followers' dreams.

But I've never found a plan I couldn't fuck up. I turned it around and shoved the knife into my own chest instead—which I don't recommend, by the way. Instead of the bond with Mictlantecuhtli strengthening, it snapped.

In the seconds I was dead Tabitha got hold of the knife and stuck it into Santa Muerte. I was too late, so I did the only thing I could think of. I yanked the knife from Santa Muerte's bony chest and shoved it into Tabitha's in a desperate attempt to reverse whatever was happening.

I don't remember much after that. Both of them burning like road flares, energy coursing between them like Hot Wheels cars on a Super Loop, then nothing. I woke up alone in the middle of the Mexican desert.

"Is she the same Santa Muerte?" I say. "Is Tabitha a part of her? Or is she a part of Tabitha? Is it a trap? The Aztec version of playing Peter Gabriel outside my window?"

"She's reaching out to you," Gabriela says, inspecting the two cards closely before handing them back to me. If she finds anything that shows they're not just card stock and ink she doesn't say. "For whatever reason, she wants to see you. Use it."

"You think I haven't thought about that? Creepy death goddess wife notwithstanding I don't even know where to look for her."

"Bullshit," Gabriela says. "You know exactly where to look. There's that church on Alvarado, that bullshit botanica on Melrose, and at least three pharmacies Downtown that if you go in the back you'll find a shrine of hers you can talk to. You know she'll show up. You're just too chickenshit to do it."

She's right on both counts. "Fuck me. There's got to be another way," I say, even though I know there isn't. Gabriela tosses the cards onto the surgical table behind me.

"Maybe you'll figure one out on your way to church."

# Chapter 5

**I didn't have time** to look over the Cadillac after Malmon put bullets into it. I'll have to get the driver and passenger windows replaced. Probably the mechanism to roll them up and down. And definitely the locking mechanism on the driver's side door. Fuck it. I'll just replace the doors. Where the hell am I going to find doors and windows for a '73 Cadillac Eldorado?

I brush shattered glass off the seats. It's a wonder I didn't shred my ass when I jumped into the car. The Caddy's a convertible. There's nowhere to anchor anything at the top, so I can't even get plastic and duct tape to cover the windows.

Just as well. The air conditioner's shot and in this heat I'm driving with the top down most of the time, anyway. But at least it gave me the illusion of keeping all the brushfire smoke out of my lungs for a bit.

"I'm not sure what surprises me more, that you're still driving it, or that it's still drivable," Vivian says. I didn't hear her come up behind me. To be fair, I was around gunfire earlier. My ears are still ringing a little.

"Hey, this car and I have seen a lot together."

"I'm sure you have," she says, an edge in her voice.

"Oh, there it is."

"What?"

"The disdain. I thought we were past that. Or at least I thought we weren't going to bump into each other again, so it didn't matter. What happened to your plan for leaving L.A.?"

She wraps her arms around herself as if to ward off a chill in this triple digit heat. "I'm still going. I just haven't, yet."

"Okay, sure. None of my business. Might want to do it sooner rather than later, though."

"What's happening?" she says. "You show up at Gabriela's bleeding out and poisoned and then the two of you have some hushed conversation when I leave the room. Something's going on."

"No shit," I say. "Honestly, I don't know why she wanted you kept in the dark. She's funny that way. Here's the short version. A pissed off Aztec wind god is framing me for multiple homicides and arsons, probably just to fuck with me, and is probably responsible for most of the wildfires going on right now, too. Anybody near me is going to get caught in the shitstorm. I'd really rather you not be one of those people. Again."

She doesn't say anything for a long time, her eyes getting that thousand-yard stare. "I'm afraid to leave," she says. "Except for college and med school, I've spent my whole life here. All of my memories about Alex are here. I'm afraid if I leave I'm going to lose all of them. I have to look at his picture every day to remind myself what he looks like."

I wasn't expecting that. It comes out of her like water from a burst pipe. Things must be bad if she's telling me this.

"I'm sorry," I say, not knowing what else to say. I wish

I could forget what Alex looked like. Best friend growing up and my last image of him is his possessed body
strangling me right before I had a zombie put a bullet in
his head. I keep telling myself he was already dead, but
it doesn't matter. Either way I killed him.

"I know," she says. "Maybe I'll just leave town for a
little while. Go up the coast."

"I think that'd be a good idea."

"Do me a favor, would you?" she says.

"Sure."

"Don't get hurt. As long as I'm on Gabriela's dime I'd
probably be the one to stitch you up. And I don't want
to see you again."

"I'll do my best."

———

There comes a time in every person's life when they
have to take a long, honest look back on their life choices
and admit that they really fucked it all up.

I didn't expect to run into Vivian again, like ever. I'd
made peace with that, with the guilt, with the fact that I'd
destroyed somebody's life and there was no going back.
And then I wake up on a table with her patching me up.

Seeing her threw me. I can't imagine how she reacted.
Not well, probably. I wouldn't blame her if she'd just slit
my throat while I was passed out, but I know she wouldn't
have. That's more my style than hers.

I've fallen into complacency. With nobody trying to
kill me and no oblivion hanging over my head, I stopped
paying attention. I might have been looking for signs that
Quetzalcoatl was coming for me, but I never really believed it. Or at least I didn't want to believe it.

I pull the Cadillac onto the 101 Freeway and head
toward Alvarado. One of Santa Muerte's churches is

there, in a strip mall between a nail salon and a Chinese fast food joint. I haven't been there in a long time, not since I first came back to Los Angeles.

The church is part of that special L.A., the schizo-phrenic one that can't decide what it wants to be. While the tourists are busy looking for movie star houses and waxed porn stars, life is happening all around them. Messy, filthy, violent. And they never see it.

I hit the Four Level, a series of Downtown freeway interchanges that cross over and under each other like an Escher painting connecting the 101 to the 110. It's a complicated knotwork of concrete and steel and almost everyone driving it doesn't know that it's literally a knot.

It's a protection spell that was laid down in the forties during construction by a group of mages. Nobody re-members what it's protection from, though. It sure as hell isn't earthquakes, violence, and drought. And why doesn't anyone know what it's for? Because the mages who designed it all killed each other about a month later. Friendship is magic.

I head down the 110 and get off at 8th. You can watch the money fade away like a disappearing shore the fur-ther you get from the high finance of Downtown. Steel and glass towers give way to bricks and bars on win-dows, strip mall donut shops and signs offering payday loans in English, Spanish, and Korean.

Every street has something like this. Twists and turns of culture if not geography. Walk across the street, turn a corner, you're in a different L.A. Like how Skid Row is within walking distance of the mayor's office, or the Police Protective League, the LAPD's very own union, sits directly across from the ACLU.

In fact, it's sitting at a stoplight between those two buildings when I get ambushed.

I barely have time to register the spells going off, the same flavor of magic coming from three different directions. I slam on the gas, 280 horses under the hood shoving the car through the intersection. But it's already too late.

The entire back end of the Cadillac shears off just behind the driver's seat, and explodes. Metal and glass turn into a fireball of shrapnel behind me. The front of the car drops onto the pavement, throwing up sparks with a noise like God's own belt sander.

The car's front wheel drive and I haven't let up on the gas. It continues down most of the block. Then, like a man realizing his heart has stopped, the engine dies from lack of fuel. Hard to drive a car when the gas tank's a shower of confetti behind it.

The car spins. There's no power in the steering and it's like trying to control a panicked bull. The car plows through a chain-link fence surrounding a basketball court and finally comes to a stop when it hits one of the basket poles.

I feel like I've been body slammed by a luchador with anger management issues. The seatbelt won't unlock, so I pull my straight razor and slice through the strap. I fall through the open doorway out of the car and onto my knees. I'm not sure where the driver's side door is.

I pull myself up, wipe blood out of my eyes from a cut on my forehead. Everything hurts so much I'm not focusing on my wounded arm and I can't tell if my hammering heartbeat is the remains of the poison or just adrenaline. So that's a plus.

I don't see anybody, but whoever blew up my car will be here in a second. That or the police, paramedics, or maybe some random normals, and I'll have all sorts of new and enjoyable problems.

I don't have to wait long. Three people in thick,

hooded robes step over the wreckage of the chain-link fence and stand in front of me like executioners. The hoods hide their faces better than normal hoods should. The formless robes are black and covered with golden sigils, most of which are the equivalent of getting a kanji tattoo and finding out later that it means "ramen."

Still, they're real mages, even if they can't spell right. I can feel the magic they're drawing from the pool, the spells they're crafting. They're sloppy. I'm not sure what the spells are, though I can guess, but I can tell that they're struggling. It's like watching toddlers put together a five-thousand-piece Lego set.

I'm not topped up myself, but I've got plenty of power. No reason to draw from the pool, and if I need a spell, I can think of a dozen I can pop off with barely a thought. Just because they showed me theirs doesn't mean I have to show them mine.

"Wool robes?" I say. "In this heat? You lost a bet, didn't you?"

"Shut up," one of them says, fists clenched, a blue glow building up around them. "You're a murderer and a monster and we're here to pass judgment on you. I declare you guilty." The other two chime in with their own cries of "Guilty!"

"Wow. That's some high-pitched squeaking you got going there. Okay, either one of you is a girl, or you're a boy whose balls haven't dropped yet. I'm going with option two. How's puberty treating you, Junior?"

The first one throws off their robe. It's a man, white, early thirties, maybe. "You killed my wife, you sonofabitch." The other two drop their robes.

One's a black woman about the same age as the guy, and the third is a gawky, acne-riddled Latino kid with a rage in his eyes he's finally figured out what to do with.

"My husband," says the woman.

"My mom," the boy says.

"Holy shit, am I a real bastard, or what?" I should be talking them down, not goading them on. They really think I killed their families. But the fuckers blew up my car. *My car.* Okay, yeah, it was stolen, but the guy who it belonged to was already dead. And yes, admittedly, I'm the one who killed him, but he was a very bad man.

"I'm gonna fucking kill you," the kid screams and, instead of letting loose a spell, he does what every angry young man does. He rushes me. I put up my shield. The kid smashes into it, bouncing to the ground, slamming his head on the blacktop hard enough I don't think he's getting up any time soon. His spell, a fireball by the looks of it, goes off.

I twist the shield around fast to keep the kid from char-broiling himself and push the fireball up until it explodes above us.

My moment of magnanimity is rewarded by the other two letting loose their own spells, and since I've got my shield angled to protect the kid, it isn't protecting me.

I get a double whammy of a freezing spell and a simple invisible hammer. Ice forms on my chest, my clothes going brittle. The pain is intense. But it's not as bad as the hammer that follows.

I fly back a good five feet before skidding and rolling on the blacktop. My tattoos take the brunt of it, and they're already thawing me out, but it still hurts like a motherfucker.

I get up. They're both so stunned they just stare at me. They must have figured they could show up with a big gun and take me down with one shot. Probably didn't expect things to get this far. If I hadn't gunned the Cadillac when I felt the magic they might have gotten me.

But they didn't. And now it's my turn.

Did you know everybody is covered in a cloud of their own bacteria? It's pretty gross when you think about it. Every time you breathe, every time you fart, burp, talk, move, take a shit, you're putting out gut bacteria. Settles on your skin, your hair, your clothes, other people, the ground.

A lot of that bacteria doesn't last very long. It dies fast. We're all surrounded by a constantly dying cloud of shit germs. And if it's dead . . .

I animate every dead thing surrounding them. Bacteria are small enough that it doesn't take much to do. I add a little color to the mix. I want them to see what's happening to them.

A dark wall of dead germs solidifies around them, covers their skin like ants. They both scream, clawing at their faces, their hands. I make the swarm crawl up into their nostrils and mouths. Their screams choke off as the solid mass of germs fills their throats. I constrict the ones around their necks.

Their eyes roll into the back of their heads and they fall to the ground, unconscious. I pull the swarm of re-animated germs back. It flows out of them, a disgusting black river of muck. I only have about ten seconds before they come to, and I don't need them causing more trouble.

I run back to the remains of the Cadillac. Fortunately, I had my messenger bag in the front seat with me, not in the trunk. I go back to the unconscious pair, pulling out a pair of rune-etched zip-ties that I bind their wrists with. They'll act as short-term blockers for their magic. I'm betting they're weak enough not to be able to break through. I do the same to the teenager out cold on the ground.

I tap the woman's face. Her eyes snap open, bleary, unfocused. Then she remembers where she is and what just happened. I know that look, so I step to the side and let her vomit out a thick black stream, the remains of the dead germs I had clogging her pipes.

"Feeling better?" I say. She lunges at me. I step easily out of her way and she ends up falling forward onto her face, cutting her forehead.

I pull her back up to her knees, letting her figure out where her magic went. The guy is coming to and does his own puking routine. Once he's done he starts cursing me. Real curses, like turn-into-a-newt curses. Too bad for him they won't work.

"Zip it," I say and snap my fingers. His mouth closes, his lips glued together. I turn back to the woman.

"Now," I say, "you and I are going to have a little chat."

# Chapter 6

**"You gonna kill us** like you killed our families?" the woman says, the look of defiance on her face losing some of its effectiveness with the dribble of black drool coming off her chin and her constantly blinking blood out of her eyes.

"Jesus, what is it with you people? I didn't kill anybody. Why would I?"

"Bullshit," she says. "You're building an army of the dead. I saw it."

"Where? In a dream? For fuck sake. If I'm building an army of the dead, why am I leaving bodies behind? Why not raid the morgue? You have any idea how many people die in this town every day?"

"I—I don't know. I'm not some sick fuck who plays with corpses."

"Fine. Whatever. How about this, then? Where would I put it?"

"What?"

"My army of the dead. Where would I put it? I'd need a lot of corpses for an army, right? That'd take a lot of space. So, what, I'm gonna stack the bodies like cordwood inside all the industrial freezers in Los Angeles? And nobody's gonna notice that?"

She's starting to question, and she's not liking the answers she's getting. "Fuck you," she says with renewed conviction. She's too far gone down this road to argue with.

"So, what do I do with you?" I say. "I'd normally stick you in my trunk and drop you off at a phone booth in the desert, but seeing as I don't have a trunk anymore, that's not much of an option."

I look back at the wreckage of the Cadillac. Okay, the front half of the Cadillac. The other half is littering the street in a block-long trail behind it. Dammit. I liked that car.

"You kill me and you're going to have so much shit rain down on you," she says.

Right. Like it's going to get worse than all the mages of Los Angeles hunting me down now. "Lady, I'm not gonna ki—"

Her head explodes.

It takes a second for me to realize what's just happened. Somebody's shot her. Either they were going for her—which bravo, nice shot—or they've got really shitty aim.

Her buddy next to her screams through his sealed lips and tries to crawl away. He doesn't get very far before the shooter pops his noggin like a ripe melon at a Gallagher show.

I finally pull my head out of my ass and duck, scanning the area for the shooter. I see a shadow duck behind cars across the street, the shape of a rifle in their hand. I start to follow, but don't get very far, because that's when the reinforcements arrive.

Three cars pull up, one of them driving over the chain-link onto the blacktop. Fuck me. I run for the Cadillac—I'll drink a toast to you later, buddy—and take some half-assed cover behind its smoking ruin.

This time I do pull in power from the pool. So do the people in the cars. I feel eight, no, nine, all drawing a lot of power, fast. Something tells me they're not the newbies I just ran into. Wonderful.

I hear car doors open, people step out. There's no gunfire or spellwork, yet. I'm not sure why and I expect I probably won't like it when I find out.

"Mister Carter," yells a voice. Older, educated. "My name is Attila Werther. I don't know if you know who I am, but I knew your parents. I was very sad to hear what happened to them." Werther, Werther, who the hell is— Oh. *Werther*. Yeah, I remember him. He's one of *those* mages.

As a general rule, we don't organize well. Get half a dozen equally powerful mages into a room and it's a pretty good bet they'll kill each other inside of an hour.

But then there are these guys who have not only power, but money and resources, on their side. I can get cash whenever I want by hexing an ATM, any mage can, but guys like Werther never have to. They're not just rich, they're wealthy. They can afford to buy an army of normals, supernaturals, mages, whatever and get unwavering loyalty. It also helps that he's something like a hundred and fifty years old.

"Yeah, I remember you. We had you over at the house a couple times. I recall you shitting on their idea of going after Jean Boudreau. You know he killed them, right?"

Werther heaves a sigh. "An unfortunate business, that. I merely felt that waiting would ultimately lead to his criminal enterprise imploding in on itself. It was a prudent course of action."

"Prudent. Oh, hey, look. I learned a new word for chickenshit today."

"Be that as it may, I have been asked by some of the

more prominent families in the city to speak to you about the recent fires. There's quite a bit of evidence suggesting you did it."

"Yeah, I keep hearing that. Bullshit then, bull-shit now."

"I see. And these two here? I suppose you didn't kill them?"

"Believe it or not, no, I didn't. I figure once you look 'em over you'll realize that they were taken out at dis-tance, probably with a high-power rifle."

"Perhaps," he says. "Perhaps. But you see, they're not my concern. You are. You've made a lot of noise in the last couple of years here. The seers and scryers have been watching you, as much as that panoply of protec-tion tattoos will allow, at least. They see something com-ing. Something big. And you are at the center of it."

"Have I upturned the apple cart one too many times?" I say. I know where this is going. Knew as soon as their cars pulled up.

"Oh, far more than one. Out of respect for your fam-ily, I can make this easier and faster if you just come out and don't resist."

"And if not?"

"Then my men here will have to kill you more pain-fully. And slowly. I have seven, and you, well, you have just yourself."

Seven? With Werther that makes eight. But I felt nine people drawing magic from the pool. Where's that ninth person? Is Werther fucking with me?

"I can always fight them with witty insults and double entendres."

"I'm sure they will be very biting," he says. "Now, will it be the clean way, or the messy way?"

I can hear shuffling feet. Underneath the Cadillac I

can see the legs of Werther's personal kill squad. They fan out quietly, trying to flank me. I do a quick count. Yeah, with Werther, that's only eight.

They already know where I am. Time to show I know where they are, too. I draw the Browning, take a bead on one of the sets of legs, and fire. It hits, exploding the guy's tibia. He goes down screaming. Once he's eye level to me I put another one in his head. He stops screaming pretty quick. The Browning feels like it's laughing.

The rest of Werther's men are on the move, scattering and looking for cover. I can still see Werther's legs. He hasn't moved. Yeah, I'm not falling for that one. He's standing there because he doesn't believe I can touch him. He's probably right. The bullets might stop dead, turn to steam, or just change course and come after me.

"Was that the clean way or the messy way?" I yell. It occurs to me that the cops should be here by now. Of course, they won't be, because Werther has either put some spells down to keep them away, or paid them off.

I can get out by jumping over to the land of the dead and popping out somewhere else. At this point I can do it in my sleep. I look around for ghosts, try to get an idea of what I'll have to deal with when I cross over.

But there aren't any. Much like freeway noise, there is no place in L.A. that is free of ghosts. Whether they're Echoes, Haunts, or Wanderers, there's always something. The only way to drive ghosts off is to throw something at them that scares them. Or eats them.

If Werther has driven off the ghosts and I pop over to the other side, I'll run into whatever fucked up thing he left for me.

"It's the unfortunate way," he says. I feel the magic as he throws a spell. The remains of the Cadillac fly into the air like they're being flipped by a hurricane.

His men step out from their own cover and open up, ugly machine guns barking bullets. My shield spell goes up, but I won't be able to keep it there very long. With all the bullets it's soaking up it's all I can do to keep it running.

As his men are firing, Werther is slowly walking toward me. Now that I can see him, I remember him better. Looks to be in his mid-fifties, white hair slicked back, blue bespoke suit. I can feel the magic radiating off of him. This is one of those times I kinda wish I still had a god's power to pull from. Once he gets to me it's game over.

If I run, I'm dead. If I stay here, I'm dead. If I jump over to the other side, I'm dead. I think that about covers it?

Five feet away from me, Werther stands there, smiling. Gloating motherfucker. Well, it was a fun ride while it lasted. I wonder where I'll end up when I die.

A speeding F-150, with ridiculously oversized tires for a ridiculously oversized truck, jumps the curb and plows into Werther. There's a tremendous crunch, like a bag full of china being beaten with a shovel. Werther goes flying.

The passenger door flies open and the driver, a black woman who looks vaguely familiar, yells, "Get in here."

My momma told me not to get into cars with strange people, but I don't know anybody stranger than myself, so I jump in. I'll worry about who I've gotten a ride from once people aren't shooting at me.

She slams the gas before I even get the door closed. If she's hitting the street, she'll need to turn around, and a truck like this isn't exactly known for agility. Then I realize she *is* going for the street. The next block over. Through a Catholic school.

"Um—"

"Jesus, you look like shit," she says. "I mean, I've heard stories, but man, you look like twenty miles of rough road."

"A shower, a shave, a 55-gallon drum of Bactine, and I'll be just peachy. You do know that there are buildings in the way, right?"

"And stairs right there." She's right. Between two buildings there's a wide stairway that leads to a grassy area and then out to a parking lot.

She hits the stairs and gets air. The truck hits halfway down. Just ahead of us and off to the side is Werther, slowly picking himself up. He flew quite a bit when she hit him. Probably broke every bone in his body.

"Didn't I run him over?"

"You did. Thank you, by the way, now—"

"But he's standing like nothing happened."

"Magic. Is there nothing it can't do?"

We pass Werther, who's still trying to get his body back in order. All of his limbs are at funny angles as they reknit and rebuild themselves. His neck is cocked to the side in a way no neck ever should be.

He glares at me. I give him a big smile and wave.

"Okay, who was that?"

"I got a better question," I say. "Who are you?"

"You don't recognize me?"

"In my defense, people were shooting at me." Now that I get a really close look at her, I do recognize her. "Holy shit. Letitia?"

"That's Detective Letitia Watson to you, sunshine." She unclips a badge in a leather flip case from her belt and shows it to me. No shit.

Letitia Watson and I met in the equivalent of mage high school. Until we're old enough to not spontaneously set shit on fire, most mages are homeschooled. Then, to hopefully not have us all turn into a bunch of sociopathic little shits, which usually happens anyway, we go to school and learn to interact with other human beings.

Letitia and I weren't friends. We didn't know each other so much as knew of each other. Mage school is less Harry Potter and more boot camp. The important thing isn't to help you grow your magic, it's to help you not blow yourself up.

"Detective? You took a job as part of the Cleanup Crew?"

"Sort of," she says. "Not quite. And it's voluntary. Somebody needs to fix the messes people like you make. It's in all our best interests." I'm about to say that she sounds like a brochure when we hit the bottom of the stairs and bounce into a football field, the truck's tires blowing out chunks of sod behind.

Mages give a fat fuck about the normals' business until we have to. If too many normals really believed in magic, they might want what we've got, and we're not into sharing. We don't want too much out in the open.

But that's unavoidable. So some of us go into jobs to help keep this shit under wraps. Police, politics, journalism. They spend a lot of time covering the tracks of fuck-ups.

If that doesn't get the fuck-up to pull their head out of their ass, you'll see one of the rare times mages work together, and that's to curb stomp that motherfucker into paste.

Huh. I just realized. Today, I'm that motherfucker.

"Who the hell did I run over?"

"Attila Werther," I say. Her eyes go wide.

"Oh."

"Yeah."

"Do you think he saw me?"

"No, but I'm sure he can find you. I mean, it's Werther. And he's looking for me. And I'm with you, so . . ."

She slams her hand on the steering wheel. We tear through a chain-link fence and into the school's parking lot. The parking lot that's completely filled with cars.

"Goddammit," she says. "This whole thing was not supposed to go this way. You have your seatbelt on, right?"

"You're asking me now, after we did a Dukes of Hazzard down the stairs?" I pull the seatbelt across my chest and click it in, wincing. The crash in the Caddy's left some serious bruises where the seatbelt caught me. Maybe I'll get lucky and get a matching set on the other side now. The Bruise Bandolier. All the cool outlaws will be wearing them this year.

"I figured now's a good time," she says, "since we're probably gonna crash."

# Chapter 7

**We don't crash.** Not as such.

We carom off bumpers, slam into car after car. Headlights shatter, alarms go off. But the truck's built to take abuse and Letitia is giving it plenty. We slam a swath through the sea of cars and hit the driveway leading out to James M Wood Boulevard.

I've never understood naming streets after people. Wood was some big-time L.A. union leader in the seventies nobody remembers. You're dead now, congratulations. Have a street.

Letitia slows down before getting on the road and merging with the rest of the cars. Like she's trying to blend in. Good luck with that.

"Where the hell did you get this monster truck, anyway?"

"Stole it off the street." She doesn't look happy with the admission.

"Tsk. And you a police officer."

"That's just my day job."

Behind us we can hear sirens. Whatever magic Werther was doing to keep everyone away from our little imbroglio must have shut down once Letitia bounced him into the air with the truck.

A few blocks further on I say, "So what now?" I'm wondering why Letitia is here. Why she came to my rescue. And how she knew I was here in the first place. I'm still not convinced I haven't jumped from one fire into another.

"If any of Werther's people are looking for us we'll lose them in heavier traffic then ditch the car," Letitia says.

"Wasn't what I was asking, but it's kinda moot at the moment."

"Why?"

"Because they're about half a block behind us." She searches the rearview until she sees Werther's three cars.

"Shit." She slams on the gas and shoves her way through the traffic. She pops the curb, mowing down parking meters until she finds a clearer patch of road and really guns it.

Car chases in L.A. are both fun to watch and pointless to be in, so they're already one up on golf. Nobody actually gets away in a car chase.

First, you're gonna get helicopters on you, mostly news crews. Then there's L.A.'s roads. They're not exactly easy to navigate. Some are laid out in grids along old Rancho property lines, others are leftovers from when a neighborhood was an entirely different city that got swallowed up by L.A., and still others look perfectly fine until you realize they curve to avoid the river and you're heading back the way you came.

Eventually it comes down to the question, do you stay on some shitty little side street that might dead-end around the next corner, or hit the freeway? Never hit the freeway. Oh, sure you can go faster, for a bit. People get out of your way once they see the lights of the cop cars chasing you, but gridlock is gridlock and no amount of panicking behind the wheel is going to make that change. And then what? You can't hide on the freeway. Too many eyes on you.

Everybody is watching your poor decision-making skills play out on television, smartphones, computers. They're taking bets on when you're going to crash, filling out their bingo cards with all the stupid shit you do.

The only reason the cops don't gun your ass down or ram your car is there are civilians in the way. Easier to stay on you and wait them out. The only way to win a car chase is to not get into one.

And Letitia knows it. So why is she doing it?

"Shit, shit, shit."

"Hey, officially nothing's happened yet," I say. "They're still back there, we're still up here. Keep it cool and we'll be fine. You've got to know some hidey-holes we can get to where they can't find us." I've never met a mage who doesn't have at least one.

"I don't," she says.

Until now, apparently.

"Okay then," I say.

"What about you?"

"Not near here, and not ones you'd want to go to."

"That's what I thought."

She turns right on Union and I can feel her cast a spell. She guns the engine, weaving in and out of traffic with more agility than this truck has any right to have.

"What are you doing?"

"I'm a cop," she says.

"And that's important how?"

"I can get more cops."

Of course. There's an LAPD station up here some-where. Which one? Rampart? Except.

"Are there more mages at Rampart?"

"Not as far as I know. I'm stationed at Central, and I'm the only one there. Werther won't try anything out in the open."

"Right. Because a basketball court at a Catholic school across the street from the ACLU and the police union is the definition of discretion."

"You don't think—"

"Yes, I do."

We're coming up on 6th Street and Letitia slows down. "Something's wrong," she says.

I can see that. Sometime in the last few seconds all of the cars and people have found better places to be. The street has become eerily silent.

"This is the same shit he did when he hit me. He's keeping all the normals clear. How much you want to bet that when we get to the station the parking lot'll be empty?"

Whatever Werther had done to drive the ghosts away, though, isn't happening. Wanderers and Echoes, a handful of Haunts tied to the street corners where they died. That gives me an idea.

"Speed up," I say. I haven't felt a draw on the pool. Hell, I didn't even feel Werther casting, so he's using his own power. Probably just to make some dickhead "look what I can do" point.

The most efficient way to not tax his reserves would be to center the spell around himself. He can keep the borders of the effect set and the only drain on him is maintenance. Which means as long as he's close by we've got no one to see us, and no one in our way.

Letitia guns the engine. The three cars have been keeping their distance even though there's no one between us and them. Now that we're putting on speed, they're moving closer, but still staying behind us.

With no one watching, all the rules of car chases have gone out the window, except one. He can still wait us out. The question is, can he keep the spell going longer than we have gas to keep driving?

"We want to end this, we need them to catch up," I say. I check the ammunition in the Browning. I've still got over half a magazine.

"Yeah, I figured that," Letitia says. "Only what happens when they do?"

"You're a mage," I say. "Do magic." I slide open the window at the back of the cab, and sight for the least expensive looking car, a BMW with blackout windows, and pop off a few rounds. Though none of them hit, and if any had it'd be a miracle, the formation breaks. The cars spread out.

I sight along the Browning's barrel at the same car. It's pulled to the left into the next lane. Instead of pulling the trigger, I focus on the car, weave a spell together, and let it loose.

"Bang," I say.

The front of the car explodes, throwing chunks of the engine out onto the street. With Werther concentrating on his mass go-away spell, any defenses he has covering the cars aren't going to be as strong. I figured putting some distance between them left the other cars out of the zone and wide open.

I try it again at the second car, which has just pulled into the lead, covering the third. The spell goes off fine, but about 30 feet behind them. They're close enough for Werther's protection spells.

"You got one?" Letitia asks.

"Yeah. But the other two are still on us." The seeds of an idea start to grow. "Hold on to something in case this doesn't work."

"In case what doesn't work?"

I target the street just behind the truck's tailgate and in front of the lead car. I let off the same spell. The explosion happens in mid-air outside the defenses, and the lead car drives right into it. Flames blow out the windows, thick, black smoke billowing out. A couple tires blow, putting the burning car into a skid. It careens away onto the sidewalk and slams into a bus stop. I don't see anybody get out.

Werther must have decided that this shit won't stand because the remaining car, a jet-black Mercedes SUV, shoots forward. Letitia maneuvers the truck, trying to keep it behind us, but the truck handles like a slug, and in no time the Mercedes is alongside.

"Keep driving," I say. "Don't turn, don't slow down. I'll be right back."

I focus on the truck's door hinges with a spell, blowing them out. The door rattles in the frame for a second and then falls out onto the street, almost hitting the Mercedes.

"What the hell are you doing?"

"Just keep driving."

I have enough power to pull this off, but it doesn't hurt to top up the tanks, and it'll get Werther looking in the wrong direction. I draw in as much energy as I can. As soon as he notices he does the same, trying to block me from the source.

With his attention split between his spells and his attempt to lock me out, everything he's doing is going to take a hit. The next spell, I cast on myself. I feel the palms of my hands shift.

I jump out of the truck, reaching for the roof of the Mercedes. My left hand hits, sticking like a gecko, my right missing by a few inches. But those inches mean I'm hanging off the side. My left shoulder feels like it's on fire, and I can feel the hot wetness of blood spreading into my shirt from popped stitches. I pull myself up onto the roof just as the window rolls down and bullets come out. I'm hoping Werther likes his Mercedes too much to punch holes through the roof.

I've done this spell hundreds of times, but this particular way only once. I ended up losing the Cadillac for over a year when I did it, but I was weaker then.

I focus on cold, empty streets, dark skies, the howl of oblivion, images running through my brain like high speed film. I reach out my senses until I can feel the entire car below me, and let the spell loose.

The air shatters in between heartbeats with a noise like a jet engine fucking a wood chipper. Day goes to twilight in a split second and the air turns cold and sucks away at my energy.

I can't see Letitia's truck anymore, though I can see a bright glow speeding alongside us that's Letitia herself. The only solid items on this side are things that have been around long enough to imprint on the place. Most of the buildings are missing, and the few that aren't have been there for decades. I can't stay long because the environment will kill me, not to mention the ghosts, whose attention we've already gotten.

I thump on the roof with my fist. "Welcome to the land of the dead," I yell. "The premier tourist destination for assholes like you. Whattaya think? Like it?" They answer with a few shots through the roof that come a little too close for my taste.

"Well, if you're gonna be that way about it, I'll just

leave y'all to your business." I reverse the spell, jumping from the car at the last moment before shifting back.

I don't bring Werther's car with me.

Jet engine noise, bright, blinding sunlight, and I slam into the side of the truck. My gecko hands snag on the edge of the cab and the side of the truck bed, legs dangling dangerously close to the ground. I hook one leg up into the cab and Spider-Man my way from the back of the cab to fall into the seat.

Letitia stares at me. "Where did they go?"

"Somewhere else," I say. My breath is ragged. I haven't had to do shit like that for a long time. It was easier than I expected it to be. Well, the spell was.

My body, however, feels like I've gone a couple rounds with a bear. Pretty sure my arm is bleeding again, and my hands ache from hanging off the cars.

"Are they coming back?"

"Guy like Werther? Count on it. But we have more important things to talk about." I draw the Browning and shove the barrel into Letitia's side. "You want to tell me what the hell you're doing here, Letitia? I'd hate to have to kill you before I find out what's going on."

# Chapter 8

**Letitia keeps her eyes** on the road and doesn't say anything. I push the gun harder into her side. I'm running out of patience and I'm not in the mood for anyone's bullshit.

"Either you're thinking of how much to tell me, how to tell it to me, or coming up with a whopper of a lie. If you go with Option C, I'll know. And then I'll just shoot you. I might even shoot you just because I assume you're going to pick Option C anyway."

"After I saved your life?"

"Very conveniently, too. You just happened to be in that spot at that time with a stolen truck. You've changed, Letitia. I don't recall you having a taste for larceny."

"Yeah, I've changed," she says. "You haven't."

"I've changed plenty," I say. "Got my anger management issues under control and everything." She raises an eyebrow in disbelief. "If I hadn't, I'd have shot you already. Now talk, or I might have a relapse."

"You've been getting a lot of people's attention lately. Not all of them want to kill you."

"That's a relief. I can rest easy knowing that it's only most people who want to kill me. But you're part of the

Cleanup Crew. If everybody else is gunning for me, it's in your best interest to do the same. So how come you aren't? If you're one of the people who doesn't want to kill me, why?"

"Me, and a couple of . . . associates . . . have a proposition for you. Mutually beneficial. I was trailing you since you left the warehouse. When I saw what was happening, I swapped cars and came to help. By that time Werther was already doing his thing, and I couldn't think of anything to do but run him over."

"A woman after my own heart," I say. "Mutually beneficial, huh? Okay, I'll bite. What's the offer?"

She shakes her head. "We need the others. I only know the gist of it. They've got the details."

"All right, let's start with the gist, then."

"We know who's framing you and we want to help you get her."

That was unexpected.

"Her?"

"No," she says. "No more questions until we get there."

"Where is there?"

"David Chu's house." She says it like it should mean something to me.

"Never heard of him."

"L.A. City Council? Running for mayor? Nothing?"

"You're making noises with your mouth, but I'm not sure you're actually speaking English."

"Jesus," she says, shaking her head. "You don't pay much attention to the world around you, do you?"

"I figure the world can take care of itself. Mostly I'm focusing on not dying. I'm not a fan of mage politics. Tends to get you dead. Goes against my core ethos of not dying."

"You're not going to have a choice," she says.

"Dying? Eventually, sure. But that sounds like a threat," I say, looking at the gun in my hand. "What do you think Mister Trigger Finger? Does it sound like a threat to you? Mister Trigger Finger thinks that sounds like a threat."

"Maybe Mister Trigger Finger needs to reel it in a bit and calm the fuck down. Jesus, how has nobody murdered you yet?"

"Oh, you know. That which does not kill me needs to up its game."

"I'm talking about politics. Like it or not, you're political just by being you. People know about that earthquake a couple years back, about the Bruja's hotel burning down, about the people who died on the train. Stories are coming out of Mexico. Dead cartel leaders, heroin distribution lines cut. Sounds like you put a dent in the Mexican drug market just by being there. But that's not the most interesting thing."

"Oh, what is?" I don't like this. People are keeping tabs on me. I don't like being tracked and I don't like being talked about.

"Bullshit stories about gods and goddesses. Love triangles. Real telenovela stuff. Nice wedding band by the way," she says. "I can't wait to see what the kids look like."

"We haven't really discussed it," I say. "You know, newlyweds." Interesting. She's digging. There are rumors but nothing that people are believing just yet. Well, some people.

"You're seriously expecting me to buy that you're married to a goddess?"

Belief's a weird thing with people, normals and mages alike. We can accept all sorts of weird shit, but you go just one step too far and they're all like, "Nope.

Don't buy it. I can believe in amazing cosmic powers that can bend reality to my will, demons, spirits, horrors from the spaces between time. But an invisible man in the sky who grants wishes and judges me based on how many times I've masturbated is where I draw the line."

"Am I? Huh. She told me she was a stripper from Tijuana."

She gives me this look that I can't quite decipher. Horror, acceptance, nausea. Then she pulls it back. "I hope they don't take after their mother."

"I dunno. You haven't seen her pole dance."

"I know it's bullshit," she says, but she sounds a little deflated. "A lot of people know it's bullshit. But there are plenty of gullible assholes out there who believe. They think you're some kind of king of the dead making zombie armies."

"Yeah, I heard that one earlier today. But then we necros hear a lot of shit about ourselves. Did you know we eat babies and have sex with the dead? I mean, I don't, but everybody says we do. There was one guy in New Orleans, though. He was pretty into necrophilia."

"You joke, but whether they believe it or not doesn't matter. You're seen as either a threat or someone they want on their side. The fact that you've been in L.A. as long as you have and haven't aligned yourself with anybody makes you ripe for recruitment."

That's funny. Align myself with a group? The closest I'm aligned with would be Gabriela, and that's more a mutual "watch each other's back to make sure if anybody's sticking a knife in it we're the ones who put it there." Nobody would give me the goddamn time of day and now they want to shoot me on sight.

"What's that thing Groucho said? I wouldn't be a member of any club that would have me? I'm not much of a joiner. And neither are the rest of us. You know what they call five mages in a room together, right? A bloodbath. I don't think Werther was trying to recruit me."

Interesting, though. Worrying if true, I'm not really up for being used as a pawn. Again. Not least of which because they're wrong. I fucked up Santa Muerte's and Mictlantecuhtli's plans. I'm not the king of dead. At least, not anymore. I think.

And that bit about the bloodbath? Pretty much how it always works out. The really powerful mages, they don't want to share and they're really good at not sharing.

"It also makes you ripe for elimination," she says. "You don't have a great track record of not being in the middle of shit when it happens. A lot of people remember Boudreau, and some of the shit you got up to before you left L.A. And some shit after you left. Married to a death goddess? Not a big leap to assume you're burning people alive."

"What, I'm the boogeyman now? Come on. 'Go to sleep son, or Eric Carter's gonna get ya.' I'm a goddamn teddy bear."

"We know you're not doing it. We can help you with the situation. Get people like Werther off your back. That's at least worth listening to, isn't it?"

I admit, it would be nice to have people not shooting at me quite so often, but let's be honest, they're going to anyway. If I jump in with anybody, eventually they're gonna try to kill me. Letitia's group, Gabriela, somebody else. It's not something with good odds as a long-term prospect.

But it can't hurt to talk, can it? If there's evidence that this Councilman Chu has that I'm not setting all these fires, maybe people will calm the fuck down.

"All right, Scarecrow, let's go see the Wizard."

———

Councilman Chu lives in Encino. Letitia tries to tell me about his district, its borders, and all I can picture is reproducing amoeba, which, this being L.A., somehow seems to fit. But then she won't shut up about it and my eyes glaze over and I finally have to tell her to stop talking or I'll shoot her.

Chu lives in the hills above Ventura Boulevard among the twisting side streets where the houses are hidden by overgrown ivy and shade trees that have been there since the thirties.

We ditched the truck. It was a little conspicuous, what with the dented, blood-covered hood and the missing passenger door. The thought of stealing another car made Letitia a little sick, so I took that hit. A snap of the fingers, a little bit of magic, and we were on the road in a gray Honda Accord in no time flat.

She's not sure what to do with me. I'm giving off mixed signals by keeping the gun in my hand with a round in the chamber, but the safety on. I might shoot her. I might not. Who can tell? Certainly not me. I haven't made up my mind, yet.

She pulls onto a tiny side street off of Hayvenhurst and onto a steep driveway. At the top it widens into a circular patch outside a two-story mansion with a three-car garage. One car, a nice, but not too nice, Volkswagen SUV sits to one side. Letitia pulls up the Honda behind it and parks.

"Real man of the people, this Mister Chu. So down to Earth and humble. How many bedrooms does this place have? Five? Six?" Don't get me wrong, I've got nothing against money. I'm a fan of money. I steal it whenever I get a chance.

But I'm not a fan of the rich. I don't know if it's irony, chutzpah, or my own Holier-Than-Thou-Angry-Young-Man shtick that's let me ignore the fact that I'm just as much the privileged, moneyed elite as this guy, but since I found out I've inherited more money than I can count, it's harder to lie to myself.

Money, like magic, is power. And like any power, you can do something cool with it, or you can wave it in everybody's face like a drunken frat boy swinging his cock around. I don't know this Councilman Chu, but I already don't like him.

"He's one of us," she says, as though it explains everything. Sadly, it pretty much does. With so many mages it's all about power, presentation, influence. Anyone worth a damn wouldn't be living in a series of motels across the city like I do. They'd buy property, cement their positions, grow their network.

There's that annoying cognitive dissonance again.

"Who owns the krautwagon?" I nod toward the VW. It's clearly not Chu's. Too shabby, no flash and dazzle. This is a car that actually gets used, probably for a commute.

"Peter Sloane. He's an Assistant District Attorney."

"What? No circuit court judges? Senators? The President? And I thought this was a professional circus." We get to the door and she rings the doorbell. "You don't need the gun," she says.

"Probably not, but it gives me a warm, fuzzy feeling."

The door opens up to a young man in a blue pinstripe suit. Blond, mid-twenties, one of those smiles always plastered on a politician's face. He steps to the side, waving us in.

"Mister Carter," he says. "It's nice to finally meet

you. I'm Peter." He puts out his hand to shake and then notices the gun in mine. "Oh. I see. I imagine you must have some questions."

"You could say that." He might be an ADA, but everything about him screams mook. Whatever he is in this line-up, he's expendable help. You can almost smell the redshirt on him.

"Hopefully we can give you satisfactory answers."

"For your sake, I hope so, too." He turns the smile up a couple thousand watts, but I'm not buying it. If Letitia and Chu are mages, I'm sure Peter is, too. Privilege, money, and power give people a confidence they don't deserve. I should know.

I don't know how powerful he is, or what his knack might be, but I'm pissed off enough not to care. If I have to beat the crap out of Chu and these two, I will and I won't look back.

I follow Letitia and Peter into a cavernous foyer and on to a living room that looks like an old Victorian gentlemen's club. Bar on one side, a group of thick, leather-upholstered chairs around a coffee table.

David Chu gets up from one of the chairs. Tall, Asian, a Mister Rogers sweater, and movie star good looks that I assume he intends to convey honesty and youthful energy. To me it makes me think of those deep-sea fish that are all teeth and a glowing lure to pull in other fish to eat them.

"Mister Carter," he says. "I'm so glad you could make it. I hope your drive over was uneventful." He doesn't try to shake my hand, seeing the gun and taking it in stride.

"Some gunfire, some magic, some people dead. You know the drill."

"Sadly, I do," he says. "I was Downtown during the riots helping protect businesses from looting." He raises the t-shirt under his sweater and I can see a couple of puckered scars from what look like bullets, a surgery scar up to his belly button, and one that looks like a bad burn.

"I lost about a foot of my large intestine and a kidney," he says. "Some of our people took advantage of the chaos to try breaking into other mages' homes, labs, and hiding places. There was a lot of fighting. And a lot of dying."

"I remember," I say. The riots sucked for everybody, and of course all the magic types decided it was the perfect time to act on old grudges, grab territory, remove rivals. "Shit happens."

"Indeed, it does. Have a seat. Can I get you a drink?"

"Nah, I'm good." I gesture with the gun and Letitia and Peter get the hint and sit in a couple of other leather chairs. I stay standing.

"Tish? Peter?"

"I could use an iced tea," Peter says, as if having a suspected arsonist waving a gun around happens to him all the time.

"Nothing for me," Letitia says. "Thanks." There's a tremor in her voice, but I don't think it's fear. At least not fear of me. One of her "colleagues"?

"He killed Attila Werther," she says.

Chu raises his eyebrow. "Really? Now that's a feat."

I wave it off. "He's not dead. He's just someplace he doesn't want to be. He's a smart boy, he'll figure a way out before he gets eaten."

"Your mercy knows no bounds," Chu says. Two glasses slide into the room hovering at about waist height. They float down to rest on the coffee table, coasters sliding out from a stack to catch them. It's showing off. It's a little thing, but I get the feeling that Chu's the sort of guy who'd use a handshake to assert dominance, or some such bullshit.

He showed me his, it'd only be polite that I do the same. But I resist the urge to slip over to the other side and pop out behind him with my straight razor.

"I notice you don't seem to have a lot of wards covering this place," I say. I felt a few when I walked through the door, but nothing impressive. Mostly low-level alarm type stuff. Nothing that would fry an intruder's brain, say, or melt their eyeballs in their sockets.

He shrugs. "If I'm not here I don't much care, and if I am, well, I handle it myself." That tells me pretty much everything I need to know about this guy.

I holster the Browning. There's no point keeping it out. If things get hairy it's all going to be tossing spells at each other. If I'm reading him right, keeping it out is just going to be seen as a weakness, and that leads to the kind of fallout that's more of a pain in the ass than I'm really up for right now.

"All right," I say. "I'm here. I'm told you had a proposition for me."

"You spent some time in Mexico recently," Chu says. "I hear you caused quite a stir with some of the cartels. Must have made some enemies."

"Oh, you have no idea."

"Why did you do it?" Peter says. He takes a sip of his tea, blue eyes locked on me like missiles.

"Since I was in Mexico, I figured I'd murder a bunch of cartel assholes." Letitia gives me another one of those looks like back in the car, like she doesn't want to believe me, but does, anyway.

"But why did you go to Mexico?"

"To murder a bunch of cartel assholes." Now Letitia smiles and leans forward. I can see the cop in her eyes. I get the feeling that she's very good at her job.

"You don't need to tell us if you don't want to," Peter says.

"So glad to have your permission. We were talking about enemies."

"Have you heard the name Jacqueline Sastre?" Chu says. Shit. Now it starts to make sense.

"La Niña Quemada," I say. "Yeah. I heard about her in Mexico. She kills a lot of people. She's really good at it."

# Chapter 9

"Jacqueline Sastre's a high priced sicaria, an assassin, for the cartels," I say. "They call her The Burning Girl, La Niña Quemada. She's very good at what she does. She'll do the beheadings, the sniper attacks, garroting, whatever. But she really likes to set people on fire. Last I heard she was working for Cartel del Golfo."

I also heard that she's a demon or a Bruja, but I'm doubtful. The Federales can't catch her because the ones who aren't corrupt are incompetent as fuck. They named her after a couple dozen burnings and the demon/Bruja story stuck.

Chu manifests a thick manila folder in the air in front of him. It glides over to my side of the table and I have a really hard time not rolling my eyes. Dude. Just use your fucking hands.

I open the folder to a series of reports and photos from various agencies and police departments in Mexico and the U.S. In the most recent photos, she's a bottle-blond, light-skinned Latina, tall, with dancer's legs and model looks. She's been at this job for only a few years as far as anyone has evidence. They say she started as some narco's girlfriend, and when he wouldn't kill the snitch his betters told him to, she picked up a gun and put two in the snitch's head herself. Then she put two in her boyfriend.

From that point on, the story goes, she gets plenty of work. Young, pretty, charming, ruthless. For a while she specialized in killing cartel rivals in what you'd think are safe places, their homes, their clubs, their beds. Nobody checks you for weapons if they know you're blowing the boss.

The photos show the progression of both her career and her inevitable jump off the deep end. Cartel violence is brutal, cruel, and messy, but she really cranks it up to eleven.

I've seen worse than what's in these photos, but man, this is some harsh shit. Beheaded bodies hanging from meat hooks off freeway signs, coolers filled with body parts, severed heads with the victims' genitals stuffed in their mouths.

A few of the reports talk about Santa Muerte, how police think Sastre worships her. The thought fills me with an anger I can't quite place. Yeah, I know I went to Mictlan to kill her and all, but at least I didn't make up some Satanic Panic bullshit about her.

Or maybe I'm angry for another reason that I don't really want to look at.

Then we get to the bodies that gave her her name. Corpses in barred cells burned down to blackened bones, elaborate tables covered in thick metal straps holding half-burned bodies, eyes wide, faces contorted in agony. She didn't just kill people, she hunted them down, caged them, tortured them with fire and burned the skin off their bodies until they couldn't take anymore.

A more recent set of photos have names at the bottom in letters made on a label maker and stuck to the prints.

When some of the names are people I've heard of, Travis Niesler, LeAnna Bruce, Joy Bennett, I know they're the mages she murdered. There are others I recognize, more for their last names than their first, members of L.A.'s more influential mage families.

Like all the others, their corpses are barely recognizable as human. Ash and split bone, cracked teeth scattered like popcorn kernels. If I went to each of these places, would I see their ghosts? Could any of them talk to me? Maybe, maybe not. I doubt they'd have anything useful to tell me other than how much it hurt.

The final page is a zoomed-in surveillance photo from a month ago showing Sastre after she's just crossed the border into San Diego. She's smoking a cigarette and smiling at the camera.

Considering how many watch lists she's on it's a little surprising. Looks like the person who compiled this file felt the same way. There's a Post-it note stuck to it that says "WTF?? HOW DID THIS GET MISSED?" They don't understand. They never will. But I do.

My eyes hang on her, her just-lit cigarette, her brazen attitude. I close the folder. "Fascinating stuff," I say. "But how do you know she did it? I see the corpses, I see a picture of her coming in through San Diego, but that's it. What do you have linking the two?" I'm fishing. Curious to see what they know, what they don't.

"Witness reports," Letitia says. "You hear about a warehouse club fire last weekend?"

"Must have missed it."

"Sixteen dead, sixty-four injured. We talked to over a hundred people trying to figure out what happened. The details are sketchy on when and in what order, but they all roughly match up. A woman came into the club, shot a girl in the head, then lit her on fire."

"But how—" Letitia cuts me off by shoving her phone in my face. There's Sastre in the background of someone's selfie. And another. And another. And another. Letitia scrolls her finger, zipping through photo after photo. She's shot from multiple angles in dim light and bright. Photobombing selfie after selfie as she makes her way toward her target.

Thank fuck for Millennials.

I already know that she did it. It was that last photo in the folder, the one taken at the border crossing. She had that taken for my benefit, because I'm the only one who'd know what it meant. Standing there, defiant, looking into the camera, smoking a cigarette.

Which she had lit with a battered Zippo inlaid with an elaborate jade and turquoise pattern on its side. I know that lighter. It's the one Quetzalcoatl gave me to burn down Mictlan. The lighter holding Xiuhtecuhtli's fire.

"The girl she shot and burned," I say. I think back to the photos. Most looked to be in houses, or on sidewalks, but only one looked like it happened in a warehouse. Takes me a second to remember the name. "Amanda Werther, right? What's her relation?"

"Attila Werther's granddaughter," Chu says.

"Wait a second. I don't get it. If there's all this photo evidence, why the fuck does Werther think I killed his granddaughter? And everybody else?"

"First of all, he doesn't. Not about his granddaughter," Peter says. "He's seen these selfies. He knows it was a woman. He just hasn't made a connection to the rest of the murders, yet. Second, he hasn't seen the rest of the file. We're part of the Cleanup Crew. It was easy to copy photos off phones and the internet and wipe them clean."

"We wanted to isolate this and find the murderer before Werther and the big families got involved," Chu says. "There would have been a bloodbath. The last thing we need are mages trying to kill each other in the streets of Los Angeles."

"Yeah, because that never happens," I say.

"Look," Letitia says. "We didn't make the connection at first. Everybody figured it was a rivalry, and as far as the Werthers and anyone outside this room knows, it was. Nobody thinks you did that one."

"But they think I did all the rest? Then give them all this and get them the fuck off my back."

"We can't do that," Chu says. "If we do, then whatever plan she's got either goes down the drain or is accelerated. And given her predilection with magical fire, we'd really rather not push her into lighting up the whole city."

"Fuck you," I say standing up and heading toward the door, the folder in my hands. "Fuck all of you." I get to the door and the folder evaporates into smoke.

"That's not going to work," Chu says. "The folder's merely a projection. The real one is in a safe place."

"Why are you doing this?"

"Because you're the perfect bait," Chu says. "She clearly wants to make your life miserable and she can't keep killing people and expect that no one's going to figure it out eventually. I don't know if she's hoping you'll be dead by then, or if she has something else in mind. But if we want to keep people safe, we have to draw her out."

"I'm wondering how you're gonna spin this into campaign rhetoric. You do know that most of L.A. isn't made up of mages, right?"

"Is it wrong of me to want to save my city?" he says.

"No. But that's not what you're doing," I say. "You want to hang me out to dry and use this to get a feather in your cap among the mage families. Even if you lose the mayoral election because the normals don't vote for you, you're going to get more respect from them. And they've got a lot more power at their disposal."

"Eric, if there are any personal benefits, they're all incidental. We're trying to save lives."

"Then where's everybody else?"

"Excuse me?" Chu says.

"There are only three of you. If you saw this as a city-wide problem, you'd be calling in the big guns. And why you three? What the hell got you together? I can see you and the lawyer connecting, but what's with Letitia?"

"We met at—" Letitia starts.

"That's not what I mean."

"There are only three of us because we're just getting started," Chu says. "We're looking for similarly minded individuals in the mage community that have different areas of expertise. As I'm sure you're aware, getting mages to do anything is like training a toddler to poop on command. So, we're taking things slow. But if we had a group of people in various positions of respect among both normals and mages, imagine what we could do. We could unite—Is there something funny about this?"

I can hardly breathe I'm laughing so hard. "Oh my god, you're trying to make a Mage Council."

"What we're doing is important," Peter says, his pale cheeks going red with anger.

"You know why there's no high organization of mages?" I say. "Because they always fuck it up. The last time they tried that shit out here was in the 80s. Some of the most powerful mages in the city. Best of intentions."

"What happened to them?" Letitia says.

"They disbanded," Chu says, waving it off.

"That's a nice way of saying they all murdered each

other," I say. "Backstabbing started almost immediately as everybody vied for control, made alliances to undercut the others. Within three months the killings started. By the fourth they were all dead."

"How do you know this?" Peter says.

"My parents were asked to join. They declined."

"If I recall," Chu says, "they tried to organize the big families themselves against Jean Boudreau."

"And we all know how that turned out. They were idealists. Idealists get killed. You three want to start yourselves a little magic circle jerk, knock yourself out. But if you want to use me to raise your profile, you can fuck right the hell off."

I slam the door on my way out. I start the car I stole with a spell and turn to head down the driveway. I don't get very far before Letitia runs out after me. Against my better instincts, I stop and roll down the window.

"Get away from these people, Letitia. They're gonna get you killed."

"Look, I know what you're thinking because I've thought it, too. And you're right, what they're trying to do is going to end up looking like the Bolsheviks raiding the Winter Palace. But there's a reason I'm here, and we—I need your help."

Letitia and I never knew each other well. Different circles, different friends. But when high school is 50 hormonal kids all capable of leveling the building when they have a tantrum, they force you to hang out with each other and learn to cope.

You can't avoid cliques, but if you can get people to stand being in the same room together, there's a better chance nobody gets turned inside out because somebody didn't get a Valentine's Day card.

Plus, she stabbed me in class, and once somebody

sticks a knife in you, you gain a whole new respect for them. I may not know her well, but I know her well enough that I don't think she's lying to me.

"What do you want me to do? I'm not gonna be bait. I'm not their fucking puppet."

"I know that. Can I show you something? It'll explain a lot."

"I've got half the mages in the city coming for my head. I don't have time."

"It'll be an hour, maybe two tops."

"Fine. Get in." I pop the door open and she slides into the passenger seat. "Where are we going?"

"Home," she says.

# Chapter 10

**Letitia's house in Burbank** is one of the ubiquitous single-story bungalows that fill the Southland. A sort of yellow-creme color with white trim. Big bay window, a garden filled with rose bushes lining the lawn. It's . . . cute.

There are a lot of words I could use to describe Letitia. Angry, capable, vaguely Amazonian. She used to wear steel-toed boots and a green army-surplus trench coat in high school, her head shaved in a mohawk. But cute? Never.

"That's, uh . . . a nice place," I say. "Don't take this the wrong way, but it doesn't exactly scream you."

"People change, Eric."

"You telling me you don't still have a pair of curb-stompers sitting in your closet for special occasions?"

She smiles at that. "Yeah, okay. Maybe I haven't changed that much." Her face gets serious. "But I've changed enough. And that's what I want to show you."

I pull into the driveway and we get out. The sky is an angry yellow haze, thick with smoke. With so many nearby brushfires, I can't tell which one I'm smelling. Griffith Park? Wildwood Canyon? Verdugo Mountains? Flames peek over the tops of the hills while helicopters and tanker planes fly overhead. In the distance I watch a plane dump a couple thousand gallons of red flame retardant over Verdugo. I wonder how effective that's actually going to be.

Letitia unlocks the front door, and it's yanked open from the other side by a short Filipino woman with bobbed hair, high cheekbones, and a scowl on her face that could melt steel.

"Annie," Letitia says, surprised. She looks behind her into the street. "Where's your car?"

"In the shop. Which you'd know if you'd read any of your fucking texts. Where the fuck is yours?"

"At the station," Letitia says. She waves at the stolen car behind us. "This one's for undercover work." The lie flows out of her like water.

Annie narrows her eyes, but doesn't question it. Then she turns her scathing look onto me. "Who the fuck is this?"

"He's from the Police Commission. I told you they're riding my ass."

"I am," I say, trying hard not to make it a question. "Routine ride-along. All good."

"Now I have to get some stuff," Letitia says, "but tonight we'll talk."

"You've been saying that for the last three weeks," Annie says. "I'm tired of the secrets. I'm tired of the dancing around the subject. You tell me what's going on tonight, or I'm gone."

"Oh, baby, don't be like that."

"Don't fucking 'baby' me." She turns her glare my way. "You."

"Uh, yeah? Me?" I say. I'm staying as far away from this conversation as I can. I can twist reality into knots, command the dead, and walk in the twilight lands, but domestic squabbles? Fuck if I'm getting in the middle of that.

"You gonna tell me what's going on?" Annie says. "You've been her excuse for a month and a half now. Are you fucking her?"

"Whoa, hang on. No. No no no. Look, you want the truth?" Letitia freezes, eyes growing wide as I keep talking.

"Magic. It's simple. I'm a necromancer. Letitia just saved my ass from a hit squad for some pissed off mages that were trying to kill me because they think I've been murdering people by lighting magical fires. People trying to kill me isn't actually all that unusual. Kind of par for the course, really. In fact, Letitia tried it in high school. That's how we know each other. High school. She stuck a big old butcher knife right in my back. Skimmed off a rib, so it wasn't too bad.

"I probably deserved it. I'd been drinking and raising dead squirrels to run up girls' skirts. I was an asshole back then. Anyway, she's brought me here to prove to me why I should trust her now after all this time, and I think the reason might be you." I stick my hand out to shake. "Hi, Annie, my name's Eric."

Annie stares at me, that scowl never leaving her face. "You think you're pretty fucking funny, don't you?"

"Frequently," I say.

She turns her attention back to Letitia. "This guy's an asshole. I don't like being made fun of. Now I got an Uber coming to pick me up in two minutes and I'm going to meet it at the end of the block. Because I don't want to fucking see you right now. Tonight. We talk. And if I don't like your answers I am out the door. You understand me?"

"Yes," Letitia says, voice quiet.

"You know I love you, but I can't do the secrets." She pushes past us, stalking out of the house.

I turn and wave at her. "Ta!" She answers me with two immaculately manicured middle fingers.

"I don't think she likes me much," I say.

"I am going to fucking kill you." She stalks inside the house and I follow, closing the door behind me. I notice discreet wards carved into the threshold, the door jamb, next to the windows. The magic coming off them is surprisingly loud. I felt them a little from the street, but now that I'm inside it's like a constant hum of white noise. She's got this place locked up tight, and the wards very well hidden.

"You're with a normal."

"I almost wasn't thanks to you."

"You live with this woman and you've managed to keep magic a secret from her? I'm impressed. There are plenty of normals who know about us. Why not just tell her?"

"That's a stupid question," she says.

It is, but I'm genuinely curious. We all have our reasons to hide ourselves from the rest of humanity. Some of them are better than others. Magic isn't something you tell just anybody about. Not only because we try to keep a tight lid on that shit, but because it's dangerous. Normals and mages are complicated.

Take my sister, for example. Lucy had next to no power in an influential family of mages. All that did was paint a target on her back. We hid her away like Bertha in Jane Eyre. Changed her name, made up a bullshit story that she was an orphan our parents had taken in. We distanced ourselves in public as much as possible from her.

If you're with a normal you have two choices. You can keep them safe, or you can tell them the truth. I prefer option three. Don't get involved with them in the first place.

"Okay," I say. "So why don't you cut her loose?"

"I—Goddammit." She throws herself onto the living room couch.

"She's your reason, though, right? That's why you want me to help? You're afraid your girlfriend's gonna get caught up in this."

"My wife," Letitia says. "I wasn't expecting her to be here. I was going to show you our wedding albums, and tell you about her and—Fuck!" She slams her hand down on the arm of the couch.

"Annie's all I've got," she says. "I can do my job with the normals, I can do my job as part of the Cleanup Crew. But I can't fucking do it if I don't have somewhere to come back to where I'm not constantly reminded about all of it."

"I can understand that," I say. "But you made a choice, and there are consequences. Trust me, I know all about consequences. You think Sastre's going to come after her? Why?"

"We fit the profile," she says. "Everyone who's died has lived with one other person they're close to. A single father and his son, twin sisters, an adult daughter taking care of her grandmother. Even Werther. His granddaughter was the only family he had left here. Everyone else is in Europe waiting for him to bite it so they can loot his corpse. These are people who are so close to the victims it breaks them. If people actually stopped to think about it, they'd know this isn't what you'd do. People are after you because you're a convenient target for their grief. And nobody likes you much."

I sit in an easy chair across from her. "Shit." I wish I could say I think she's wrong. But she does fit the profile. And nobody likes me much.

"You're afraid Annie's going to be killed."

"Yeah," she says. "I don't know if I could go on without her. I've worked serial cases before, but I've never fit the victim profile."

"Leave town," I say. "Take an extended vacation. I did piss somebody off when I was down in Mexico, and if it were just some cartel boss I wouldn't be worried about it. If it was just Sastre coming after me, I wouldn't be worried about it. But there is more going on here than you know, and if you get in its way, you're gonna get hurt."

"Eric, this is my wife." She points to the ring on my finger, even though she's conspicuously missing one of her own. "You understand that, right? Help us," she says. "Help me."

If I laugh I'll have to explain my being railroaded into marriage with a death goddess and we'll be here all day.

"Okay, say I throw in with you and your politician buddies. What's the plan? And don't say to just do what I would normally do until she shows up, except that you'll be following me." She doesn't say anything. "It is, isn't it? Goddammit."

"But you'll be surveilled," she says. "And you'll have a wire. There will always be someone nearby, another mage."

Aside from the fact that having anybody looking over my shoulder freaks me out, what happens if Quetzalcoatl goes after whoever's watching me? And how do I know whoever she has watching me isn't blaming me for these murders too and takes a shot?

"No," I say. "It's a stupid plan. It'll get me killed, whoever is watching me killed, and probably several bystanders. I'll keep you updated when I find anything out, but it's better if nobody knows where I am."

My phone rings in my pocket, cutting off whatever she was about to say. It's Gabriela.

"A little bird told me you had a car accident on the way to see your honey bunny," Gabriela says.

"Please don't call her that," I say. "I'd like to keep my breakfast down. Yes, I did, and no, I haven't seen her yet. But I did find some things out." I fill her in on Sastre, taking care to circle around Quetzalcoatl, and the lighter.

"I take it you're not alone," she says, catching on.

"Ran into an old high school acquaintance. She helped fill in the blanks." Letitia gives me a questioning look, but I ignore her.

"And her knowing that gods are involved might not be prudent?"

"I'm still figuring that one out."

"Got it. Come on by the warehouse when you get a chance. All this Secret Squirrel shit over the phone gives me a headache."

"I'll see you later tonight."

"Who was that?" Letitia says as I slip my phone back in my pocket.

"A friend." I stand up, fighting a wave of dizziness as my heartrate jackrabbits for a second before calming down. Between the poison, the stab wound, having my car blown up behind me and doing moving car gymnastics, I think maybe I need to take a nap. Like that's gonna happen.

"I really can't convince you to let me put surveillance on you?" she says.

"No. But you'll try anyway. So, know this. If I find anybody tailing me I'll assume they're trying to kill me. Don't let it be one of your people."

# Chapter 11

**Sometimes you have to** take a moment to take stock. Look around, get clear on the things you have, the things you don't, for good or ill.

Things I have: a gun, a straight razor, a messenger bag holding the accouterments of my craft, a leather-bound ledger that has more secrets in it than I know what to do with, an assassin in league with a pissed off wind god, a shit-ton of corpses, mages who want to put me into the ground, a stab wound in my shoulder, and the lingering effects of a really nasty poison in my system.

Things I don't have: a lead.

I don't know where Sastre is, I don't know where she's going to strike next, I don't know which mages want my head on a stick, and I don't know when this fucking poison making my heart play bongos in my chest is going to finally run its course.

And I don't have my Cadillac. Pieces of it are sitting in a Catholic school basketball court, or being sent to storage for the police to comb over. I wonder what they'll find out about it.

Of all the shit that's happened today, that's the thing that pisses me off the most. I really liked that car. Now

I'm stuck in this shitty Honda that whines every time it shifts gears. Sure, the Cadillac wasn't mine to begin with, but I murdered a mage in Texas for it.

Okay, that sounds bad, but he was eating the souls of young Loa, Voodoo spirits, children really, and he had it coming.

Finding Sastre is my next step, but the question is how? I could summon some Wanderers, ask if they've seen anything, but that could take hours and might not get me anywhere. I doubt Gabriela's going to be much help on that front. She has informants and lackeys and some decent divination, but her street cred is in the shitter right now and she doesn't have the eyes and ears she used to, not to mention Q fucking with the divination airwaves.

I could go where I was originally going, to get an audience with Santa Muerte, whoever she is now, but I really don't want to. Asking favors of gods and spirits hasn't really worked out for me lately, and the last thing I want is to find myself in debt again.

I pull a tracking charm from my messenger bag, a small hematite pyramid carved with runes and hanging from a string. I used this in Mexico a few times. I don't know if it'll work, but what it does should at least give me a better idea of what I'm up against. Quetzalcoatl might have a lock on questions about the murders so everything points back to me, but how well is he hiding her? Does he know that I know about her?

If the charm can find her it will lift toward the direction she's in. If it doesn't, it won't do anything. If she's being shielded and it can't get a bead on her, it'll spin in slow circles.

I dangle it from the string and concentrate on Sastre. At first nothing, then it begins to slowly spin. Okay. That's good to know. He's got her protected from scrying.

The pyramid spins faster, cranking up the speed until it's a blur at the end of the string. It starts to glow red and the string catches fire. I open the driver's side door, almost slamming into a truck speeding by, and toss it out, where it goes up like a Roman candle.

Okay. That didn't work. She's got warding guarding her that's more powerful than the charm. Honestly not that tough. It's a pretty weak charm.

But that means I need some major mojo to punch through Q's tampering enough that I can get some useful information. I think I know where I might find something like that.

When my parents died, they left my sister and I property that neither one of us had ever heard of. I was gone just after the bodies were in the ground, and didn't find out about any of it until I got back from Mictlan. With my sister dead, everything came to me. Some houses, a piece of property in the Mojave that I haven't seen yet, storage units dotted across the Southland, and a ledger detailing everything in them. The ledger is a large leather-bound book filled with pages and pages of listings that read like a junkyard inventory in a Harry Potter fanfic.

It lists spell ingredients from the mundane to the esoteric: dried herbs, manticore teeth, bottles of chupacabra venom. Magical devices and thaumaturgical instruments, most of which I couldn't even tell you what they're for. Spirit bottles, summoning coins that don't list what they summon—always a bad idea—keys that open doors that only exist for seconds at a time. There are staves and wands. Wands. Nobody's used wands since the 19th century. It goes on and on.

I've skimmed the book. That's all I could do. It's the size of a folded Sunday newspaper from when newspapers mattered, three inches thick and a good five pounds.

I pull over to the curb, pull the ledger from my messenger bag, and flip on the car's overhead light. When I open it, it seems to have more pages than it should. It probably does. The handwriting on the pages is a spiderweb scrawl of tiny letters written by a dozen different hands. The fountain pen ink is faded to a grayish brown at the beginning. Then comes jet black ballpoint, typewritten notecards, and finally computer printouts pasted to the pages.

Pity the only organization it has is by date starting in the 1890s. There's no W for wands, A for amulets, or S for Shit That Will Kill You if You So Much as Look at It Funny. All of the items are scattered throughout the pages.

On the plus side, it lists everything's location. Storage unit addresses and numbers, safe deposit boxes and banks, GPS coordinates for things buried in the desert. Some have been updated two or three times as they were moved.

I remember seeing some items for locating lost things: amulets, a compass, a kewpie doll that spins its head in the direction of the thing you're looking for and screams. I turn pages until I get to the late 1940s, looking for the kewpie doll. Not the best for stealth, what with all the screaming, but that's the only one I can remember a date for. There are no entries between 1939 and 1946 during the war, and then a flood of items from late '47 to '52.

My eye snags on an entry. It's not what I'm looking for, but it's interesting nonetheless. The entry reads, "Browning 9mm Hi-Power—Nazi artifact—MELT DOWN ASAP—DO NOT LISTEN TO IT." That's slightly alarming. But there's nothing here that says why, or what it would say. As far as I can tell, the Browning just makes much bigger holes than normal, feels disgusting to hold, and gives off an air of disappointment whenever I don't kill someone with it. There are times I've wondered if it had a mind of its own, and now I'm pretty sure it does. But you can say that for any magical artifact. I get the same sense from my time-twisting pocket watch, though I'm never creeped out over picking it up like the Browning.

I found the gun in the attic of my parents' house when I was fifteen. If it's listed here, then what was it doing there? Who took it out and why? A mystery for another day, I guess.

I keep going until I find an entry for a compact makeup mirror that shows an image of what you're looking for and tilts in its direction. There's a note next to the entry. "V. POWERFUL." That sounds like just what I need. And thank fuck it's not the kewpie doll. I got enough of creepy dolls in Mexico to last a couple lifetimes.

The mirror's in a storage unit in Sherman Oaks. I haven't been inside this one yet, but I know where the keys and codes for it are, including instructions to get past the wards keeping it safe. When I got them, I put them all in a safe deposit box in Van Nuys. For once I won't have to slog across all of L.A. to get where I'm going. When I get a chance I really need to see if there's a teleportation charm somewhere in the ledger.

It doesn't take long to get to the bank in Van Nuys and then to the storage unit in Sherman Oaks, a nondescript two-story box covered in stucco with a gated-off parking lot. There's an office, surveillance cameras, a loading dock. Everything you'd expect to see.

I punch a code into a keypad next to the gate and it slides open, too silently to be normal. The office is closed. There are no hours posted. I peer in through the glass doors and see everything I would expect to see, only it looks too clean, too uniform. In fact, now that I'm looking, everything looks too clean. The parking lot asphalt is too black, the painted parking lines too white. There are no scratches on the doors, no dings in the paint, chips in the stucco.

If I didn't know better, and I'm not entirely sure that I do, I'd think this was a trap of some sort. But trap or not I need to get in there. I punch the code into the keypad next to the loading dock, and it rolls up on tracks. A light goes on automatically. In for a penny and all that.

Inside is no worse than the outside. No smells of dust or age, no stains on the floor, just a big empty room with a door at the far end. There's no keypad here, but the door won't budge. I consider an unlocking spell, but stop. I may not be able to feel them, but there have to be wards against that sort of thing. The last thing I want to do is try to break in and end up a smoking smear on the floor.

Instead I try the unit key. As the door opens, the loading dock door lowers. When it closes I feel a flood of magic that wasn't there a moment ago. The lights past the doorway turn on. And I can't believe what I'm seeing. There are no storage units here. There is only one, and it is the entire building.

There are shelves, crates, safes, desks. Every horizontal surface holds labeled knick-knacks and tchotchkes that radiate magic the way uranium throws off neutrons. Spiral staircases at each corner lead to a second-story catwalk that hugs the walls and holds nothing but bookshelves.

It's one part warehouse, one part magical antique store. *Raiders of the Lost Ark* and *Willy Wonka* all rolled into one. The magic coming off all of these items is unimaginable. There must be some really heavy-duty wards on this place to hide it from the outside.

I wander between narrow halls made from the gaps

between crates, taking care not to touch any of the artifacts left out in the open. Who knows what they'll do if I handle them wrong? The artifacts have paper tags with dates written on them, but no descriptions. I have no idea if they're in the ledger or not. I think the items without tags—pens, letter openers, stray books left on desks—are normal.

Each crate has a date stenciled on it, and they go backward the further into the room I go. The object I'm looking for is dated June 13th, 1947. I find the crate showing the date along with several others stenciled on the side, each item inside too small to warrant an entire crate on its own.

It takes a few minutes, but eventually I find an unlabeled letter opener that looks reasonably safe and sturdy enough to pry the top of the crate open. It snaps halfway through, but by then I've got the top wedged open enough to get my hands under it and shove.

The crate groans as the nails bend, and in a few minutes I've got the entire top up, exposing smaller boxes with their own dates. June 13th is near the top, underneath a box containing a cut-glass doorknob that the ledger tells me opens doors that aren't there into places you don't want to go.

The mirror is brass with mother-of-pearl covering the top and bottom. It opens with a click and the inside is just as innocuous as the outside. The makeup's gone, but the mirror is nice and shiny.

I concentrate on the remains of the Cadillac. I don't expect it will work. This place is massively shielded. I can't even feel the local pool of power.

The second I finish that thought, though, the pieces of the Cadillac sitting in a police impound yard appear in the glass. The mirror tugs in my hand, pulling itself to the right. If it can punch through this place's wards, it might work to punch through Quetzalcoatl's.

I try test runs on Gabriela, Letitia, and Chu; I get nothing. I think about Letitia's house, and there it is, with Letitia and her wife arguing on the doorstep.

Okay, things only, not people. I concentrate on Quetzalcoatl's lighter. The mirror tugs toward the southeast. In the glass I see Sastre in a dark, industrial-looking space, the lighter on a worktable in front of her. She's wearing a tank top, hair pulled back, sweat on her brow. She's tightly wrapping bunches of sticks into bundles the size and shape of ice cream cones and placing each one carefully onto an enormous stack of them on the table. The floor is piled high with twigs, a heap of thin leather straps next to them.

She's in a factory to the southeast tying piles of sticks together. Not what I was expecting, but it gives me a place to start. I check my phone to call Gabriela, but of course there's no signal. This place is locked up tight. I flip through more of the ledger looking for descriptions of other items in the room.

> *December 3rd, 1893—Monocle (1): Gives wearer ability to discern provenance of any wine.*
>
> *January 11th, 1921—Walking Stick (1-15): Creates multiple versions of itself in various colors and styles until the user picks one, locking in that style until placed in a corner for half an hour, after which it resets to its original appearance.*
>
> *6/12/62—Moonstone Amulet (1): Protection against charging minotaur. NOTE: Does not appear to protect from any other attack by a minotaur.*

So much of this is useless junk. Sure, it's magic, but it's still trash. What's the use of an amulet that only protects against a charging minotaur, but not against, say, being punched by one? How many people died before they figured that out?

*9/14/92 Insect Killing Jar (1): traps and devours the souls of anyone within at least fifteen feet, possibly more, including the user, when opened. DO NOT OPEN. Attempts to destroy have so far been unsuccessful. SERIOUSLY DO NOT OPEN THIS THING.*

Great, it's not just useless junk, it's fucking dangerous useless junk. I close up the crate, find a massive book left out on the desk titled *Esoteric Mysteries of the Spheres: Newtonian Physics and the N Dimensionality of Subjective Reality.* Any book with a title like that's only good for using as a hammer, so that's what I do with it.

I leave *Subjective Reality* on the top of the crate and shove the ledger back into my messenger bag. I go out the way I came. As soon as I'm past the door and into the loading room the magic cuts off. The loading door slides smoothly open, as if there wasn't enough magical energy in the room I just left to level a city. It closes on its own once I'm outside, an airlock for magic.

I look into the hand mirror, feel it tug toward the southeast. She's still at it, bundling twigs. Now I just need to figure out where it is, and what to do when I find it.

# Chapter 12

**"I have a proposition for you,"** I say once Gabriela answers her phone.

"You're not my type," she says.

"Thank fuck for that. I found a way to track down the Burning Girl. She's in some factory or something. Up for some recon?"

"Why, Mister Carter, are you flirting with me?" she says.

"I take the babes to all the best places. I'll be there in ten."

When I pull up, Gabriela's waiting for me in the warehouse parking lot. She's got a Benelli shotgun with a pistol grip slung over one shoulder, a bandolier of shells over the other, and her machete on her back.

Behind her, half a dozen of her people, men, women, and if I'm reading things right, a vampire or two, stand with AKs in their hands. Most of them don't like me. Can't really blame them. They had a sweet setup at Gabriela's hotel, and the minute I show up it all goes to shit.

They may not like me but we have an agreement. They don't fuck with me, I don't drag them off to the other side and confront them with the horrors of the grave. Doesn't work as good on the vampires, though. Go figure.

"Nicely nondescript," Gabriela says, raising an eyebrow as I roll down the window. The Honda I stole with Letitia was running on fumes so I stopped to steal a BMW hardtop Z4.

"This is L.A. Nondescript comes with a price tag. Besides, I got tired of being chased and not outrunning anybody."

"Losing that Cadillac was the smartest thing you've done since I met you," she says. "Too bad you don't have any taste in replacement vehicles. I'd have stolen a Porsche."

"I didn't exactly lose the Cadillac," I say. "And what part of recon did you not understand? You're loaded for bear. If I'd known you were bringing heavy ordnance, I'd have stolen something bigger. I'm not sure it'll fit."

"Oh, I dunno," she says. "It'll be tight, but I think I can shove my big gun into your tiny car."

"Are we still talking about the shotgun?"

"Shut up and open the door."

I lean over and push the passenger door open. I feel a flare of magic as she slides into the seat and the Benelli, machete and bandolier are gone.

"I don't even want to know where you put those," I say.

I fill her in on what happened with Werther, Letitia, Chu, and Chu's pet lawyer, Peter. I hand Gabriela the compact. "The mirror'll only show things, not people," I say. "Concentrate on Quetzalcoatl's lighter, it should give you a good view of where it is. Last I looked she was right next to it. And hang onto it. It'll jump in the direction of whatever you're looking for."

I don't want to say it, because she knows her shit, but

I have to. I'm a little nervous about this whole venture. "You get that this is more of a stake-out than a frontal assault, right? I'd really like to come back from this one in one piece."

"I don't think I like this new cautious you," she says.

"Yeah, well, I don't usually have to worry so much about some rando on the street shooting me, poisoning me, or blowing up my car while I'm still in it. When people try to kill me they tend to space it out over a few days, not shove it all into one afternoon."

"I can take care of myself, Eric," she says.

"Yeah, I know. I've seen it. And that's not what I'm talking about." I nod toward her crew watching us. None of them look happy. "What about them? Look, I got nothing to come back to. If I die, big fuckin' whoop. But you?"

"I'm not risking their lives," she says, an edge in her voice that makes me start to wonder if this is really about going after Sastre for her. "If you didn't want my help, why did you call?"

"I do want your help," I say. "And I know you've got a vested interest in this. But I also want to get you back here in one piece."

"Jesus, Eric. I know my way around killing cartel sicarios." She's right. She can take care of herself better than almost anyone I've ever met.

"Sorry for bringing it up."

"Just shut up and drive," she says, pointedly not looking at me.

I pull the car out of the parking lot. There are all sorts of things that can go wrong with what we're doing, and I'm not sure Gabriela and I have the same idea about the point of this trip.

I don't want to go after a professional assassin who's got a god on her side when she's gone to ground. There could be all sorts of shit in there that I don't know about, wards, booby traps. Hitting a tripwire and getting a face full of buckshot is not my idea of a good time.

But if I know where she is, then I can follow her when she leaves, and maybe catch her before she sets anyone else on fire.

I try to tell Gabriela this as diplomatically as I can, but I don't think she's listening. She just grunts and stares at the mirror.

"She's bundling sticks," she says. "Why is she bundling sticks?"

"I haven't been able to figure that out. She's been at it a while."

"Maybe we'll get a chance to ask her," she says.

"If we get a chance to ask her then this whole thing's gone to shit."

"You're making that sound bad," she says.

The mirror tugs in her hand toward the south. "Head east," she says. "If we can triangulate it we might narrow it down by a couple miles."

Gabriela used to have a crew of techheads. They did this with a different tracker that went brighter or darker depending on where and how far away the target was. But they had software on their side and GPS and nailed a location in half an hour. We're going to have to do this the old-fashioned way.

We take the 10 and cut through Boyle Heights into East L.A. before the tugging on the mirror shifts direction. I take the car south on the 710, over the 5 and past the train tracks. When we hit the outskirts of Vernon, a tiny industrial town that's all factories, train tracks, and smog, the mirror yanks in Gabriela's hand, leaning due west.

"Looks like she's in Vernon," she says.

"About fucking time." We've been driving for almost

two hours, the sun setting on the slow-moving snake of white and red lights. Traffic slowed us to a crawl despite a spell designed to make people want to get out of our way. It only works if there's somewhere else for them to go.

"Okay, she's not bundling sticks anymore," Gabriela says. "She's dipping the ends in some kind of liquid and putting them on a rack."

"Whatever it is, it can't be good." I get off at Atlantic and cross the river. Between the dead fish smell of the bare trickle of the river, the stink of the factories and trucks, and air you can chew, Vernon is not what you'd call a nice place.

Vernon was built for business. Only about ninety people live in it, but thousands come in every day to work at one of the factories. Right now there should only be a percentage of those people around. Night workers, security guards, that sort of thing. It might as well be a cemetery.

The mirror points to a small, gated factory with three buildings behind the fence. We drive around it a block away a couple of times, watching the mirror tug to keep the lighter in its sight, until we're sure that this is the place.

I park around a corner. So far I've kept the car as unobtrusive as possible. A dozen or so you-can't-see-me charms are scribbled onto the car door in Sharpie, and I've kept our distance. If there are cameras, they shouldn't even pick us up.

I pull a roll of HI, MY NAME IS stickers out of my messenger bag and write I'M NOT HERE on a couple, pumping them with as much magic as they'll hold without bursting into flame. I hand one of them to Gabriela. She slaps it onto the front of her shirt. She's got her own charms, but it doesn't hurt to have extras.

"I thought you wanted this to be a stake-out," she says.

"I do. But do you know which building she's in? We have to get close enough to—"

I'm cut off by Gabriela throwing the door open and running toward the gate. Goddammit. I get out of the car and chase after her.

The parking lot gate is padlocked. I get there before Gabriela can pop the lock open with a spell, or more likely blow it off its hinges.

"The hell are you doing?" I don't want to use any magic just yet. I don't know if Sastre is a mage, but if she is, we're close enough that she'd feel it. I don't want to take any chances and warn her we're coming.

"Shit that needs to get done," Gabriela says. She spies a dumpster nearby that we can climb to get over the gate. She starts toward it.

"No, seriously," I say. "What is your problem? I get it. Neither one of us wants what's coming if we don't do something, but running in and getting gunned down isn't gonna do either of us a goddamn bit of good."

Gabriela glares at me. "No, you don't get it. You're not trying to save the city, you're trying to save your own skin. And I'm not so much of an asshole that I can't admit that I'm doing the same thing. I need this, Eric. Everything I built has gone to shit, and I need a goddamn win. Now you can either nut up and come kill this bitch with me, or you can stay out here like a pussy and let a grown-up do her fucking job."

I don't know what to say to that, so I don't say anything. After a moment, she climbs the dumpster to get over the gate. Well, shit. I hop the fence behind her.

Gabriela hands me the mirror. It points us toward one of the smaller factory buildings. I'm not sure what they make here, if they make anything. There's no signage beyond the usual, saying to keep out. There are holders for cameras, but the cameras are gone. I start to notice other things, missing pipework, rust on the building's metal siding.

Businesses in Vernon come and go. It costs money to demolish an unused building. Easier to leave it alone, move somewhere else, come back when things are better. Rinse and repeat in four years when the economy goes tits up again.

And that's not even talking about the buildings so filled with chemicals that they've been condemned, but nobody has the money to clean up. There are places around here leaching toxins into the groundwater, poisoning nearby communities. I remember hearing about one factory closing because of it, but there are hundreds here.

There are four entrances to this building that I can see, a loading dock with a door next to it, a door leading to what looks like an office, and a door in the side that looks like it might be an emergency exit. With a final look in the mirror to make sure our target's still there, I slide it into my pocket and draw the Browning.

As usual it feels like insects under my hand, but there's something different now. Like it's paying more attention. Like it knows what I read about it, and it'd really rather I not know. So help me, if it starts whispering some Son of Sam bullshit, I'm melting it down for paperweights.

Gabriela kneels at the door and runs her hand a few inches above it, not touching. She makes a complicated hand gesture, like she's pinching two pieces of air on either side and pulling them together to tie a knot in the center.

"I've bypassed the wards and any alarms that might still be active on this door." Glad she caught that. I suck at wards, and unless they're big enough to trip over I hardly ever see them. My own attempts at wards and traps are shoddy, amateur-hour work at best.

Magic has a way of making you think you're invulnerable. That nothing can touch you. I have several years' worth of scar tissue and badly mended bones that say the opposite. I've tended not to just jump through doors if I don't need to. As mages go, I'm more cautious than most, and that's saying something, considering the stupid shit I've done.

Gabriela doesn't seem to have that restraint. I'm not sure if she has a plan beyond "break in and start shooting," but whatever it is we're doing, it's not mine anymore. It's Gabriela's. I wanted information. She wants validation. Who knows what the hell that's about? She might not even know.

She has responsibilities, people depending on her, territories to defend. She needs to show strength. Her standing's already hurting, and taking down somebody like Sastre would send a message that the Bruja's still somebody you don't fuck with. But it feels like there's more to it than that.

Gabriela angles herself off to one side of the door, the Benelli ready to fire if anything so much as sneezes. I position myself to the other side and pull it open on her mark.

The creaking of the hinges might as well be a scream in the nighttime quiet, but we don't stop moving. We go in low, watching and listening. The door slowly closes behind us with a rusty creak. What little light was coming in from the streetlights outside disappears.

This part of the factory is a confusing chain of conveyor belts, cobwebbed machinery, smelters gone cold. I can't see very far into the gloom. There are a few

Echoes around, but no Haunts, and the nearest Wanderers are the dead hobos down in the riverbed, people who'd set up camp and drowned when the L.A. River turned from a trickle to a torrent.

Now that we're inside, we need a better idea of the layout of the place and where Sastre might be holed up with her bundles of sticks.

I pull the compact from my pocket and click it open. I hold it close, covering the glass with a cupped hand. When it works it gives off a dim glow that in here would be like setting off a flare gun. I concentrate on the lighter.

Nothing happens.

Like people everywhere have done throughout the ages when faced with critical failures of important equipment, I employ a tried and true method. I shake it. Gabriela looks back at me, and even in the dimness I can see the question on her face.

I answer with what I hope are expressive shrugs and gestures at the mirror. I shake it some more, mime smacking the side of it. She finally gets it when I show the mirror to her and all she sees is her own reflection in the gloom. We both come to the conclusion at the same time that this is a very bad situation and now would be a good time to be somewhere else.

Which, of course, is when Sastre opens up on us.

It's easy to say that we should have expected it, but that ignores that fact that we did expect it, hence the guns. I just didn't think we wouldn't see it coming.

Gunfire splits the air, muzzle flashes leaving blind spots in my eyes. Bullets erupt out of the darkness and ricochet off the conveyor belts.

We duck and split into two different directions to flank Sastre. Then I have a thought. We haven't actually seen her. If I were setting a trap, what would I do? I'd rig up something that would fire into the darkness so who-ever was after me thought I was where the gunfire was.

Another fusillade from the same location. It's got to be rigged. She wouldn't be stupid enough to stay in one spot.

Gabriela's figured it out, too. A blast from her shot-gun draws fire from another location, and from the flashes I know where they both are. Instead of shooting and giving away my position I concentrate and find a handful of Echoes of people that have died over the years in accidents. No Wanderers, no Haunts. Good. I'll have more time before they come for me.

I slip over to the other side, my ears filling with that jet engine sound as I pass over, the air going cold and dead around me. From here I can see where both of the women have taken positions to fire, but they're both moving closer to each other. On the living side it's a nightmare show of ducking under cover, taking potshots, jumping out of the line of fire, inching ever closer.

But over here it's like watching ballet. The factory is new enough that it's not on this side. There are no block-ing walls, annoying machinery, or conveyor belts to run into. It's just one giant stage. They duck, slide, pirouette. Shimmering lights of life and death.

I make a beeline toward Sastre, holstering the Brown-ing and drawing my straight razor. One quick slice through the throat and it's all over. They've gotten close enough, or run out of enough ammunition that they've moved on to hand-to-hand. Gabriela's going to have that monster machete of hers, but I don't know what Sas-tre's got.

I make my move, running through them both to get behind Sastre. I'll have to time it right, so that she's not ducking a slice from Gabriela that I'll take in the face. I get close behind her, ready to move back to the living side when everything lights up in the bright orange glow of a raging inferno.

A blast of power throws me back as the flames blind me. I skid across the floor, passing through barely visible industrial equipment that doesn't exist on this side. My straight razor skitters in the opposite direction. After a moment my eyes clear and I freeze.

"Hello, Eric," Quetzalcoatl says, an enormous winged serpent of flames hovering above his assassin. "I've been waiting for you."

# Chapter 13

**Q's come a long way** from the literal trash fire I met in Zacatecas. He had built his form out of random garbage strewn across a hotel parking lot, accreting his body out of discarded items. A throwaway god made of bike parts, soda cans, bits of string, all held together with burning hatred.

But now he is conflagration, devouring star, angry god of fire and blood. Before, it was just his eyes that glowed, but now it's his whole body, fifteen feet tall, wings of fire beating lazily to keep him aloft.

"If I knew you'd be here I'd have brought you something," I say. "Like a fire extinguisher."

"You betrayed me, little necromancer. I could have had Mictlan and you cheated me out of it."

"If by cheating you mean not murdering countless souls in an afterlife, okay. I'll take that hit."

On the living side I can see Gabriela and Sastre going at it. Strike, parry, spin, pirouette. If it weren't so deadly and I wasn't faced with incineration myself, it'd be beautiful to watch.

Gabriela's holding her own, but I can see she's slowing down, while Sastre isn't. I need to get back and help her. Except I don't know if Q will be able to follow me over.

I don't have much power over here. I can't tap the pool on the dead side and can only use whatever I've already got. It's a lot, but I don't know if he has the same limitation. On the living side I saw him torch twenty guys with a thought. Is he as strong here? I really don't want to find out.

I get to my feet and slowly circle him, a little closer, a little further away. He watches, occasionally shifting his wings to keep me in his line of sight. I want to make him think I'm scared, which isn't the case. I'm fucking terrified. But as long as he's paying attention to me and not to where I'm going I might be able to get out of this.

"I could have destroyed you," he says, "and I did not." His voice the sound of brushfires and dry kindling. "You owe your life to me."

I can't help but laugh. "That's like proving this new deodorant I'm wearing fends off elephants because there are no elephants around. I could have destroyed you and didn't. I guess that means you owe your life to me." I stop when my foot connects with my dropped straight razor.

I start to pull together the bits and pieces of a spell in my head. It's such a stupid idea that it's just got to work. When I grab the straight razor I'll be ready to go.

"Your life is forfeit, worm," he says.

"Blah blah blah. You realize that's all you do, right? Just yammer on and on and on and not actually get anything done? I mean, look at yourself. You're not made of trash this time, but you're still a wreck." And this close, I can see that he is. The fire wings are tattered. His glowing serpent form is missing scales.

In the distance I can feel Wanderers edging closer.

I've been here long enough to have caught their attention. The first ones should start showing up any second now. If I don't time this right it could end very badly.

"You dare—"

"Oh, blow it out your ass. I'm the one who got into Mictlan. I'm the one that kicked the shit out of your weird talking cat-thing when you sent it after me. I'm the one who took everything you wanted to do and shit all over it. So yeah, I fucking well do dare."

His body swells, expanding and growing hotter. His energy is a lighthouse in a storm surge, but it's not something I can use. Not yet.

The first Wanderers melt through the walls. They have my scent, but they're caught in his glow. All that power, all that blood spilled in hundreds of years of sacrifice.

I duck and scoop up the straight razor. Quetzalcoatl responds by expanding further, putting himself between me and his assassin's glow on the living side to protect her, and totally misunderstanding what I'm trying to do. He should really be more worried about himself.

Before the Wanderers realize that they can't eat him, I run the razor quickly across a scarred patch of my forearm free of any tattoos. I've spilled a lot of blood from that spot, to the point where I almost don't feel it anymore. Almost.

Blood wells thick and fast from the wound and before any of it can spill to the ground I fling my arm out wide, spattering my blood into Quetzalcoatl's flames, where it sizzles like butter on a hot pan, and set off my spell, pumping some of my own life energy into him.

Everything changes in a heartbeat. The bright orange of his flames goes a dim, dusky blood-red. I fall to my knees, hoping I haven't lost too much of myself. I don't know what doing that will translate to. Shorter lifespan, maybe? I've done it once before and it didn't kill me, but it sure as hell wasn't fun.

The Wanderers know they can feed on the life in my blood, and they know that they'd really rather feed on the life of Quetzalcoatl. And now I've mixed the two. As far as the ghosts are concerned, they might as well be the same thing.

They fall upon him with the speed of lightning, tearing holes through his burning form, totally ignoring me. He counters by burning as many ghosts as possible. He'll win, eventually. I don't plan on being here when he does.

I run at Sastre, straight razor in my hand. Her back is to me. I can take her down and get the lighter, which is right there on a table next to her. I slip back to the other side at the last second, the sound of the living world— the clanging of metal on metal, cursing, yelling—loud in my ears. Dark grays and blues give way to vibrant blacks and flashes of orange sparks.

And take a back kick to my forehead. The force of it drops me to the ground, but my momentum carries me forward, sliding past her and across the floor, a few feet away from Gabriela. I try to roll under one of the conveyor belts, or stand up, or do fucking anything that isn't lie here on the floor with a concussion. I won't be down for long, my tattoos will see to that, but you get your bell rung, you're not doing much of anything right away.

Gabriela isn't quite as surprised as I am, and she recovers quickly. While Sastre's attention is split, Gabriela slashes out with the machete. It should take her head off, but at the last moment it bounces off a shield. Sastre looks as surprised as Gabriela, but not for long.

Sastre sinks her knife, a wicked looking Bowie, deep into Gabriela's chest. A look of surprise and shock flits across Gabriela's face. The machete falls from her fingers. She drops like a puppet with cut strings.

Sastre bears down, knife ready to do the same to me, but I'm clear enough and fast enough to get the Browning out as she reaches me. Her eyes go wide as she realizes the Browning's barrel is in her mouth, clinking against her teeth. She freezes, the blade barely an inch from my chest. She backs away slowly and I follow her, neither my gun nor her knife wavering.

She lowers the knife, and I pull the Browning back, but don't lower it. "Where is Quetzalcoatl?"

"I fed him to a bunch of ghosts. He's not coming to your rescue."

"And I have mortally wounded your friend," she says. "What are you going to do?"

"I was thinking I'd shoot you, seeing as I've got a gun and all you have is that pig sticker. Speaking of which, why not drop it?"

She laughs. It was worth a shot. "You first. Do you think I'll trust you enough that you won't shoot me? Killing me won't be easy. If you succeed, you'll pay for it. Go ahead, pull the trigger. I won't die. Not right away. I have charms and protections. And I can promise I'll last longer than your friend."

There's an unspoken "or" hanging in the air. I can see where this is going and I don't like it one bit. Sastre is hurt, but up close I can see that her clothes are marked with holes tiny and huge, tears from buckshot and slashes. She's taken a lot of hits, but very little has gotten through.

Even if I pull the trigger this close, whatever magic is protecting her will likely keep her going for a little while. She'll outlast Gabriela.

"I'm listening." I know what she's going to say. I've

already done the math and I'm not sure I can refuse. Every action I can think of might end with Sastre dead, but definitely ends with Gabriela dead. All except one, and it's looking like the only viable course.

"Leave with your friend. Get her help. Let me go. We finish this up another time."

It's a tough call. I could end this here and now. Not forever. I can't kill Quetzalcoatl by throwing ghosts at him. But I can slow him down, get the lighter, get this assassin out of my hair.

All for the price of one dead Bruja.

"What are you doing with the sticks?" I say, stalling for time I know I don't have.

A sly smile on her lips. "Let me go and you'll find out."

Fuck. "We will finish this," I say. "Soon."

"I wouldn't miss it." She steps back, puts her Bowie knife on the ground, hands on top of her head. I keep the Browning aimed at her as I stand. I pick up Gabriela's machete—she'll be pissed if I leave it—and put her over my shoulder in a fireman's carry. Hot blood pours out of the wound in her chest, soaking my shirt and the back of my pants. She's unconscious, but her breath is a raspy wheeze and I can feel her heart hammering. Punctured lung, massive blood loss, at the very least.

I back out of the factory, reaching behind me with one hand to open the door while balancing Gabriela on my shoulder. Sastre watches as I leave. I stop just outside the doorway, one foot holding it open.

Aw, fuck it. I pop off two shots and bolt, not bothering to see whether I hit anything or not. I round the corner of the building, glancing behind me to see if she's following or if Q has gotten the ghosts off him, before I shove the Browning into its holster. I get a better grip on Gabriela and run hard for the car. I only hope it's not too late.

I get Gabriela into the BMW's passenger seat, shoving the machete next to her. I can't heal her, but I can keep her from dying. More or less. I drip a couple drops of blood in her mouth and cast a spell that mimics death. It slows her heartbeat way down, cools her metabolism. Stick her in a morgue drawer and you won't be able to tell the difference. But it only slows down death. It won't stop it.

I grab my phone in a hand so slick with blood it takes me three tries to dial the warehouse. I tell the guy who answers that they need to get Vivian to the warehouse right fucking now or their precious Bruja's going to bleed out in this car. I hang up without waiting for an answer and stomp on the gas.

I'm weaving through thinning traffic on surface streets, blowing through stop lights at a hundred and twenty, when the first cops show up behind me. I don't have time for this shit. I dig one hand through my messenger bag until it snags on the thing I'm looking for, a small mirrored globe about the size of a golf ball.

I put my hand out the window and squeeze the globe until it pops. A blast of light fills the air. My left eye goes blind. My vision will come back in a minute, but in the meantime, I'm driving one-eyed past cars that suddenly can't see me anymore.

It's like the you-can't-see-me charms, but bigger. The cops are still coming, but as far as they and everyone else knows I've disappeared. A mage will see right through it, but it'll keep the normals and any recording equipment from seeing me. As an added bonus it mimics whatever car it's going past every few seconds just to make things more confusing.

It'll only last a few minutes, but at this speed that's all I should need. I come up onto the warehouse and brake too late, spinning into the parking lot. The only thing that keeps me from being road pizza is the fact that they opened the gate before I got there.

Three of her people run over with a gurney to help get Gabriela out of the car. Vivian's a step behind them with an EMT trauma bag. She checks Gabriela's pulse and goes pale. In a flash she's on the gurney starting compression and it takes me a second to remember what I did in the car.

"Hang on, no, she's not dead. Just really, really asleep."

Understanding dawns on her face. She's seen me do this trick before. "Got it," she says. "Let's get her upstairs. How long will this last?"

"Couple hours, but once I pull her out she's gonna go downhill fast."

"Then let's hope a couple hours is enough."

# Chapter 14

**Every day,** over seven thousand people die in America. More than two thousand of them in hospitals. Trauma wards, ICUs, ERs, posh rooms with cable and internet and machines that sing one note dirges when you're gone. Rich, poor, men, women, the just and the sinners. They all die eventually.

You want to find ghosts, you spend a lot of time in hospitals. Searching for the newly dead, waiting for the about-to-be-dead, hoping to dig up an old spook who's been hanging around the site for the last fifty years.

I'm not a fan of hospitals. They're like charnel houses. Sure, people die all the time, but in a hospital nobody dies easy. And all the rest of us can do is sit around and wait for it to happen.

I hate waiting.

Strictly speaking, this isn't a hospital, but it might as well be. Some of Gabriela's crew and I are all on the top floor outside her makeshift surgery suite waiting for her to die.

I've seen all the emotions on display here before. Pre-emptive grief, fear, anxiety, anger. More than a few throw glares in my direction, knowing that I got their leader, their hope, their protector hurt, if not killed.

A few see something else in me. They offer me coffee, or a place to wash up, worry writ large in their eyes. I know I look pretty bad. Even after washing the blood off my hands and arms, the spatter from my face, I'm still covered in gore. My shirt and pants are soaked through, stiff from dried blood.

I've spent a lot of time covered in blood. You do death magic, you get used to it. Only this is different. This is the blood of someone who shouldn't die, someone who cares about the world more than I ever have. I've only run into that a few times, and never like this. By the time they get to a hospital, they're DOA.

I'm worried, but it's a distant thing. Pushed aside along with everything else by a singular, blazing-hot thought: How do I kill Quetzalcoatl and his pet assassin and make it hurt?

About an hour and a half after they disappeared through the door of Gabriela's makeshift surgery, Vivian comes out, stands in the doorway. She looks exhausted. I've never seen her so tired. She waves me over.

"Okay," she says. "I've patched her up, but she's still under that spell. You need to bring her out and I'll be ready in case anything goes wrong. I'm not going to know for sure that what I did helped until she's a little more alive."

I follow Vivian inside and she closes the door behind us. Gabriela's lying unconscious on the surgical table, intubated, hooked to a ventilator and an IV, a blue sheet covering everything but the wound. The conditions aren't ideal—hey, it's a warehouse—but Vivian's a professional and she knows her shit.

"I don't know how this works," she says. "When you bring her out will she need to be sedated?"

"I have no idea," I say. "I've never done this on an injured person. She could come back and still be unconscious, or she could wake up screaming."

"Joy. Well, I can knock her out with a spell and then dose her with fentanyl if I have to. She's closed up, and I've got an antibiotic enchantment on the room, so she'll be fine, but scrub up, anyway. You look disgusting."

"Unless you've got a power washer I don't think it's gonna make much difference. Do I need gloves?"

"You sticking your fingers in her intestines?"

"Not today."

"Then no, you don't need gloves."

I tear open a sponge packet at the sink, scrub the dried blood out from under my fingernails, dig into the crevices of my palms. No matter how hard I try, I can't seem to get the last of the blood out. Funny. I always thought that was just a metaphor.

When I'm done I go over to Gabriela, stand at the head of the table, and put my hands on either side of her head. Vivian wheels over a crash cart.

"You ready?" she says.

"I just did it." The monitor next to the bed begins to beep as everything returns to normal.

"You ass," Vivian says. "I thought her head was going to explode, or something."

"Hey, I wasn't sure it wouldn't."

"Goddammit, Eric." She turns her attention to the monitor. "Vitals are looking good. You think she'll be out for long?"

"I've only brought someone out of it once, and that

was more on a timer. I wasn't actually there for it. Could be minutes, hours, I don't know."

Vivian frowns and I can see the gears turning as she puts things together. When I first got back to L.A., her fiancé, my friend Alex, was kidnapped. Vivian wanted to come with me to get him, only I had a better idea of what we'd be up against.

I wasn't about to see her get killed. So I sort of knocked her out with the same spell I used on Gabriela. Yes, it was a dick move. And if I had to do it over again, I probably would.

The gears finally click into place and Vivian says, "Is it the same spell—" But she doesn't finish, because a massive jolt slams through the building, almost knocking us down. I hear glass shatter, car alarms go off. I throw open the door to see shattered glass, a few injuries, and the entire top floor bathed in a red-orange glow.

The building's on fire. They followed us back here and set the place alight. Then I realize no, that's coming from outside. Through the shattered windows I watch a fireball the size of an oil tanker billow up into the sky.

I note the direction, estimate the distance. Sonofabitch. When Gabriela and I got out of Vernon, Quetzalcoatl and Sastre set the factory to explode. A blast like that must have taken out the whole facility at least. We're only about three miles away. Far enough away to be safe, but not so far we can't feel it. Fire crews will be swarming the place soon. It's going to take them hours to put that out.

But as I'm thinking that, another explosion just as large erupts near the first. It happens so fast and it's so bright that I don't quite register before the shockwave hits. I feel it punch through my chest, pushing me back.

Then there's another, and another, and another, and so many more I lose track and all that's left is a two-mile wide, five-hundred-foot tall wall of flames that dances and shimmers in multiple colors lighting the night up brighter than daytime. Reds and oranges, greens and blues. All those toxic chemicals cooking off, blowing up into the air.

We all stand there watching the flames. Watching Vernon burn in stunned silence, letting the sounds of car alarms and sirens fill the space. Let's be honest, it's not a huge loss. I mean, it's Vernon. You think about L.A., you don't think Vernon. There are only a couple hundred people who live there. The same kind of blasts along Hollywood Boulevard would kill thousands.

I can't see anything besides the flames, it's still three miles away, but with the power of those blasts I can't imagine there's anything left standing. Buildings are going to be rubble, anyone inside them dead. Night workers, security, that one guy who just had to stay late to get the spreadsheets done. They're nothing but burning paste spread across shattered concrete.

I wonder how bad it will get before the night is over. How many neighborhoods outside the blast are going to catch fire as burning debris rains down onto a city of tinder? How many foundations will have cracked a mile out from the shockwaves? How many fallen homes?

A massive twist clenches around my heart and squeezes, almost taking me to the floor. At first I think I'm having a heart attack, but it's a familiar feeling. It's so strong, stronger than I've ever felt, I don't realize what it is for a moment.

Every necromancer I've met, at least the ones who didn't try to kill me and I was able to ask, can feel when somebody nearby dies. It's a twinge. Barely noticeable. We're attuned to death the way a lawyer is to car accidents.

One death, enh, no big deal. Thirty or so, like what happened on a Metro train I was on a while back, that stings a bit.

This is hundreds.

I take deep breaths, let it wash through me. I almost have my breathing under control when I see it. A giant form in the flames that, if the normals noticed it and took a photo, would end up on a tabloid headline come morning. A winged snake of fire two hundred feet tall flows out of the flames and hovers there. I can't tell for sure, because its eyes are just tears in the surface of flames, but fuck if he isn't looking right at me.

And then I'm hit with another wave of death as more explosions rip through the distance. I can feel the body count rising. In the days and weeks ahead, survivors will die from their wounds, infections, and toxic gases. Suffocate on a pocket of escaped cyanide gas, vomit themselves to death from arsenic, go slowly insane as mercury eats through their brains.

Every new explosion brings with it more hammering against my chest, like I'm getting slammed with a shovel. I'm not sure how far away I need to be to not feel it, but this is definitely way too close to ground zero.

"You all right?" Vivian says, coming out of the surgery and seeing me on the floor clutching my chest. "Shit, you're having a coronary."

I shake my head no and manage to hiss "I'm okay" before another wave of deaths washes through me. Not everyone leaves a ghost, even in a situation like this, but with so many dead, you're going to get a lot. And I feel them tearing away from their souls, confused, hungry, scared. Hundreds and hundreds of them. L.A. will be infested by morning, not that anybody but me is gonna care, or even notice.

"I'll be fine," I say, my eyes never leaving Quetzal-coatl's form burning above the flames. Then another explosion erupts, swallowing him up in its flames, the death toll landing one last sucker punch before I pass out on the floor.

# Chapter 15

I **wake up** on a couch on the second floor of the warehouse, dirty yellow light streaming in through the blown-in windows. What little air conditioning has been running is shot, with no way to keep it all in, and the heat is even worse than before. My shirt sticks to my skin despite the dozen or so fans placed around the room, losing a war against the smoky air that has drifted inside.

I sit up, groggy, hungover, my mouth tasting like pennies, my body feeling like I've gone a few rounds with a pissed off skinhead. I wipe sweat from my face and forehead. It must be a hundred degrees in here.

I've never been near that many deaths before. That split-second moment between living and dead has always left a bad taste in my mouth, but this. Jesus. I try to estimate how many, piece apart the individual ones, but they're all a nightmare blur of burning agony, crushed bone. And then there are the ghosts. I can feel a clot of them in the distance, an itch I can't scratch, a noise I can't shut out.

The fire's still burning, though in the daylight and the haze of smoke it's harder to see. I can't tell if it's spread or not, but it's definitely still kicking. Thick clouds of smoke rise up along the horizon. Helicopters and tanker planes drop water and retardant from above, and I can barely make out streams of water from pumper trucks.

"Hell of a sight, isn't it?" Vivian says. She comes up behind the couch, eyes sunken, pulled-back hair matted with sweat. Like everybody else here who isn't me, she's changed into something for the heat, shorts and a tank top. I'm the only one here wearing pants.

"How long was I out?" I say. She takes a cigarette from behind her ear and lights it with a flick of her fingers. She takes a long draw before exhaling. I didn't know she smoked. But then, there's a lot I don't know about her these days.

"Twelve hours, give or take," she says, voice flat and empty, eyes never leaving the fire out the window. "Once I knew you weren't having a heart attack, I had a couple of the guys toss you onto the couch to get through whatever the fuck it was you were going through."

She finally looks at me. "What the fuck were you going through?"

There are things about necromancy I never talked to her about when we were together. Some were things I didn't know, hadn't learned yet. Others were things I didn't want to talk about. Like this.

"I can tell when people die," I say. "I feel it. Half a dozen I don't even notice, but you start ratcheting up the numbers? Well, a lot of people died last night. It was . . . unpleasant."

"Looked it. You always been like that?"

"Yeah. Usually I can ignore it."

"Never told me about that."

"Yeah, well, that's like bringing up a wart on your asshole. It's not something that makes for good sexytime talk."

She takes another drag on her cigarette. "The news says estimates are at about 800 dead. Mostly night shift workers in Vernon, but some residents in Alameda and South Park. Houses and apartments collapsed from the shock waves, some burned down. They're saying it's the worst disaster L.A.'s seen. They've declared a state of emergency and are trying to evacuate people from areas around the fire. Hospitals are swamped."

"Kinda surprised you're not helping out in an emergency room." I've never seen Vivian like this. There's no animation in her voice. She's not angry, not sad, not manic. The hell is wrong with her?

"I don't do that anymore," she says. I want to ask why, but something in her tone tells me that's a bad idea.

"It's gonna get worse," I say.

"They'll get it under control."

"That's not what I mean."

She considers that. "Did you make this happen?" she says. "Did you and Gabriela do this?"

"How's she doing?"

"Fine, but she's still out. Answer the question. What did you do? Did you kill all those people?"

"No," I say, but I honestly wonder how true that is. "We definitely triggered it, though. All that smoke and fire? All those dead? They're a great big double-fisted fuck you. I told you the basics of me going to Mexico, but a lot more happened than I've talked about."

I tell her about Quetzalcoatl, his blaming me for his not getting to fulfill a 500-year-old revenge fantasy, his connection to the mage murders, La Niña Quemada, what happened last night.

"She's the one who stabbed Gabriela?"

"Yeah. I had a choice to make: take her down and let Gabriela die, or let her go and get Gabriela back here."

"You made the right choice," she says.

Did I? Ask the hundreds who died last night, or the ones who are going to die today and tomorrow. Ask the survivors if they think I made the right choice. That fire's gonna burn for days, if not weeks. If they're lucky it won't spread. But it won't be the last one.

"Maybe," I say. "They'll do it again, though."

"This—I can't believe I'm saying this—this god hates you that much that he'll burn the city down just to fuck with you?"

"Honestly, I don't know. I have a hard time thinking this is all just petty revenge. But they don't think like people. Or, fuck, maybe they do."

"I still can't wrap my mind around that. Gods, goddesses. Quetzalcoatl. You know, that's the only Aztec god I remember. And he's real. I'm fine with magic because I use it every day, but actual gods? When you told me about Santa Muerte, I figured she was just some demon. I don't know why I'm okay with demons and I'm having so much trouble with gods."

I think about telling her that it's because they raise uncomfortable questions. Demons are like cockroaches. They're all over the place and mages learn to deal with them early or we don't live long. We've seen them. Some of us, unfortunately, have touched a few.

But gods are different. Gods mean maybe you're not in control. Maybe you don't have your shit together like you thought you did. Nothing will piss off us magic types more than not being in control. We can twist reality like fucking balloon animals, but there's something bigger and badder than us out there.

And Vivian wonders why I never told her half the shit necromancy is about. She has trouble with gods? Imagine if I'd told her the real story about ghosts.

"Existential crisis?" I say.

She barks out a laugh that's just this side of panic. "Yeah. And then some." She finishes her cigarette, and vaporizes the butt with a gesture.

"If it helps any, he's a real asshole. From what I saw, so's the rest of his family."

"You mean your family," she says. She nods at the ring on my finger. There's no anger, no bitterness. Just a statement of fact. Pissed off at me, hating me, never wanting to see me again. Those I can handle. But this? Vivian has her shit together. Vivian always has her shit together. Something's wrong. I don't know what it is. I doubt she'd welcome any help I might give her.

She closes her eyes and rubs her temples, a bone-weary sigh escaping her lips. It's the most emotion I've seen from her since I woke up. "What now?"

"You remember Letitia Watson?"

"High school, right? Barely. Didn't she stab you?"

"Yes, and yes. She's part of the Cleanup Crew now. Working with the LAPD. Has a side thing going with a lawyer and some guy running for mayor. Councilman Chang, or something."

"You mean David Chu?" she says. "I've heard of him. His office keeps calling me for donations."

"Yeah? He a good sort?"

She shrugs. "He's a politician."

"He is that. Turns out there's a whole file on the murders I'm getting blamed for showing that I didn't do any of them."

"You're fucking kidding me. Why am I just now hearing this?"

"Because they're not telling anybody. They want to bring down the assassin who's doing it, and want to use me as bait."

"Do they know she's with Quetzalcoatl?"

"If they do, they didn't say anything. I'm not inclined to tell them either. It's one thing to have some people trying to kill me out of misplaced vengeance, it's another to have everybody trying to kill me to get rid of Quetzalcoatl."

"If you're dead he's got no reason to stick around," she says, producing another cigarette and lighting it with her fingers. "It would solve the problem."

"I think you and I might have differing opinions on that. More to the point, if Chu and his Merry Mages know she's behind the Vernon fire, they might be more inclined to let everybody else know about her. Having L.A.'s mages pointed at her instead of me might slow her down a little."

"You think they'll do that?"

"Not Chu," I say. "He's looking for political capital with the mages and wants to be at the center of whatever takes her down. He's been making Mage Council noises."

"Oh, for fuck sake," Vivian says. "Is he that much of an idiot? Those always end with corpses."

"I think he's just fine with the idea so long as he's not one of the corpses. Anyway, he wants to use me as bait. If he controls this information, he probably thinks he can control me, too."

"You'd think Letitia would have warned him about that."

"Letitia has her own reasons," I say. "I don't think she wants to rock the boat too much. And honestly I can't blame her. I think it might also make her the best person to talk to. We at least have history."

"Yeah. If you consider her stabbing you in high school history, sure."

"I have low standards. Besides, she's with Chu

because she's afraid of what will happen to her family if she gets targeted."

I stand up from the couch, my legs wobbly, my body filled with overlapping pains. I swear I can feel every bruise, puncture and abrasion. I'm a little afraid to see what I look like in a mirror. The tattoos help me with the worst of the damage, but they don't make it feel any better.

Between being poisoned yesterday morning, jumping off cars out of the void, getting the shit kicked out of me by a cartel sicaria, and feeling the deaths of 800 people like a gut punch for every single one of them, I'm not exactly at my freshest.

"There a car in the lot I can borrow?"

"What, you're not stealing one?"

"Ugh. Too much effort. I'm tired."

"Here," she says. She pulls a set of keys out of her purse on a nearby table and tosses them to me.

"You're trusting me with your car? You do know I'm pretty hard on cars, right?"

"It's insured, I don't much like it, and I'm going to report it stolen as soon as you walk out the door." She gives me a smile that doesn't reach her eyes.

"Good to know."

"And before you see anybody," she says, "take a shower. Maybe change your clothes."

She's got a point. My clothes are more red than anything else, and the fabric has gotten stiff from dried blood.

"Fine. But pretty soon everybody's gonna be wearing blood-crusted clothes and you'll see the genius of my fashion forward sense."

"That's actually what worries me," she says, and turns her attention back to the fires on the horizon.

# Chapter 16

**You'd think after** being back in L.A. a few years and actually owning property I might spend some time in it. I don't. My sister's house in Venice is vacant, the other properties my family left mothballed and covered in dust. A few were nothing but empty lots, and stay that way.

Instead I move from hotels to motels to trailer parks to Beverly Hills mansions empty while the occupants are summering in the Caymans. I never stay more than three, four weeks in the same place, the same neighborhood. Shake up my routine on how and when I go in and out.

Right now I've got a room at the Biltmore in Downtown under my own name. But I'm staying about three miles away at a ramshackle motel on Third and Alexandria right at the edge of Little Bangladesh.

Yes, I know. It's called paranoia. With a load of mages, a pissed off god, and a cartel assassin after my ass, not having a fixed address is something of a bonus. Anything with my name on it might as well be a bomb site.

Paranoia's also one of the reasons I keep a handful of burner phones around. The one I used for my room at the Biltmore is ringing. Caller ID shows me that it's coming from the hotel desk.

"Hello?"

"Mister Carter, this is Kevin from the front desk at the Biltmore. I'm calling to let you know there's been an incident in your room."

"What happened?"

"Two people tried to break in, but were stopped by our . . . by security measures, before they could enter. We've called the police and they'll be contacting you soon, I'm sure."

That didn't take long. "Did they catch them?"

There's a long, awkward pause on the other end. "They . . . were found on the floor outside your room. I'm afraid the police will have to give you details."

"My god, I hope they're all right," I say, knowing they're not.

"I really think you'll want to speak with the police about it. We merely wanted to let you know so that you didn't come back to an unfortunate surprise."

"I appreciate it. Thanks for the call."

"If there's anything we can do—"

"No, I'm good. Thanks, though."

If things went the way they were supposed to, what Kevin from the Front Desk isn't telling me is that these people were found turned inside out. It's a really nasty ward I learned a couple months back after I almost got gunned down in a hotel in Zacatecas. I put it on the door. If anybody used a key it wouldn't have triggered. The last thing I want is a couple of dead housekeepers outside my room.

But try to jimmy the lock or break the door or whatever and off it goes. The really horrible part is that you'll stay alive for about five minutes before all your organs shut down and you go into hypovolemic shock from blood loss. I kind of feel sorry for whoever had to clean them off the floor.

I pull the battery out of the phone as soon as I hang up and toss the phone into the wastebasket. I take my pocket watch out. The watch speeds up time drastically. It's effective, if difficult to control. It doesn't always work the way I want. I don't know if it can do anything else, and I only figured this out with trial and error and more than a few dead cats. I'm just fine not experimenting any more with it.

I point the watch face at the phone at the bottom of the wastebasket. I wind the crown a couple notches and push it down with my thumb. The phone goes brittle, the glass cracks. Stress fractures appear across the surface and the plastic flakes away until there's nothing but a pile of plastic shavings and bits of metal at the bottom of the wastebasket. There's a rusty hole in the bottom of the wastebasket, too. The watch doesn't have great aim.

The first time I tried disposing of a burner phone like this, I didn't take the battery out first. Turns out rapidly aging batteries explode. The more you know.

I shower, washing off Gabriela's blood, counting the cuts and bruises, finally stopping when I can't tell where one bruise ends and the other begins. Everything hurts: muscle, skin, bone. It's usually a little difficult to see the bruises under all the tattoos, but these are fresh and clear as crystal, deep purple marks going green at the edges.

I change my clothes, tossing the blood-covered ones into a trash bag I'll burn later. At this rate I could probably just leave it lying around and let Quetzalcoatl burn it for me along with the rest of the city.

Once I feel a little more human, I call Letitia. It takes a few tries to get through to her, and when she finally answers I hear telephones ringing and raised voices in the background.

"Letitia," I say. "Busy day?"

"Jesus, Carter, haven't you heard? A couple miles of industrial buildings in Vernon went up last night."

"Yeah, about that."

Silence. Then, "You know something?"

"Oh, and then some. And you're gonna want to hear it. And I don't know if you're gonna want to tell your boss about it."

"David's not my boss."

"Yet you knew exactly who I was talking about when I said it. Can you get away for a bit? We've got some things to discuss."

"For this, yes. Where at?"

"You're operating out of Downtown, right? Meet me at the King Eddy in an hour. And remember, don't tell your boss."

"He's not my—" But I hang up before I can hear the rest.

Talking to her is a risk, but she's my conduit to Chu, and Chu's got that file. I give it a couple of hours after I tell her what's going on before she calls him. If she skips the bit about Quetzalcoatl, I'll be pleasantly surprised, but I don't expect it. I can only hope he's as much a politician as I think he is.

I can see why Vivian wants a new car. This one's a dinky little Fiat that looks like it wasn't built so much as shit out of an incontinent elephant. I may set it on fire once I'm done with it. Maybe I'll toss my bag of bloody clothes in first.

I head Downtown, passing by the Biltmore. I watch as two black body bags are loaded into the coroner's vans. I wonder who they were. This might be the thing that bothers me the most. If someone's going to try to kill you, you should damn well know their name. This random stranger bullshit is getting on my nerves.

The King Eddy is a Skid Row bar that was there long before Skid Row was. It was a no-name bar for the King Edward Hotel in the early 1900s and when Prohibition hit it turned into a basement speakeasy using Downtown L.A.'s maintenance tunnels to smuggle in illegal hooch.

Not that anybody really cared. Prohibition didn't really take out here like it did in some places. Mostly because everybody in the city government was on the take. And then when Prohibition ended, the bar came out from behind the piano store it was using as a front and went legit.

After the War things went to hell. The Red Car stopped going down 5th, the hotels all turned into flop houses, cheap rents pulled in the kind of crowd that cheap rents pull in. Next thing you know, you've got Skid Row, junkies, drug deals, beat poets. The King Eddy was a survivor.

But the one thing it couldn't survive was gentrification. Eventually it closed down, then got bought and opened back up. Now it's a hipster version of a Bukowski dive bar with eight-dollar Budweisers.

I liked it better when people were doing coke and shooting heroin in the bathroom stalls, getting into drunken fights out on the sidewalk. Yeah, it was a mess, but it was real life, messy, and visceral and full of drama. Even the ghosts were more interesting back then.

I park Vivian's Fiat in a lot on Main, slapping a Sharpied sticker that says STEAL ME on the windshield, and walk the two blocks over to 5th and Los Angeles where the King Eddy sits as a cornerstone of the King Edward hotel.

The bar's just opened and it's still quiet. Not even the jukebox is playing. A handful of regulars who came back after they re-opened sit at the bar. I score a table in the back with no one else around. My back to the wall, paying attention to the flow of magic around me, the people walking by on the street outside, feeling for any disturbances, spells, draws on the pool. It's quiet on the magic front, too.

About twenty minutes later Letitia wanders in. By then I've already downed two cups of coffee and am contemplating a third. She's given in to the heat and is wearing a skirt that doesn't seem like the sort of thing the LAPD would be okay with for on-duty detectives, and a blue blouse that's already staining in the armpits.

She sits down opposite me and starts to talk, but I stop her with an upraised finger. I pour the table salt out into a pile, spread it with my hands, and use a finger to draw a rune through it. There's a sudden silence as all of the sounds outside our table go away. It's a simple spell, small and unobtrusive enough that anyone walking by probably won't notice. It's also a pretty crappy one. No one can hear in, but we can't hear out.

"Okay, spill," she says. "What happened last night? What did you do?"

"Don't look at me. Your sicaria did it. I just spooked her." I don't mention Gabriela. She's already mixed up in this bullshit and I don't want things getting worse for her than they already are.

"You spooked her enough that she blew up Vernon?" she says, eyes going wide.

"I think it was more that I pissed off her boss, who's also in town, by the way."

"No shit," she says. "We've been trying to find her for weeks. All the scrying comes up empty."

"I found a loophole. Unfortunately, one that's probably been plugged up tight since last night. I went looking for something I know she has. I found that, I found her."

Letitia narrows her eyes, doesn't say anything. It's adorable when police try to do the silent intimidation thing on me. Most people hate silence. They'll say all kinds of shit just to fill the hole.

I lean back in my seat and sip the last of my coffee. One of us is going to start talking soon, and it isn't going to be me.

She breaks after about two minutes. "All right, before I go on to who her boss is, I'm going to ask how you knew what she had."

"It's a lighter. It's what she's using to set everything on fire. If you look at one of your border surveillance photos you'll see it in her hand after she's lit a cigarette. She made a point of having it in that shot while she was looking directly into the camera. She was sending me a message."

"What message?"

"I assume something along the lines of 'They're coming to get you, Barbara.' Maybe she just wanted me to know the chickens are coming home to roost."

"I knew you were lying," Letitia says. "You said you didn't know why she would be killing all these people and trying to pin it on you."

"It's one of my superpowers. So here's the truth. I wasn't in Mexico taking down cartel bagmen. They just happened to be in the way. This sicaria, she goes by La Niña Quemada, is working with an Aztec wind god named Quetzalcoatl who I managed to piss off while I was down there. Now he wants to get back at me. And it looks like everybody else is in the middle of it." I sip more of my coffee and enjoy the stunned silence.

# Chapter 17

**Letitia makes a face** like she's just bit into a really nasty lemon. "A god. Not a nature spirit, or a demon? It's really a god. Okay."

"That was awfully easy." Alarm bells are going off. Did she already know? I don't think so. That's not the vibe I'm getting.

"Just because I don't like it doesn't mean I think you're lying to me. Why did you go to Mexico to piss off a god?"

"I didn't. I went to Mexico to kill two other gods and ended up pissing off a third. You ever hear of Santa Muerte?"

"Yeah, I know about her. Narco saint. Cartels worship her or some shit. We had a week-long course in gang suppression and she came up a lot. Creepy as fuck."

"She's my wife."

Letitia stares at me waiting for the punchline that doesn't come. "Okay," she says. "I'd heard stories, but . . ."

"Well, I think she's still my wife. I'm a little afraid to find out. It's complicated. She started off as the Aztec death goddess Mictecacihuatl and was married to Mict-lantecuhtli, who was supposed to be dead but wasn't.

They were both playing me for a patsy so I went to kill both of them."

"Did you?"

"Sort of, but that's not the point. The point is that I'd accidentally made a deal with Quetzalcoatl and agreed to burn down Mictlan."

"Mictlan?"

"Land of the dead. Aztec souls, cartel guys, lots of Catholics oddly enough. Burning it down would have destroyed them all, and I wasn't about to commit genocide. When I refused to burn down Mictlan, he said he'd get back at me."

Letitia puts her face in her hands, like if she can't see me this will all go away. "I want to get this right. You're married to a skeleton in a wedding dress who you killed—"

"Sort of killed."

"Sort of killed?" She parts her fingers so she can look at me between them.

"It's complicated."

"You said that."

"I think it bears repeating."

"Okay. Sort of killed, and her husband—"

"Ex-husband. He was dead. Then I killed him."

"Don't you have that backwards?"

"No."

"Now this Quetz—fuck, I'm not even gonna try to pronounce that. This other god is pissed off because you wouldn't burn down all the souls in the land of the dead. Why the hell did he want that?"

"It's—"

"Complicated. Got it. Okay, so you didn't burn the place down and now he wants to get back at you by burning L.A. down."

"That I'm not sure about. I don't know what he gets out of that. He tried to have me killed in Mictlan and that didn't work out so well for him. But I was expecting it then. I don't know why he doesn't just kill me now instead of trying to pin me for a bunch of murders. He's got something else going on, but I don't know what it is."

"I think I'm gonna be sick."

"Welcome to the wonderful world of necromancy," I say.

"I like my knack better," she says. "But I really wish I didn't have it right now."

"What is it?"

"Alethemancy."

"I don't know that one," I say, which isn't really surprising. There are so many ways to categorize and subcategorize magic I'm bound to have missed a few.

"Truth magic," she says. "Like how you see the dead, I can tell when I'm being lied to." That explains the weird looks she was giving me the last time we met. If she can tell when I'm lying to her, can she tell when I'm not telling her everything, as long as I keep it truthful?

"Good to know. Am I lying to you now?"

"I really wish you were."

"Me too. Now that that's out of the way, I found our assassin in Vernon. Ran into her and Quetzalcoatl. Barely made it out in one piece. Later that night, blocks of factories go up in massive fireballs."

"Maybe it's a coincidence," she says.

"I saw Quetzalcoatl in one of the fireballs."

"Shit," she says.

"Accurate, if understated."

"So, what happens now?"

"I need that file. Or it needs to get out there. If everyone knows about her it'll make it a lot harder for her to move around. The less she can maneuver, the safer people are going to be." And the less likely some random asshole with a grudge is going to come after me.

"I know that," she says. "It's just— Fuck it. Fine. I'll get the file."

"Thanks," I say. I'm not sure how to ask this next part, but I need to know, so I just say it. "Why the fuck are you working with that guy? Chu? You're not the minion type. I get why you're working with him now. But you've been with him a while, not just since these murders started. I don't get it. The guy's a fucking narcissist."

"What's that thing with pots and kettles?" she says. "I know he's a narcissist. He also gets shit done. And he has a vision for this city, and for everybody in it. Not just mages, everyone, especially the people on the fringes. I believe we can make it better.

"Eric, I'm a black lesbian LAPD detective and closeted witch, married to a Filipino woman who I have to lie to every day about who I really am, while making sure my day job doesn't find out about all the magic shit, and doing my real job to clean it all up. You don't get much more on the fringes than that."

"You really think he can make a difference?"

"I know he can."

I tried idealism once. Gave me a rash. Cynicism is just pattern recognition. And no rash. But it's not exactly doing me any favors. I wish I could believe the way Letitia does.

What really is the difference between Chu and Gabriela? His methods might be different, but he's pretty much doing the same thing she is; trying to make things better. She's just ruthless and bloodthirsty about it.

I don't get the same vibe off Chu that Letitia does. Or

the same vibe I get off Gabriela. For all her murderous badassitude, I believe her when she says she wants to improve things because I've seen it. I think she's batshit to try, but hey, not my pig, not my farm. But there's something wrong with Chu, I just don't know what.

"Fair enough. You do you," I say. "Let me know when you get that file, would you? The sooner we can get this out, the better for everybody."

"What about you? What are you doing?" she says.

"Need to go see someone." A pit opens in my stomach just thinking about it.

"Who?"

"Honestly, I'm really not sure."

———

I park in front of a strip mall just south of MacArthur Park on Alvarado. It's pretty much what you'd expect from a strip mall on Alvarado. Parking signs in English and Spanish, a Chinese fast food place, nail salon, coin-op laundry with a hand-painted LAVANDERIA sign above it.

Wedged between the nail salon and the laundromat sits a church to one of the fastest growing religions in the Western Hemisphere.

The storefront could just as easily be a donut shop or a taqueria except for the hand-painted sign above it: Sanctuario De La Santa Muerte. A drawing of La Dama Poderosa herself looks down upon the parking lot and the cars speeding down the street. I get out of the car and look up at the sign above the Mylar-covered window. Never thought I'd be here again.

Well, I've put this off long enough. Time to go to church.

An electronic chime sounds as I push the door open. Tepid air blows through a vent from an air conditioning unit grinding against the sweltering heat. For all the grime of the parking lot outside, the inside is a rainbow explosion of color. Bright yellow walls, shelves in blue, green, red, and on every surface prayer candles to Santa Muerte. Candles for protection, love, revenge, each in its own distinct shade.

Santa Muerte shrines and statues break up the rows of candles. Everything from four-foot-tall resin-cast skeletons down to dashboard models with black plastic gems for eyes. Keychains, jackets, t-shirts, scapulars. It's Santa Muerte tchotchke heaven in here.

A Latino man stands behind the counter and nods as I enter. I recognize him as the man who was here when I first came in a couple years ago. I've always wondered about him. When Santa Muerte killed my sister, she either had someone do it or possessed someone. She couldn't completely manifest physically in the living world.

Did he do it? If he did, should I kill him? Does it matter anymore? Did it ever? She's still dead, and I've exorcised her Echo, and I think I kept Santa Muerte from being able to walk the Earth.

"Eduardo, right?" I say. "Shrine open?"

"For you? Always. Go on in. I'll keep the riffraff out."

"I thought I was the riffraff."

"I won't tell if you don't."

"Fair enough." I stop as I pass by the counter toward a curtained-off area near the back. "Hey, I just gotta know. Did you kill my sister?"

"What if I said yes?"

"I'd kill you slow, cut off your head and wear it as a party hat."

"She picked you well," he says, smiling. "You already know who did it. You're asking if I was the vessel. No, sorry, chief. Wasn't me. Don't take this the wrong way, but I kind of wish it was. Then you could kill me and get some closure. Stop holding on. It's not doing you any favors."

I'm too tired to get a good rage going. Everything feels distant, drained. When I think of Lucy now I feel a cold, dull ache, an unshakeable exhaustion. The anger's been burned out of me. He's wrong about closure. There are some things you move on from. This isn't one of them.

"If I find out you did it, I'm coming for you."

"If I find out I did it," he says, "I'll hand you the knife. I hope you find what you're looking for."

"I don't," I say, and step through the curtain.

It's like going from a Willy Wonka funhouse to a Goth's wet dream. White Christmas lights are strung along the black painted walls, casting everything in a hazy glow. The wrought iron candelabras spaced every few feet are the same as last time, but the folding table and plastic benches that were here before have been replaced with an intricately carved altar and short wooden pews.

And then there's her. A life-size Santa Muerte. A skeleton in a white wedding dress, scythe in one hand, a globe in the other. Bottles of tequila, packs of cigarettes, half-smoked cigars, bunches of roses all lie at her skeletal feet.

Last time I was here I made an idiot of myself and actually prayed to the damned thing trying to get her attention. Then I got sick of it, drank her tequila, smoked a cigar, and put it out in one of her eye sockets.

This time I sit in one of the pews. She'll either show up or not. I don't really care beyond hoping she can give me some insight on what her cousin might be up to.

No. That's a lie. I want a lot more than that. I want to

know what happened in Mictlan. Did Santa Muerte take Tabitha, or did I get to her in time? Is she alive? Is that a concept that even applies anymore?

A thick scent of smoke and roses fills the air. "I was wondering when you were going to show up," I say.

"Funny," Tabitha says, sliding into the pew next to me. "I was wondering the same thing."

# Chapter 18

**Tabitha looks like she always has,** a completely normal Korean woman with long black hair. No sign of the Bony Lady that I can see other than a silk-screened drawing of her on the front of Tabitha's red t-shirt. I look into her eyes for any trace of Santa Muerte, but I couldn't see it before and I can't see it now.

I don't know what to say. Hi? How've you been? So, are you actually you or are you Santa Muerte wearing a Tabitha suit and should I try to kill you right now?

I settle on, "I got your cards. They were kinda cryptic."

"They're open to interpretation. That's the point," she says. "Good to know you got them, seeing as I put them into your pockets, on your dashboard, in the bathroom."

"You could have just shown up," I say. "Not that I wanted you to. Let's just get that out of the way right now."

"I know you didn't," she says. "That's why I didn't do it. But I figured we should talk eventually. I'm sure you have some questions." She glances at the ring on my finger. "So do I."

She's right, but I'm not going to ask most of them. I can feel myself getting spun up just being in the same room, and I'm not sure why. I feel nervous and confused more than anything else. Who is this person? Why do I even care about her? I'm free and clear, and I know what I need from her, so what the hell is my problem?

I want to get in and out as soon as possible. But before I can ask about Quetzalcoatl, there are a few things I need to know.

"Who are you?" I say. "Tabitha? Santa Muerte?"

"Yes," she says. "And no."

"Oh, for fuck sake. Can I just get a straight goddamn answer? Enough with the cryptic bullshit."

"That is a straight answer, Eric. I'm both Tabitha and Santa Muerte, and I'm neither of them. When you interrupted the ritual and pulled the knife from Santa Muerte and shoved it into Tabitha, you sacrificed them together. The knife did what the knife was supposed to do. It killed them. Like it killed you."

"It didn't kill me," I say, but I'm starting to wonder. She's right that the obsidian blade was designed to kill anything it cut. So what makes me think I survived? Besides a deep sense of denial and a remarkable facility for rationalization.

"Just because you're alive now doesn't mean you didn't die then," she says. "You were a sacrifice. It split you from Mictlantecuhtli. It's a simpler version of what Tabitha and Santa Muerte went through."

"You're talking about yourself in the third person," I say.

"No, I'm talking about them. When I said I'd given you a straight answer, I did. Tabitha's dead, Eric. So is Santa Muerte. Things didn't work out the way they were supposed to and instead of having one or the other, there's both and neither. Who they were has made me. I have their memories, their desires, their fears. I'm both of them and neither of them at the same time. I have pieces of their personalities in me, but I'm not them. I'm something brand new."

It starts to sink in that I'm talking to a complete stranger, a total unknown. Is she the Machiavellian goddess who orchestrated a five-hundred-year long con to get out of Mictlan? Or is she the woman who got taken in by it?

"La Reine est mort, vive La Reine?"

"Something like that, yes."

"So why the Lotería cards? El Valiente, La Corazon, the others? Those aren't random. Those are the cards Tabitha drew from her deck in Tepito. They're a message, but I don't understand what. You're not Tabitha and we don't have a connection. You said it yourself, you're brand new. What fucked up head game are you trying to play?"

"Let me ask you a question," she says. "Why are you still wearing the ring?"

I've been asking myself that same question for months. I can take it off whenever I want now. So why haven't I? I can feel the energy in it, the connection to Santa Muerte. Was I holding out hope that Tabitha had somehow taken her place? Is wanting a connection with someone who understands what I saw in Mictlan, who understands how it works, such a powerful draw that I'd ignore her own role in Santa Muerte's plan, or my sister's death, even if she was as much a victim of Santa Muerte as anyone else? It's stupid and fucked up, I know, but I think the answer is yes.

I felt like an ass before, and now that I know I was holding out hope for someone who doesn't exist anymore, that there's somebody else sitting in her place, I feel like an even bigger ass. This is how things go to shit. We let our feelings get in the way, make shit up about other people whether we know we're doing it or not.

"It's a reminder that it was a huge mistake and to never let it happen again," I say. "Like a scar, or herpes." She looks at me, and for a moment I can see Santa Muerte in those eyes, the pupils pulling me in, swallowing me up.

"You're right about the cards," she says, breaking eye contact. "They were a message. A lot of the logjam of souls in Mictlan has been eased because of you, but it's still a broken place. Mictlan still needs a king, now more than ever. And since you killed the other one, you're the only candidate left. You are El Valiente. I'm offering you La Corona."

"And La Corazon?"

"I think that's something we'd have to work out."

"Is this the hard sell or the soft one? I'm the only candidate? You can't find a replacement out of how many billions of people on this planet? Five hundred years of planning and you and Mictlantecuhtli never came up with a backup if it all went to shit?"

"It wasn't my plan," she says. "It was—"

"Santa Muerte's, I know. Who you aren't. If you're not Tabitha and you're not Santa Muerte, the fuck do I even call you?"

She pauses, confusion crawling across her face. "I—I need to think about that," she says.

"Have to think about that? How about Santa Pain-in-My-Ass? La Niña Multiple Personality Disorder? You have their memories and their desires? That's gotta be a headfuck. Which of them wins out if they don't agree? Do you flip a coin? Does she get the body

on holidays and weekends, or do you alternate during
the week?"

"It's not that simple," she says, gritting her teeth. She's
getting mad. Good. I'm fucking furious, my anger pouring out of me like a busted water main.

"Oh, it isn't? You're supposed to be La Dama
Poderosa, La Flaca, the Bony Lady herself. But you're
actually some dead girl necromancer who kicked because she believed somebody else's bullshit. I didn't
come here to talk to her. I came to talk to a fucking
avatar of death, and if she's not in there, then I'm wast-
ing my time."

"Oh, fuck you," Tabitha says, standing and getting in
my face. "You killed me, Eric. You stabbed me in the
heart."

"Really? I thought you weren't Tabitha."

"I—she. Goddammit. I have her memories. I know
what you did. You shoved that knife into my chest . . . her
chest, and then you—" She lets out a frustrated noise
somewhere between a groan and a scream.

"What did I do?" I say. "Because I sure as hell don't
remember."

"Nothing," she says, a little too quickly. "You were
just gone. Kicked out by Mictlan. That's not the point.
You murdered me."

"To save you."

"Well, it didn't fucking work, did it?"

"Oh, do not give me that shit. I should have just killed
you outright instead of letting you yank my chain
thinking—"

"What, that you were more than just some guy I was
told to fuck? Because that's what you were, Eric. I had
marching orders and I followed them. When I came on

to you, you'd just gotten the shit kicked out of you. You really think a girl's gonna go for a guy with a busted nose, covered in bruises? Yeah, that's hot. You think I have that little respect for myself?"

"Clearly, or you wouldn't have done it in the first place."

One second she's Tabitha. The next, her face splits open with cracks like dried mud, flames glowing behind her eyes. And then she's Santa Muerte, an eight-foot-tall skeleton in a dress with a burning scythe in her hand, a screaming goddess of vengeance.

"Oh, there she is. The star of our show. Outstanding performance. Brava!"

"You know nothing," she says, her voice a tear in the fabric of the universe. The full force of it slams into me, a freight train made of sound, pushing me back in the pew.

But now I'm on familiar footing. I might be confused about Tabitha, but a pissed off death goddess? That I can handle. Whatever came into being out of Tabitha and Santa Muerte, the binding between the personalities can't be that tight. It didn't take much at all to get Tabitha talking about herself in the first person. And it didn't take much to draw out Santa Muerte.

I don't doubt that I'm confronting something brand new, built out of both of them. But it doesn't matter. I had a reason for coming here, and all this bullshit about Mictlan, rings, Tabitha, and my own fucking stupidity clouded it over. But I remember now.

"Oh, blow it out your ass," I say. "I killed you once before, I'll fucking do it again."

She tips her head back, neck bones creaking, and laughs. Without flesh it should be comical, but everything about her is terrifying.

"With what?" she says. "You don't have Mictlante-cuhtli's knife, anymore. That ridiculous razor? Foul language?"

"Xiuhtecuhtli's fire," I say. "Quetzalcoatl's in town. And I bet he'd just love to get his hands on you."

# Chapter 19

**That stops her.** "You're lying," she says. "I would know if he was near."

"You sure about that? 'Cause I had a lovely chat with the guy last night. He's got a minion lighting shit on fire. You hear about the Vernon disaster? That was them. If the lighter can do that to a whole chunk of the city, just think what it can do to you."

In Mictlan she was terrified of Xiuhtecuhtli's fire. It could burn the whole place down and she knew it. It might not have quite the same power here as it does in Mictlan, but she's not from here. At least the Santa Muerte part of her isn't.

"Why, I bet you'd go up like gasoline-soaked cardboard. I'm betting if one of you goes, you both do. What would happen to Mictlan then? Neither one of you would be there to protect it. Quetzalcoatl could stroll right in and burn the whole place down."

Santa Muerte shudders, her body shrinking, twisting, half her and half Tabitha straight down the middle. Tabitha's skin melds bloodlessly into the bone. She pushes aside the wedding veil with a skeletal hand and I can see anger in Tabitha's eye. But more importantly I can see fear.

"He's here for you," she says, her voice a resonant harmony between Santa Muerte's and Tabitha's. "What do I have to worry about?"

"Yeah, he's here for me. So why hasn't he killed me, yet? Instead he's murdering other mages and pinning the killings on me. That sound like him? There's something else going on. It can't just be me he's after. Maybe he's hoping I can lead him to you, too."

"I know this pitch," she says. "You want something, Eric. Tell me what it is."

"You sure you don't want me to be all cryptic and subtextual and shit?"

"Just fucking tell me."

"I need to know what he wants, and to do that I need to understand him. And you're the only one left standing who I can ask. What the hell was his beef with you and the rest of his family? He turned on all of you and helped the Spanish wipe your people out. Why did he do it?"

"Because he's an asshole," she says, her voice more Tabitha than Santa Muerte.

"No," I say. "I'm an asshole. What he did is so far outside the realm of asshole I don't even know what to call it."

"He betrayed us all for more power," she says, her voice shifting back toward Santa Muerte's. "He wanted to rule over everything, he wanted to be the only god. He thought to use Cortés to get that power for himself. But he was outwitted by the Spaniard after they tried to take Mictlan. Wounded and weak, he was trapped in a vessel and buried beneath the temple of Huitzilopochtli and Tlaloc. I would send what few worshippers I had left to see him every twenty years, to spit on his writhing spirit and ensure that he was still trapped."

"And then he got out," I say. "How?"

"The vessel was weak like the Spaniard who trapped him. The magic guarding it cracked over time. With the spells failing, he was able to free himself."

How does she know this? She couldn't leave Mictlan. Then it comes to me. "Your followers who were staking him out. They were there when he broke free."

"Only two lived long enough to see it. They brought me images and impressions, anything useful. The rest had died long before. I knew where he had broken through, and sensed that something in him had changed, and not for the better. He blamed me for his own betrayal. As you said, I was the last one standing. He believed I would try to kill him the first chance I got, which is what he would have done. There was nothing but rage there. Blind, pointless rage."

Pieces are falling into place. If I hadn't known before, I certainly know now. He wants revenge for what he sees as a betrayal. But is it revenge against me, or revenge again Santa Muerte? Both? Neither? What the hell is his game?

"Boy doesn't give up, does he?"

"No," she says. "His stubbornness is almost as strong as yours."

"Ha, funny. See this face? This is the face of funny."

"You want help defeating him," she says.

"I just need to know how to do it. What was this vessel he was trapped in?"

"Fired clay," she says, "ensorcelled by Cortés's monks. I couldn't recreate the spells. Their magic was alien to me. But I know it was powerful enough to hold him."

"Well, I'll just pop on down to Target and pick one up." Dammit. I suspect the vessel isn't the important thing here, but the spells that trapped him. I can think of a few, but none would be powerful enough to hold him. "Any suggestions?"

"Come with me to Mictlan and take your place by my side."

"Not what I was asking. We've already had this conversation. You tried to kill me and stuff your ex-husband's spirit into my body. What makes you think I'm going to trust you? Even if the you I'm talking to isn't really the you who tried to murder me."

"He's gone. You know this."

"Let me talk to Tabitha."

"She's not—"

"Let me talk to the piece of you that's more Tabitha than not Tabitha. Jesus. Is this new? I don't remember either one of you being so pedantic." The skeleton shifts, muscle and skin and clothes flowing up the bones until it's Tabitha again. She closes her eyes, takes a deep breath, lets it out slowly.

"I'm still getting used to . . . myself," she says.

"I think I liked you better when you were just her avatar," I say. She scowls for a moment, but then lets it go. I wonder if maybe she liked herself better that way, too.

"Do *you* have any suggestions?" I say. She starts to talk and I interrupt with, "That don't have me becoming the new Mictlantecuhtli."

"Fine. Well, you can't kill him," she says. "He's a wind god, so Xiuhtecuhtli's fire isn't going to touch him. If anything it makes him more powerful. And you don't have the obsidian blade, anymore."

"Awesome. Okay. Fire bad, killing's out."

"I think you have to trap him," she says. "Like what Cortés did to him before."

"Inside a clay jar inscribed with a bunch of old Spanish spells that I don't know how to cast?"

"Bit of a longshot," she says. "I don't know what to tell you, Eric. I think you're right. When Quetzalcoatl exacts vengeance, he doesn't fuck around. If he was really trying to kill you, he'd have just done it. There is more going on here. But I honestly couldn't tell you what."

Does this even have anything to do with me? Am I a distraction? Bait? Just a loose end to tie up? I was hoping to get some idea what he might be up to by coming here. Instead . . .

"I shouldn't have come," I say. Tabitha's dead, or maybe not dead, and Santa Muerte's—worse? Better? How would you know if someone snuck into your house and replaced everything you owned with an exact replica?

After spending time with her in Mictlan my feelings about Tabitha got confused. I went from wanting to kill her to wanting to save her and . . . maybe something more. Now I don't even know what the hell I'm feeling. Numb, mostly. I expected this meeting to be weird and awkward, but not this weird and awkward.

"I'm glad that you did," Tabitha says. She puts her hand gently on my arm. I jerk it back like I've just seen a scorpion sitting on it.

"Sorry," I say. "How much of you is in there? And you know what I mean, so please, just give me a real answer."

"All of me," she says. "All of Santa Muerte."

"Who's in charge?"

"You still don't get it," she says. "Nobody's in charge. I'm me. Just me."

"I get it," I say. "I just don't want to." She's been Frankensteined together with personalities and powers intact. Thinking of her as Tabitha is like thinking of a heart transplant patient by the original owner's name. Which reminds me. "I still don't know what to call you."

"I have to think about that," she says. "In the meantime, use my old names."

"Don't suppose you'd like to take on Quetzalcoatl for me?"

"Not if I can help it," she says. "I have responsibilities. Like you said, where's Mictlan going to be if I'm not around? I can't risk getting into a fight with him. I was serious about you coming to Mictlan, you know. If whatever he's doing needs you, removing you from play is going to be a problem for him."

If this were Tabitha, I might think about it. But Santa Muerte's shadow taints everything. Some things I can't forget, or forgive. One of these days I'll have to finish what I started in Mictlan. I'm just not sure what that is.

"You know I'm not gonna do that," I say.

"I know. But I needed to say it."

"I guess that's it, then." I stand up from the pew. I've sat too long and every muscle in my body is yelling at me for it.

"I guess so. Goodbye, Eric."

"Goodbye, whoever the hell you are."

"Oh, Eric, one more thing," she says, as I'm about to step through the curtain. A jolt of fire rips through my left hand starting from the ring. My fingers cramp and twist like knots. The pain almost brings me to the floor. I turn to look at her, wondering how I missed this trap. Her face is Tabitha, but her eyes are empty, black sockets. The pain disappears as quickly as it came on.

"Like it or not," she says, a scent of smoke and roses filling the room, "we're linked. We'll see each other again. Husband."

And with that, she's gone.

# Chapter 20

I yank the ring off my finger as soon as I'm out of the chapel. There are a few customers looking at candles and a woman behind the counter. They're all looking at me like I've just grown a second head. Yeah, fuck you, people. You try being married to a death goddess.

I storm out the front and throw the ring as far as I can. I watch it sail over the parking lot and disappear among the street traffic. And then feel a sudden new weight in my pocket.

Goddammit. Of course it wasn't going to be that easy. I pull the ring out of my pocket. Yep, same ring. Still warm from when I was wearing it. Fine. You want to play that game? I might not be able to get rid of the damn thing, but that doesn't mean I have to wear it. I slide it back into my pocket. The fuck was I doing wearing it in the first place?

But I already know and it pisses me off. Because I'd hoped that somehow it'd be Tabitha waiting for me in there and not some goddess stitched together from leftover parts.

If I hadn't pulled the knife out of Santa Muerte and plunged it into Tabitha in a split-second decision to try to reverse things, would it just be Santa Muerte wearing Tabitha's skin? Shit, how do I even know it isn't? Try to fix shit and all I do is make it worse.

Okay, yeah, not entirely true. Mictlantecuhtli is gone. Nothing left of him but a pile of ground-up jade blown away in the wind. Still feels like an epic fail.

I should just let Quetzalcoatl burn everything down. Shit, I should have burned Mictlan down for him when I had the chance. I should track his ass down and just ask him. Dude, the fuck do you want? Burn L.A.? Set fire to Santa Muerte? You want your pet assassin to put a bullet in my head?

Great. Let's fucking do this. I am goddamn tired of this. I'm just tired in general. I've got mages hunting me down, a pissed off god whose agenda I can't figure out, and a cartel sicaria intent on making everything a pain in my ass.

When the phone rings I'm not in the best of moods and instead of looking to see who it is first, I stab the answer button and yell, "What?" into the microphone.

"Mister Carter," David Chu says. "I'm sorry, did I catch you at a bad time?"

"Is there a good time these days?"

"I'm an optimist," he says. "I was wondering if you could come by the house later. I'm releasing that file to the community and I wanted to give you a copy. You might be able to see something in it that we don't."

"Come again? I thought this was all Super-Secret Squirrel shit."

"It was intended to be, but under the circumstances, I think it would be better to get the information out than have you draw out the assassin. I spoke with Letitia and I understand there are larger forces at play. She told me about Quetzalcoatl, Santa Muerte, all of that. Had I known sooner I would have done this already. I'm not your enemy, Eric. I'm doing what I think is best for the city, and for our community. I handled it poorly. I'm sorry."

"Uh, sure. Okay." I want to be pissed off, but he sounds sincere. It's also his job to sound sincere, so I probably can't trust it. I'm more disappointed in Letitia than anything else. But I knew she was going to say something to him.

"There's another reason I want to get the file out there exonerating you," Chu says.

"Oh? You find something embarrassing about yourself in there that you need to get ahead of?" Silence.

"I'm almost tempted to not tell you," he says, irritation creeping into his voice. "You'll find out eventually, anyway. But that would be cruel. The European branch of the Werther family is upset at what you did to Attila, and they— What exactly did you do to Attila, anyway?"

"I moved him, his car, and his chauffeur over the line into limbo and left him there. He's smart. If he's not out by now he will be soon. Let me guess, everybody's saying I killed him, too?"

"They are. In fact, the family has put a bounty on you. Anyone who does the deed and brings proof in the form of your head gets, and I quote, 'The full backing and support of the Werther Clan as an adopted relative.'"

Shit. Mages don't need money. We want cash, we magic a few ATMs, manipulate some stock trades, whatever. If you want mages to take something on, you offer up something better than cash. Usually it's some mystic heirloom, a spellbook, whatever.

But this is a whole other level. They're essentially telling everyone that whoever brings in my head gets the family name, the contacts, access to their resources. If they're willing to let some schmuck off the street into their family just because he walks in with my head in a bowling bag, they really want me dead. If people weren't lining up to kill me before, they sure as hell are now.

Considering what everyone thinks I've done, it might not be a stretch that some people are going to think I've managed to kill Werther. Anybody with their head out of their ass should know I'm not in his league. He's so far above me in ability that all I can see is his shining ass wiggling down from the top of the ladder for people to climb up and kiss it.

"Fantastic. So Werther's family has put a hit out on me. Until that file gets out and everyone sees it, I'm walking around with a target on my back." Provided they even care. I may not have killed those other mages, but I did send Werther over to the other side.

"That would be the size of it."

"I'll head over. Provided nobody tries to kill me, I should be there in an hour or so."

"So, we'll say two, maybe three hours, then?"

"Funny. And fuck you." I hang up the phone.

Goddammit, Letitia. When I asked her to get the file I was thinking more like, oh, I dunno, steal it? What the hell is it about Chu that rubs me the wrong way? It's not the money, the politics, the showing off, or even the ridiculously bad idea of trying to put together a Wizard's Council. He's running for mayor, everybody likes him, he's got a history of helping out the community. He feels too good to be true.

And that's it. He's too good to be true. Jesus, what is wrong with me? Am I looking at anybody who's not a raging asshole looking to line their pockets with power as a threat? Sure, he's a politician, but that doesn't mean he's a bad guy.

What's done is done. Maybe I'm just being paranoid.

If he hadn't called me I'd have had to find out about the hit on me the hard way, and I'm really tired of surprises.

I walk past old Chevys, Fords, beat-up Toyotas, towards Vivian's Fiat. The more I look at it the uglier it gets. A shiny beige turd of a car, all curves and rounded edges. I can't wait to ditch the goddamn thing. I thumb the key fob to unlock the doors when I'm about halfway to the car.

The explosion lifts the Fiat like a rocket, blowing out all the windows in the cars and strip mall shops. The shockwave picks me up and throws me ten feet. I come down hard on the cement, but keep enough of my wits about me to roll. A couple of my tattoos trigger, absorbing the blast, cushioning my landing, diverting the shrapnel.

I pull myself to hands and knees. Bits of Vivian's Fiat are raining down around what remains of it, flames crawling through its interior from the undercarriage.

"Oh, come on." I'm not upset about the car per se. I mean, it's a Fiat. But between this and the Cadillac I'm starting to wonder if it's not me people are after but whatever I'm driving.

I pull my wits together and look around to see if anyone's taking advantage of the situation. No one steps out of the laundromat with a gun to pop me while I'm down. Did they think a weak-ass car bomb was going to do it? The blast largely went up, not out, and it was mostly flash and sizzle. Anything decent would have left a crater and half the storefronts would be rubble. Fucking amateurs.

The ringing in my ears begins to clear and now I can hear muffled screams as people realize what's happened and start to panic. I don't see any bodies, and I didn't feel anyone die, so that's good. It looks like I was the only one near the cars when the bomb went off.

Sirens getting closer. I stand up and the world tilts the wrong way. I'm not running anywhere, and I'm sure as hell not stealing a car. None of these things are remotely drivable. I sit down, try to clear my head. I need to think of something before the cops get here.

I pull a HI, MY NAME IS sticker out of my messenger bag, write I AM YOUR SUPERVISOR on it, pump it with some magic, and slap it on my chest. The last time I did this when I was mildly concussed I tried writing SOMEBODY IMPORTANT and it came out SOME-BODY IMPOTENT. That didn't go so well.

A black and white screeches into the parking lot, stopping just short of the curb. One officer, stepping out of the car and calling the scene in on his radio. He sees me and I wave him over, letting the Sharpie magic do its thing.

"Holy shit, sir," he says, running over to me.

"Help me up and get me the fuck outta here."

"I think we should wait for the paramedics, sir."

"Did I fucking tell you to think?" I say, hoping the magic backs me up. The thing about Sharpie magic is that, like most spells, it's more based on intent than appearance. I could have just written COP on it, and as long as the intent was "cop in charge whose orders you have to follow," it would have worked the same. At the same time, the words shape the message. If someone has problems with authority, writing SUPERVISOR won't work as well.

"Yes, sir," he says, helping me up. He's a younger guy with puppy energy. Looks like he's straight out of the Academy. His nameplate says HEARNE.

"What's your first name, kid?"

"Kevin," he says as he helps me into the passenger seat of his car. "Which hospital am I taking you to, sir?"

His eyes are a little glazed over. I might have overdone it a little on the Sharpie magic.

"No hospital, Kevin. I need you to get me to, uh . . . a safehouse. In the Valley." I give him the address to Chu's place in Encino. When we get there I can have Letitia take over. As a cop and somebody working the Cleanup Crew she'll know how to handle him.

"On it." He guns the engine as soon as my seatbelt's locked and hits the lights. As he speeds away I can see other black and whites heading into the parking lot with a bomb squad truck close behind.

Kevin reaches for the radio to call in where he is and where he's going, but I stop him before he can hit a button. "They can't know," I say. "I'm undercover investigating corruption in the ranks. Some of the people in dispatch might be part of the conspiracy."

"Really?" he says, shock and fear on his face. He pulls his hand back and focuses on driving. I turn down the volume. The last thing I need is to have Kevin tell dispatch where we are with fuck knows who else listening.

With the lights and sirens going we're making good time. Now *this* is the way to deal with L.A. traffic. We're on the 101 coming up on Highland when I see them in the side mirror. Two motorcycles zipping through traffic toward us. Not an unusual sight in L.A., but the accompanying feeling of magic speeding toward us like a bullet gives them away. I wonder if they're the ones who set the bomb, maybe assuming I'd be unconscious in the back of an ambulance by now. I'm not sure how they found me, though. Probably staked out Gabriela's warehouse. Or one of her people talked. Doesn't really matter.

If they did set the bomb, it's not actually a bad plan. Would explain why the blast was so small. They don't want me to be a smear on the pavement. They need my head if they want to collect, and I doubt the Werthers are gonna pay up for some sludge in a baggie.

"Get off at Highland," I say. The air's a lot more smoky than I'd expected. Something close by is on fire. Griffith Park, maybe, or the Hollywood Hills. It's gotten to the point where it's impossible to keep track of all the brushfires.

"What?" Kevin says, blinking around him like he's coming out of a dream. "I—Hang on. Who the hell are you?" I was afraid of this. Sharpie magic is better at re-direction than mind control, and it can wear off pretty quickly. But there are ways around that.

I push more power into the spell, throttling it back when his eyes start to go glassy. Frying his brain doing ninety on the 101 would be bad. For me, at least. He'll already be dead.

"Get off at Highland," I say again. What the hell is around here? Then I have it. "Head to the Bowl." It's late enough in the summer that the Hollywood Bowl should be crawling with people. And cars. That I can steal. I'll have Kevin run interference and go after the bikers while I grab myself something off the valet and get the hell out of there.

"C-Can't," he says. A thin tear of blood rolls down his cheek from his left eye. His hands are shaking. Shit. I pull back on the magic. I don't want to kill the guy. "Brush f-fire in the hills. They've got it closed off."

Of course they do. They're not going to let in 15,000 people paying a hundred bucks a pop just to have to evacuate them again.

Okay, change of plan. No cars, but also no people. Losing these guys would be good. Taking them out of the game completely would be better. At this point it doesn't really matter if they think I'm a serial killer. As long as the Werthers have their bounty out on me fuckers like these will just come at me again. The least I can do is thin the herd.

Of course, that means I have to keep Kevin alive long enough to get me there, which is proving to be a bit of a challenge. "It's okay," I say, keeping my voice as calm as possible. "I'm your supervisor. I called it in. We have special clearance." The effect is instantaneous. Kevin stops shaking. He blinks away the blood in his eye, wipes his cheek with the back of his hand.

"You got it, s-sir," he says. He's not fighting me, anymore, but I think I broke something. I was really hoping he'd be able to walk away from this one. "W-what's the plan?"

"We're gonna go kill some bad guys," I say.

# Chapter 21

**The black and white careens** around the sharp turn of the freeway exit, blowing through a red light and swerving up Highland. Traffic's light for this time of day, but the only things up here are freeway onramps and the Bowl. With all the smoke coming over the tops of the hills like fog, I can see why nobody else is up here.

Kevin's not doing so hot. His hands aren't shaking and his eyes have stopped bleeding, but a thin stream of pink fluid is running out of both nostrils and his right ear. Sorry, pal, nothing personal. You were just the right guy in the wrong place at the wrong time.

Kevin turns the car to the Bowl entrance, a long street heading up to VIP parking, the bikers closing on us. When I give the signal, Kevin hits the brakes and swerves hard. One of the bikers slams into the side of the car, sending the rider over the top. The other low-sides as he tries to turn, rolling off into a messy crouch as the bike skids across the lot.

Kevin's out and drawing his gun before I can even get the seatbelt undone. His reflexes are surprisingly good for somebody who's rapidly turning into a vegetable. He puts two rounds center mass into the biker who low-sided. The guy must have protections other than just his motorcycle gear, because the bullets aren't doing anything.

I get out to handle the other biker, but I don't have to. His head hangs at an impossible angle on a neck that bulges wrong in too many places. He went so fast I barely felt him die.

I turn back to Kevin, who's fired two more shots with the same effect. Before he can get off any more, the biker lets loose a spell. I try to get my shield to give Kevin some cover from whatever's coming—I can tell it's big—but I'm too slow and the spell hits him like a freight train.

Kevin literally turns inside out. The entire front of his body from his face to his crotch splits down the middle and wraps backward, legs and arms doing the same inverted peeling action, turning everything into a bloody mass of organs and cracked bones. His eyeballs pop and his teeth shoot out like popcorn as his skull folds in on itself. He's dead before he hits the ground.

I could feel the spell burning through a lot of magic and the biker drops to one knee. He starts to pull in more magic to top off his tank.

I expect him to throw a spell at me, so I bring up my shield to bounce it back, and instead he draws a samurai sword from his back.

A sword. Really. Who brings a sword to a magic fight? The least he could do is kill me before he tries chopping my head off. He yanks his helmet off, tossing it to the side. Sweat and blood from a cut over his eyebrow is running into his eye. But I don't think that's why he took the helmet off.

"You're fucking kidding me. Dan? It is Dan, isn't it?" The kid who ambushed me outside his mom's burned-out house in West Adams is standing in front of me with a fucking samurai sword. "I brought you back to life, you little shit."

"But you killed me first," he yells.

"You shot at me."

"You killed my mom."

"I did not, I— The fuck am I doing?" I raise the Browning and pull the trigger. Whatever he's enchanted his motorcycle gear with might stop a round from a regular gun, but I can feel the Browning wanting to take a bite out of him. Kid's a fast learner, though. He's got a shield up and the bullet ricochets off into the trees.

"I killed you before, you little bastard, and I'll do it again if I have to. And this time no take-backs." I start to pull together a spell. I know I outclass him, but that shield's going to block most things I can throw at him. So I don't throw anything.

"Blow it out your ass, old man." He starts to run at me with the sword high over his head, screaming like a Florida meth addict.

"Old? Fuck you, I'll show you old." I let the spell loose just as he gets to Kevin's dripping corpse. The former Officer Hearne reaches out and grabs his foot as he runs by. Shield won't do shit if you've got it aimed in the wrong direction. And he's not looking at his feet. Dan goes down hard, the sword skidding across the ground toward me. I stop it with my foot, the cheap blade snapping in two.

"You couldn't splurge on a decent sword?" I say. "This thing couldn't cut cold butter." Dan answers me by screaming. At this point Kevin has rolled onto him and crawled his inside-out corpse up Dan's legs, pinning him to the ground.

If he were thinking clearly, Dan could throw him off with a spell, but he's panicking and trying to crawl away, not registering that that's not going to work. He's got a couple hundred pounds of inside-out, dead cop inching slug-like up his body. This is why people die in zombie movies.

I step over to them and crouch down. Dan's eyes are wide with panic. He beats uselessly against the corpse with his fists, sending up little sprays of blood and gore.

"I gave you a second chance," I say. I wipe a drop of blood spray off my cheek. "I know you don't believe me when I say I didn't kill your mother. Something tells me you're never going to believe it. I've got a whole boat-load of pissed off mages after my head right now. I don't have time for this shit. I can't have this happen again."

"It won't," he says, tears pouring out his eyes. "I promise. Please. Just get it off me." Kevin hauls himself up to Dan's chest, pushing the air out of his lungs, keeps moving up his body.

His screams turn to a wheeze and then a whimper and then nothing but a gurgle as the corpse crawls up to his face. Dan's not dead yet, but he will be soon, drowned in the cop's blood and smothered from his weight.

He's a pain in the ass. And apparently a serial killer. And he tried to kill me. Twice now. I should just let him choke to death.

Then I notice the ghosts, and now I have questions.

I have Kevin roll himself off and let go of my control. The body lands next to Dan with a wet plop. Dan takes a deep breath and starts coughing up chunks of Kevin meat, his face smeared with blood and brain matter and fuck knows what else.

"Since the last time we met I've heard some things about you, Dan." He freezes, eyes going wide. "Oh, yeah, I know your name. I also know what you've been doing with your little poison tricks." I press the Browning against his head. "You might not want to try any of them at the moment, by the way. I got an itchy trigger finger."

"The fuck is it to you?" he says. "There are mages in this town who do worse. Shit, there are normals that do worse."

"Lot of 'em, yeah. I've known a few. But we're talking about you. The folks you've killed. You do it here in L.A.? Or you go out of town?"

"Motherfucker, I do it right here under everybody's goddamn nose."

This is not news to me. I've been so focused on our own little drama that I hadn't noticed the fifteen, maybe twenty Wanderers, that have shown up, with more pouring in. Men, women, old, young. They stand around us in a circle staring at Dan, some with rage on their faces, others with confusion, like they just walked into a room and can't remember why. I have a pretty good idea why they're here, though.

"I kinda thought so. Killed a lot of people, have you?" He laughs. He doesn't care about the gun against his head, the gore he's still coughing up. He's proud of his work.

I'm not sure who I'm more pissed off at, Dan for being a fucking serial killer, or all the mages in this town powerful enough to take him out who didn't. But hey, he didn't come after one of us, so why should we care, right?

"I've killed dozens. I know how to get away with it. Who gives a fuck about a bunch of normals? They're not mages. They're not us. They're fucking toys. I can do whatever the hell I want with them. Long as I don't cross the line, nobody fucks with me."

Yeah. The Line. Always had a problem with that.

It's a balance of power thing. The last thing anybody

wants is a mage war on the streets of L.A. It'd make hunting me down look like a stroll in the park. So we don't fuck with each other. Everybody leaves each other to do their own thing, and fuck the people who get in the way. You leave them alone, they leave you alone. Don't cross The Line.

Fuck The Line.

I slash the straight razor across his face, slicing through his cheek. Blood wells out the wound. He screams and tries to crawl away from me, but I shove the Browning harder into his temple and he freezes, shrieks turning to whimpers.

I pull a spell together. One I've thought about for a while but haven't actually tried. It shouldn't be tough. When I killed Jean Boudreau after he'd murdered my parents, I grabbed him, took him over to the other side with me, and fed him to the ghosts.

Like when I moved Werther's car earlier, I had to take Boudreau to the other side with me. But this spell's a little different. With Dan here, I just send him.

He disappears, leaving a vaguely person-shaped blob of light thrashing around on the other side of the veil. I can see the ghosts fine. But Dan's not dead. Yet.

He probably has no idea where he is, or what's happening, but I bet he's recognizing a few faces.

And from the way they all descend on him, I think they might recognize him, too.

# Chapter 22

**"I thought two to three hours** was being generous," Chu says when I finally turn up on his doorstep.

"Things got a little hectic."

"I heard," he says, standing aside to let me in.

After delivering Dan to the ghosts I took the cop car far enough to ditch it on a side street and jack somebody else's ride. The Cleanup Crew can only do so much. At some point the shit I do that makes their jobs harder is going to catch up to me, but I'll deal with that when I don't have a price on my head.

I headed back to my motel to clean off the gore, get a change of clothes, and spend some quality time with a first aid kit. Bruised, scraped, cut. I blew capillaries in my left eye and it's bright red with blood. I think I bruised some ribs, and my back is telling me just how much of an asshole I've been to it.

I'm exhausted and in pain and I don't have time to be either. So I do a suburban speedball with a handful of Vicodin and some Adderall. It's gonna suck tomorrow, but until then at least I'll be functional.

"Peter," Chu calls, "can you get me and Mister Carter a whiskey, please?" He turns to me. "Neat?"

I nod and he yells back the order. Somewhere in another room I can hear the Assistant District Attorney get up and pour me a drink.

"Does he do windows, too?" I say.

"Peter's just a generous soul, Mister Carter. Can I call you Eric? By now we should both be on a first name basis."

"No," I say. I walk past him and into the room where we'd met before. Letitia sits in a corner looking at me with concern. Peter's poured the whiskey, hands me a glass as I come inside.

"Jesus, Eric," Letitia says. "What the hell happened to you?"

I down the whiskey in one gulp. "Long day at the office."

"You're bleeding," Peter says, nodding toward my chest. I don't bother to look.

"I'd be surprised if I wasn't." I'd bandaged things as well as I could. Sometimes you miss something.

Chu comes into the room. "Considering how your day's gone, I'd say you got off light. There's a been a scramble from the Cleanup Crew to cover up a few things."

"They find the cop at the Bowl?"

"Yes. He's being handled by someone in the Medical Examiner's office. Please tell me that was Sastre."

"Sadly, no," I say. "Ran into some guy who thought I'd murdered his dad. Maybe he was after the bounty. His friend probably was. The cop was collateral damage."

"Are you sure he's dead?" Chu says. "They only found two bodies. Shouldn't there be three?"

"As dead as it is possible to be," I say. "And they can stop looking. They won't find him. Doesn't really matter, anyway. We have bigger problems."

Peter gives me a skeptical look. "We?"

"Yes, we. As in the whole fucking city."

"Quetzalcoatl?" David says. Peter frowns, passing a look between us, clearly out of the loop.

"I'm keeping that quiet for the moment."

"Obviously," Peter says.

"Apologies," Chu says, ever the diplomat. "I only found out myself a little while ago and I thought it would be best if we had Mister Carter here to talk to before going into detail."

I take that as my cue. "Short version, I pissed off an Aztec god who is now up here burning shit down and blaming me for it. Sastre works for him. But I don't think I'm the reason he's here. If he wanted me dead, he'd just kill me outright."

"Why do you think he's here then?" Letitia says.

"No fucking idea. And honestly I don't really care. We just need him and his pet sicaria gone."

Peter takes all this in stride. Whether he believes me or not doesn't seem to matter. Chu believes and that's enough for him.

"He's a god," Peter says. "What does he need a cartel assassin for?"

"Something he can't do," I say.

"Like pull a trigger?" Letitia says. "Light a fire?"

"Fire he does just fine on his own," I say, remembering a crowd of Sinaloa toughs getting torched in a hotel parking lot in Zacatecas. "But the trigger, yeah. Hard to hold a gun when you're nothing but a ragged manifestation of wind and fire. I ran into her the other night. She was tying bundles of sticks together. I can't see her being big on the arts and crafts, so I figure he needs someone with thumbs."

"Sticks?"

"Yeah, I don't get it either," I say.

"What do we do about it?" Peter says.

"I'm tapped. I was hoping y'all might have some ideas."

"Could you ask your . . ." Letitia starts and raises an eyebrow at me. Okay, so she hasn't told them everything.

"I did. I got some information. After shit went down, Cortés had him trapped in a clay pot inscribed with binding spells and buried. Over time the spells faded and he cracked it like an egg."

Chu and Peter don't seem to like it. Even more loops to be left out of. Letitia'll get grilled later, I'm sure. Not like it's much of a secret, anymore.

"So, like a spirit bottle?" Chu says.

"If you mean like a spirit bottle in the same way a nuclear missile is like a bullet, sure. This is a god we're talking about here, not some pissy little poltergeist."

I've used spirit bottles before. They can be incredibly easy to make, depending on what kind of spirit you want to capture. I've got some drunkard ghost I trapped in a half-empty bottle of Stoli a few years back still banging around somewhere.

But this is so far out of the realm of what I can do; hell, what I even know how to do, I don't see any way to make it work.

"Do you know anyone who can make a spirit bottle that powerful?" Peter asks.

"If I did, you think I'd be here talking to you people? How about you? My name's mud in this town. You're the fucking golden children in here." Peter and Letitia shake their heads. Chu looks thoughtful. "You got something?"

"Actually, I think you might," he says.

"How so?" People say shit like that, it usually means

they know more than they've been letting on. I don't like that.

"There's a rumor, an old rumor, that your family had been collectors of a sort." He looks uncomfortable, gauging each word carefully.

"Spit it out," I say. "I'd like to get some sleep before dawn."

"The rumor is that the Carter family has been collecting magical artifacts, reagents, spellbooks, what have you, for decades," he says. "Nobody knows for sure because it's always been denied and nobody's been able to confirm because they don't know where it would all be stored if it did exist."

"News to me," I say. "My family and me, we weren't all that tight." I catch Letitia watching me out of the corner of my eye. She doesn't say anything, though I'm sure she knows I'm lying.

Chu nods. "Sure. Of course. But it seems to me that if this collection did exist, it might have something like that in it."

"And nobody knows where this place is?" I say.

"Not so far as I'm aware. Most people just write it off as a myth." He leans forward. "Does it exist, Mister Carter? Might it have something like what we need in it?"

"My folks must have forgotten to tell me about it before they were murdered and I had to leave town for a decade and a half."

There must be something in the tone of my voice that tells him to back off. He leans back in his chair and picks up his whiskey, swirling it in the glass before taking a sip, like nothing just happened.

"So where does that leave us?" Peter says.

"Can we do something about the assassin?" Letitia says. "If we can't touch him, what about her?"

"Mister Carter?" Chu says after a moment. "Any ideas?"

"Huh? Oh, yeah, that's probably not gonna work. Tried that. Didn't go so well. Q was protecting her."

I'm barely paying attention to the conversation. Instead I'm thinking about what Chu just said about my family's collection. I doubt he has any idea how big the thing is, though I don't doubt for a second there are rumors. Considering how old it is, I'd be surprised if there weren't any.

I wonder if he's right. Maybe there is something in there. I recall seeing lots of spirit bottles listed in the ledger. Some of them even had some promising descriptions. I stand up, bringing the conversation to an abrupt halt.

"Problem?" Chu says.

"I have to go," I say. "Gonna take me a while, but I've got some ideas. I'll swing by tomorrow when I know more."

"Call ahead first," he says. "I'm having a fundraiser here in the afternoon."

"People are actually giving you money?"

"That is how one runs for office, yes," he says. "Campaigns run on cash. Cash comes from donors. We can't all be trust fund babies."

I ignore the dig. I get it. My family had money, and apparently a hell of a lot more. But it's a bullshit insult. Any mage worth a good goddamn can get money. He's playing the self-made man angle for the normals. He doesn't need cash, he needs influence.

"Sure," I say. "Wouldn't want to frighten away the bourgeoisie. I'll show myself out."

Letitia follows and catches up to me before I get through the door. "The hell are you doing?" she whispers.

"Following through on an idea," I say. I should trust

her. She hasn't done anything but help me. But she's still working with Chu, and I don't trust him. I'm not about to tell her a goddamn thing about the storage unit.

"Is this an idea that's gonna fuck everything up?"

"Do you honestly think anything I do can make things worse?"

"Yes," she says.

"Okay, fair point. I promise I will do my best to not fuck things up worse than they already are. Happy?"

"No, but it'll have to do. Just be careful. Lives are on the line."

"You realize it'd be easier for everybody if you just shot me, right?"

"I've thought about it. You gonna at least tell us what this idea of yours is?"

"No," I say. I leave her at the door, where she watches until I'm down the street and can't see her in the rear-view anymore.

# Chapter 23

I head down to Ventura Boulevard and park in an empty lot. It's wishful thinking, but with all the crap my family's collected over the years there has to be something in the ledger that's a powerful enough spirit bottle it can hold Quetzalcoatl.

I scan through page after page, writing down every entry that looks promising on the back of a Taco Bell receipt I find in the car's cup holder.

It takes almost an hour, but I've got it narrowed down to six possibles, none of which I'm crazy about. Two don't just pull in a spirit, they pull in all the spirits around for a mile and a half. Even the ones that are still in people's bodies. They're probably strong enough to pull in Quetzalcoatl, but I don't really want to be stuck in there with him.

The third one's less a spirit bottle, more a magic vacuum cleaner. Literally. It's an old Electrolux from the fifties that was used to rid a hotel of demons. Only problem is that the bags were enchanted, too, and they all got used up.

Number four is a clay vessel that was used in Iraq to trap an Ugallu, this nasty Persian storm demon. I've heard of them, but never seen one. It starts off looking promising, but a series of addendums shows that it's not an Ugallu, it's about fifty of them, and they're still in there. To make things oh-so-much more interesting, sometime in the thirties it kind of went on walkabout and nobody's clear what happened to it.

The fifth one looks like it might do the trick. It's from the late sixties, a prototype built for the government. It's about twice the size of a bottle of Jack Daniels, made of titanium, and uses an ensorcelled piece of plutonium as a power source.

Now the downsides. It has to be kept and transported inside a lead-lined case, and if you're in its vicinity unshielded for more than a day you'll come down with radiation poisoning. Oh, and since it was designed as a prototype, it's bright yellow and covered in radiation hazard stickers and warning labels, like THIS END TOWARD ENEMY and DO NOT EAT. Not exactly subtle.

Number six looks, if not the most promising, at least not as personally threatening.

*November 19th, 1947—Spirit Bottle: Glass and metal. Unbreakable. Appears to be designed to trap and contain powerful entities. January 14th, 1948 Addendum DO NOT USE UNDER ANY CIRCUMSTANCES*

Leaving a note for mages saying DO NOT USE UNDER ANY CIRCUMSTANCES is like sticking a banana in front of a monkey and telling it not to eat it. There's no description as to why it shouldn't be used. There's nothing saying what's wrong with it. And if it were really dangerous, you'd think whoever wrote that entry might mention why.

Since that and the nuclear one are both in the Sherman Oaks storage unit, I figure I'll grab both and just not tell anybody that if they stand too close to one of them they might go sterile.

I head toward the storage unit, but double back, head a few miles out of my way. Keep my feelers out for any magic. It doesn't look like I'm being followed. So off to the building I go.

It's how I left it. Considering the wards and charms on the place, I doubt anyone could get inside without leveling the building. Heading in feels just as surreal as before, with the added benefit of having spent some quality time with the ledger, so I feel like I'm walking through a minefield.

Crates and boxes, desks and bookshelves. So much shit collected over decades, I have to wonder who organized it all, if you can call this organized. How many people know this place exists? This couldn't all have been done by my family. There aren't that many of us. My parents and grandparents had no siblings. So far as I know, I'm the last one standing.

Questions to answer another time, I suppose. I'm just thankful the place is air conditioned. After nine o'clock and it's still up in the 90s. The sooner I can get those two spirit bottles and get the hell out of here, the sooner I can get Quetzalcoatl off my ass and keep him from doing whatever crazy-ass shit he's trying to pull.

The radioactive bottle is surprisingly easy to find. It's in one of those thick steel briefcases you expect to find nuclear launch codes in, which makes a certain amount of sense. I crack open the case. There are lead panels covering the insides. The ledger entry for it went into more detail than most. It's just the way it was written, even down to the warning DO NOT EAT.

I close it up before my hair starts falling out. Fucking technomancers, man. Mages are kind of like mad scientists, always pushing what we can do with magic, but those guys are real mad scientists. Half the shit in here was made by a technomancer and it's probably the half that'll kill you out of spite. The only good thing about technomancers is they tend to blow themselves up before they cause too much trouble.

I decide to leave the portable nuclear disaster-waiting-to-happen where it is for now. If the other one doesn't pan out, then I'll give this one a whirl.

After an hour of looking, moving crates and hauling boxes, I can't find the other bottle. Even with this ridiculous lack of organization I should be able to find it pretty quickly. Everything's got tags and numbers and they're roughly in order, but the damn thing just isn't here.

I'm about to give up and go with the nuclear option when I have a thought. I've moved crates to check the ones behind them, but what about the ones against the wall?

Another twenty minutes and I find it, a safe recessed into the wall behind a stack of metal and wooden boxes. Thing's a fucking antique, but it has the ledger entry number painted on it in more modern military stencil. Gold filigree around the edges of the door, the words CARY SAFE CO. BUFFALO NY written in gothic script. Thick hinges, lever to open it. But instead of a dial, there's a metal plate about ten inches square with runes etched along the edges.

At least I don't need to figure out a combination. It's pretty obvious what the plate's for. I put my hand on it and it either unlocks or it kills me. I try the lever first. I'll feel real stupid if I die and it turns out it was unlocked the whole time. But no, it doesn't budge.

Well, shit. I press my left hand against the plate. There's a loud click of bolts disengaging. No fire, no explosion, no turning into a frog. I try the lever again. It turns easily in my hand.

Somebody went to a lot of trouble to make sure nobody found this thing and only certain people could open it. I'm starting to think I should leave the bottle where it is. But if I do that, I'll never know what the big deal is. Maybe it's exactly what I need.

I pull on the lever. The door opens like it's on freshly oiled hinges and inside . . . there's a cocktail napkin.

You have got to be fucking kidding me.

A goddamn cocktail napkin? I pull it out to take a closer look. It's from Kelbo's, a chain of old L.A. tiki bars that started in the forties. I remember the last one closing down in '94, the year before I left L.A. I turn the napkin over and written in pen is "TRinity 34778".

Trinity? The fuck is Trinity? Somebody's name? The nuclear bomb tests? Some Catholic shit? I take a deep breath, calm down, start thinking.

Whatever it means has to be from somewhere between 1947, when the bottle was found, and 1994, when Kelbo's closed. Something about the writing bugs me and after a few minutes of staring, it clicks.

The first two letters, TR, are capitals, then five numbers. It's a phone number from the old telephone exchange system, when there weren't as many people with their own numbers and you had actual operators to talk to.

The first two letters of the word matched numbers on the phone. But different cities might share the same numbers. So out of something like 32 you might get EAstgate, FAculty, and DAvis.

Or in this case, 87, TRinity. The phone number on

the back of the napkin is 873-4778. My momentary ex-
citement at figuring it out dies fast. They had area codes
back then, but they've split them up over and over as
more phone numbers were needed. Who knows how
many people have that same number in different area
codes now? There's 818, 323, 213, 310, and those are just
the ones I can remember.

I check the time on my pocket watch. It's almost
eleven. I write the exchange and number in pen on my
hand and lock the napkin in the safe, shoving the crates
back in place. It was there for a reason, and something
tells me I shouldn't let anybody else get hold of it.

Exhaustion hits me like a brick. The Adderall and
Vicodin have worn off and I'm tired and everything
hurts. I need sleep. I'll hit the motel for a few hours'
shut-eye and figure this out in the morning.

I go through the same process getting out of the storage facility as in, and once the door opens and I step
outside into the dry, too-warm air, I can feel the city's
magic again. That place is shut up so tight I can't get
anything from the outside. Not the magic, not the temperature, not even a single bar on my phone.

My phone. My phone can get me on the internet. The
internet has information. Information like old telephone
exchanges. I used to have no need for computers and
cell phones. If somebody wanted to get hold of me, I had
an answering service. But now I don't see how I lived
without them.

My exhaustion is gone, but adrenaline's only going to
last me so long. I pop another Adderall to pick me up,
and a Vicodin to smooth things out. That should keep
me going a few more hours.

I get in the car and start typing on a tiny keyboard.
Now that I know what I'm looking for, it goes pretty

quickly. Fifteen minutes of tracking down exchanges, area codes, and phone numbers, and I piece it together. That old exchange was in Downtown L.A. Once I have that it's easy to narrow down.

It's too much to hope that whoever had that number fifty years ago has the same number now. But it's the only lead I have. I dial the number. It rings a few times then picks up with the long beep of an answering machine.

"Hi," I say. "I found this number in a safe in Sherman Oaks. I don't know if you know anything about it. But I need to get what was supposed to be in there. It's a thing called a spirit bottle. And if you're the right person then you know what I'm talking about. Call me at this number if you are. It's really important." I should be doing this on one of my burner phones, but I don't have one with me.

I sit there staring at my phone, willing it to ring, but then I remember that it's after eleven. Sane people aren't crazy about getting late night phone calls from strangers.

And then the phone rings. At first I'm not sure I want to answer. All I wanted was a goddamn bottle to stick a god into, not this weird cloak-and-dagger shit.

But I've gone this far, I might as well see it through. As a great man once said, "Buy the ticket, take the ride."

"Hello?"

Silence, then, "Robert? No, you can't be Robert." A woman's voice, gravelly from age, maybe too many cigarettes. There's surprise in there, maybe even shock.

"Eric," I say. "Eric Carter. I found—"

"Oh, dear god," she says. "Eric. You sound just like him. He was right. He said you'd come one of these days and know what to do."

"I'm sorry, but I don't know who—"

"Oh, of course," she says. "I'm Miriam. You would have been too young to remember me. He said if family came looking then it would be important. And that they need to understand. We need to meet."

"Okay, where do—"

"Can you get to Union Station?" she says. "The waiting area. It'll be empty. I don't think you'll want anyone else around. And it was a special place for him. For us. That's where we met. He told me to give you, well, give whoever came looking the key." My head is spinning. I didn't know what I was expecting but it sure as hell wasn't this.

"Okay, I need you to slow this down a little," I say. "Who are you talking about?"

"Oh, I'm sorry. I thought you knew," she says. "Your grandfather."

# Chapter 24

**Back when it opened in 1939,** Union Station was the jewel of Los Angeles. People came from all over the country. Make it big in Hollywood, try their luck in the Sunshine State, hide from a past best left buried in the east.

It sits on what used to be Old Chinatown. The land got bought up and Chinatown moved to the west a bit. The problem I've always had with it isn't the place itself. Union Station's beautiful. Gorgeous chandeliers, amazing tilework. Even if you don't know you've seen it, you've seen it. Like everywhere else in L.A., it's been in the movies.

No, it's not Union Station I have a problem with. It's all the land around, and a piece of little-known L.A. history that took place there in 1871. Something like five hundred white men descended on Chinatown, ransacked buildings, tortured and murdered the residents. By the time it was all over, eighteen Chinese men hung from lampposts. Fun fact, biggest mass lynching in U.S. history. Bring that one out at your next cocktail party.

All the white folks cheered, all the Chinese wept, and all the dead left ghosts.

Whenever I come down here I try to pass by where

the massacre happened. It's a little outside Olvera Street, a historic district that's turned into a kitschy tourist trap of Mexican restaurants and south-of-the-border tchotchkes. Strong Haunts, those dead Chinese. A hundred fifty years gone and they're solid as the day they died. They're even strong enough to incorporate the lampposts into their manifestations.

Faces purple from bruising and strangulation, heads hanging from necks at impossible angles. They're close enough together that walking through is like stepping through a grove of corpses. Like the Billie Holiday song, strange fruit indeed.

I've tried talking to them. I picked up a little bit of Cantonese in the nineties. Barely enough to hold a conversation, but enough to ask a few questions. They look right at me, open their mouths, and scream. I'm just another fucking gwáilóu as far as they're concerned. Five hundred white guys loot your neighborhood and hang you from a lamppost, I wouldn't trust me, either.

I'm not sure why I pass through here to Union Station. I certainly don't enjoy it. It just feels important to remember that no matter what monsters are out there, there's nothing more dangerous than just plain people.

Union Station's always open. Most of the passenger trains are done for the night, but some of the non-stops run through, and there's always cargo. Stepping through the doors is like stepping into the 1930s. There's a pristine ticketing area to one side that they don't use anymore except as a movie set, but the waiting area, the main concourse, is huge and well used.

A peaked ceiling with hand-painted tiles, forty-foot windows on either side, rows of wide, Art Deco mahogany chairs with leather cushions. Not a lot of people come to Union Station this late at night. Before I left

L.A. you'd find at least some of the seats occupied by homeless people trying to take a nap somewhere they wouldn't get shanked. But now the station's cleared them out.

But even with the hour, I would expect to see more than one old woman sitting in one of the chairs near the end of the hall. She sits ramrod straight, a cane held in front of her. Skin marked with the deep crevasses of age, hair white and falling down her shoulders, eyes that are bright and alert. As I get close enough she looks me up and down and her eyes go a little distant.

I sit down in the chair opposite her, lean forward to get a better look. The wide aisles between rows were designed with people carrying 1930s luggage in mind, not for convenient conversation.

"You're Miriam, I take it."

"Miriam Dawson," she says. "I knew your grandfather, Robert. And your parents."

"Funny, they never mentioned you," I say.

"I doubt they mentioned that your grandfather was still alive until you were fifteen, either. The Carters and their secrets." Hearing that is like a punch in the chest.

"My grandfather died after getting back from World War II with my grandmother in a car accident. My dad was an orphan."

"Your grandmother, yes, but not your grandfather. That happened back in New York. 1945. They had your father before Robert went off to fight in 1943. He'd only been home a month when the accident happened. He came out here to start a new life, get his bearings and a place to live before he brought your father out here." She tilts her head behind her. "That's where I met him. On the train. He helped me when some of your people tried to rob and kill me. He was a good man."

"I wouldn't know," I said. "I never met him." A wave of sudden anger washes over me. Why did they tell me he was dead? Why keep that a secret? He was alive for the first fifteen years of my life and I never met him? He was the only surviving ancestor I had. My mom's parents had passed away a year after I was born.

"Oh, I know that look," Miriam says. "God, you look just like him. You're angry. Because they didn't tell you? Or because you're having to find out from a stranger?"

"I'm really not sure," I say. "More the first, I think. And wondering why."

"Your grandfather went to fight voluntarily. Very few of your people did. They didn't see the point. They knew they'd be safe no matter what. But your grandfather wasn't built that way. He knew he would be perfectly safe on a battlefield, and if he hid things well enough, he might make a hell of a difference.

"He wasn't counting on other mages fighting in the war. Did you know Eisenhower was a talent? Not a terribly gifted one, but he knew magic when he saw it, and it didn't take long for your grandfather to get his attention."

"This doesn't really answer my question."

"Young people," she says, rolling her eyes. "So impatient. And yes it does, if you'll mind your elders for five minutes."

"Are you gonna call me a whippersnapper?"

She laughs. "I just might. Now shut your hole and listen. Robert was sent behind enemy lines to verify rumors that the Nazis were using magic directly in the war effort. They were. Necromantic rituals, magical experiments on people from the camps. Robert stopped them. But it scarred him."

Necromantic rituals. I can see where this is going.

"PTSD?" I say.

"He used to wake up screaming in the middle of the night. Almost killed me a time or two waking from nightmares about ghosts and armies of walking corpses."

"So he did know me," I say. "But he couldn't be around me."

"Not after you manifested your talents, no. And you were six months old when it was clear what they were. Oh, he loved you, and he hated himself for not being there. He heard stories from your parents, heard things off the streets. The fights you were getting into. The anger. He so wanted to help you. Because that's how he'd been at that age."

"But every time he came near me he'd have a panic attack," I say.

"That's putting it mildly. We'd taken you off your parents' hands for a day when your talents manifested at six months old. You made a roadkill rabbit get up and dance. You were delighted. Laughing and clapping."

"And, what, he rolled up into a ball and shook?"

"No," she says. "He tried to kill you. I had to hit him over the head with a rock several times before he stopped strangling you and cleared his head enough to realize what he was doing."

Jesus. What the hell had he seen? A lot of necromancy is really fucked up, I won't pretend it isn't, but to do that to him? I can't even imagine what he saw. And if he tried to kill me . . .

"Did he know an old Nazi in town named—"

"Neumann," she says. "Yes, they knew each other from the war. Your grandfather tried to kill him so many times. And the other way around. But they never could. Finally, your grandfather stopped trying, and instead made a point of stopping anything he tried to do."

"I heard somebody finally got him."

"Yes. A zombie, if you can believe it. Well, not a zombie exactly. I'm not clear on the details."

"Sounds like poetic justice."

"Yes, it does, doesn't it? Robert knew that he couldn't be trusted to be entirely rational with you. He tried. Therapy, drugs, hypnosis, magic. But he couldn't get past his nightmares. When he looked at you he saw a monster, not family."

"Yeah, I tend to bring that out in people. They thought it would be better if I just didn't know?"

"Yes. It wasn't my decision. Your father never liked me much, so when Robert finally died I was largely shunned. Told not to seek you out. Robert and I never married, so I wasn't technically family. There were wards on some places and things that would only open up to family. I thought about getting hold of you anyway, but then I thought it would be better not to. I did leave you a couple of things your grandfather wanted you to have, though. I pulled them out of storage before he died and I was locked out of those warehouses your family kept all that stuff in."

"A pistol and a pocket watch?" I say.

"Oh, good, you did find them. The gun he got off a Nazi necromancer and said only another necromancer could make the magic work. The pocket watch . . . well, it wasn't always a pocket watch. When I met your grandfather it was an elaborate nineteenth-century clock weighing almost twenty pounds. Had to carry it in a suitcase. Over time it changes, or decides to change. Who knows, maybe in another twenty years it'll look like a cell phone."

"This is fascinating, and kind of disturbing, history, but—"

"The safe," she says.

"Yeah. Kind of on a timetable. Why was your phone number in there?"

"I don't know what the thing is, but it frightened him. He called it a spirit bottle, and got it when he was doing security for some local archaeologists. I'm afraid I don't have the details. He paid for the phone line and when he died I kept it up. I don't really know why. He told me to only talk about it if someone from his family called the number. I think he was hoping no one ever would and then it would simply be lost. But, in a weird way, I think he had you in mind."

"Presumably you know where it is," I say.

"Oh yes," she says. "I'm the only one." She hands me a key with a plastic, teal-colored tag that says AMBAS-SADOR HOTEL on it. There's a number on the key, 427. "Now it's your problem. You'll find it in that room in the Ambassador Hotel."

The Ambassador Hotel. Of course. Why not? It's not like anything else about this is easy. "You do know that the Ambassador was torn down a few years ago, right? It's not there anymore." She looks at me like I'm the stupidest kid in school and she's trying to teach me that two and two is four.

"Of course it isn't there," she says. "Not on the living side."

# Chapter 25

**It takes me** a second to parse what she's just said.

Items leave a psychic imprint on the landscape. Have something around long enough and it will have an equivalent on the side the ghosts inhabit. It doesn't even have to be particularly old, it just needs to be imbued with enough people's attention for enough time.

Things that don't stay fixed in one location don't stick around. Cars, for example, or any other vehicles, unless they're directly related to a haunting, like a ghost train.

But buildings, particularly old buildings where some shit's gone down, they're solid as rock. Walls are walls, floors are floors. You want to open a door, you better have the key. There are ways around it, but they're usually more dangerous than they're worth.

And just because a place has been torn down doesn't mean it's gone. The imprint's still there. People remember, wonder, write papers and books about it.

A hotel that used to host the cream of L.A. society, diplomats, kings, and even a presidential candidate who was assassinated isn't going to let something like being demolished keep it down.

Hiding something in it is kind of genius, but I see a few flaws in this plan. "Physical key, psychic lock," I say. "How's that supposed to work? And how did he get it in there? I don't know what his knack was, but it was clearly not necromancy. I don't see him wading through a sea of ghosts to get to the—" I glance at the room number on the key. "—fourth floor."

"You know, your grandfather was a pain in the ass, too."

"Must be a family trait."

"It's a physical key because it's a physical lock. The room is a pocket dimension. It's anchored to the location where that room in the Ambassador used to be, and used it as a template. The key tag is a talisman to ward against the ghosts as long as it's on your person. He usually went into the hotel, stood outside the room and then crossed over so he didn't have to deal with the ghosts. It's about the safest safehouse you can have. It even has electricity and running water. Well, it did the last time I was there. Nobody's been in since before your grandfather died."

"Jesus. All it needs now is a moat full of alligators. How did he do all that?"

"He didn't. A lot of people owed him favors. Big favors. The only thing he had to figure out was how to get over to the other side, and that was just a spell. He liked to go there and get away from things."

"And you don't know what makes the spirit bottle such a big deal?"

"Just that it scared him enough that he felt the need to hide it in the most secure place he could think of."

This feels dangerous. Like I should walk away and not look back. But there's something at the back of my mind that tells me not to ignore it.

"Thank you," I say. "For the key and for telling me about my family. If it's all right, I'd like to talk to you about it more sometime."

"I thought you might. Some of it's not easy to talk about. I loved him, but he had his flaws, and trouble always seemed to travel in his wake. We both lost a lot of good friends because of things he did."

Sounds familiar.

"Thanks. Should I call you at the number I got hold of you tonight?"

"I'm having it turned off," she says. "It was only around for one reason." She pulls out a cell phone, stores my contact information. I get the same from her.

"You need a lift anywhere?" I say. She's gotta be in her nineties by now and I'm not leaving her alone in an empty train station after midnight.

"No, but thank you," she says. "I'll be just fine."

"Look, I'm not gonna just leave—"

Her eyes flash a dim, glowing red and her smile is full of teeth. "Looks are deceiving, Eric. I'm not as old as I look. I'm much older."

Some things fall into place. "This is why my dad didn't like you, isn't it?" I say. Now that I'm looking for it, I see the signs. "Lamia, right? I dated one a few years back in New York. It didn't work out."

"It very often doesn't," she says. "But it worked with your grandfather and I. Your father didn't trust me. But Robert did, and that's all that mattered to me. Goodnight, Eric. Be safe."

She stands up smooth and graceful as a dancer and for a brief moment I can see her true self just under her skin. It's a good glamour, but then, Lamias are excellent predators.

"You too, Miriam. I'll see you around."

———

I get to the Ambassador grounds about half an hour later. The hotel closed in '89, but they kept it around a while for film shoots. That's the fate of everything in this town. It thrives, declines, gets turned into a movie location, *then* they tear it down.

They left it standing a good long time, too. Finally came down a few years before I got back to L.A., and they built a school complex on the grounds, the Robert F. Kennedy Community Schools. Needed to call it something, I guess. Kinda morbid, though, you ask me.

I slap a HELLO, MY NAME IS sticker with the words I'M NOT HERE written in Sharpie onto my chest and pump a little magic through it. I stand outside the gates of the school and peer inside. I can barely make out the outline of the old hotel in the distance. It looks a little more solid from this side of the veil than I'd expect. I can't usually see a vanished building on the other side unless it's got a lot of significance. I guess the Ambassador rates.

It's not a long walk, but I'm not sure which route would be easier. Navigate through the school until I get to the site of the actual hotel, or pop over to the dead side now and walk in a straight line.

There are a lot of Haunts and Wanderers around, though they seem to be keeping their distance. That's definitely not normal. The Wanderers at the very least should be swarming me, hoping for a free lunch whether I'm on their side or not. I walk toward a cluster of Wanderers on the street corner and they all back away from me, generally keeping about ten feet of distance.

No shit. Looks like that anti-ghost talisman works. It must only work near the hotel grounds, because I saw plenty when I was leaving Union Station and they didn't have this reaction.

That decides it, then. I slip to the other side. The color leaches out of everything, leaving it dim and blue, the jet engine noise blasts through my head, and I'm over. I head toward the hotel, the ghosts keeping their distance, though some of them are straining like mad dogs at the end of short leashes. I quicken my step. I have no idea how effective this talisman really is. It's doing its job, but it feels like the power could snap at any moment. If that happens I might not be able to get back fast enough. And with the new construction, who knows where I'll actually end up. I won't materialize into solid matter or anything like that, but I could find myself in an inconvenient spot.

The entrance of the hotel is just as grand on this side of the veil as it was when it stood on the other. It stands out from everything else on this side. Brighter, more color, not the drained look of the dead. Guests and hotel staff bustle around, most not noticing me. They look off. Too solid, too busy, too . . . alive. Are these just Echoes from the hotel's past? Not quite ghosts?

"Take your bags, sir?" a bright-eyed bellboy says, stepping into my path. Vibrant red uniform, pillbox hat. If the staff is talking to me, there's more going on here than I thought, but for the life of me I can't figure out what.

"No luggage," I say, holding up the key. His eyes flash on it and his smile grows impossibly large.

"Ah, of course! Mister Carter. We haven't seen you in quite some time. But as per our agreement we've kept the door to your suite in tip top shape. The maid hasn't been inside to clean it, obviously, but we've noticed no degradation in the spells you cast to keep things clean and in good working order."

"Uh . . . thanks."

"All part of the service, sir. Your contribution to this hotel has allowed us to keep things going for quite some time. You're paid up well into the next century."

He frowns momentarily, then the smile is back. "I'm so sorry, sir, I hadn't realized you weren't the original Mister Carter, though the family resemblance is uncanny. As part of the contract, anyone who holds the key and is a member of Robert Carter's family is allowed entrance to the suite. Do you need me to show you to your room?"

"I think I could use a guide," I say.

"Well then, follow me, sir." He snaps around like a soldier on parade and steps into one of the elevators. I follow closely, not quite sure what to make of all this.

"Can you refresh my memory?" I say. "You said something about a 'contribution to the hotel.' What was that, exactly?"

"Blood, sir," the bellboy says, his smile freakishly wide. "Gallons and gallons of it. That was the deal. And with that much blood, you've kept the Ambassador going for decades no matter what happens to the world outside."

The bellhop is clearly no Echo, and he's sure as hell not acting like any ghost I've seen on this side.

"Do you speak for the hotel?" I say.

He looks over his shoulder at me, and I figure it out just before he tells me, "Sir, I am the hotel."

Holy shit. None of these people are ghosts. Not individually. They're all part of a larger, much more powerful one: the ghost of the Ambassador Hotel itself. The Ambassador wasn't just a building, wasn't just masonry, glass, and wood. It was the people who slept there, worked there. It was Bobby Kennedy's assassination and the Rat Pack's performances.

This Ambassador isn't just an imprint on the psychic landscape. It's the soul of the hotel itself.

The elevators ride smoothly and in moments we're up on the fourth floor. He points to the far end of the hallway. "There you go, sir. I'm sure you'll find everything to your satisfaction."

"I'm sure I will," I say and hand him a five spot as a tip. He graciously tips his hat and disappears like the Cheshire Cat, only it's his hat that lingers instead of his grin.

The hallway is empty and I half expect to see two little axe-murdered girls asking me to play with them forever and ever. Which actually happens more often than you might think.

The door at the end of the hall is different from the others. I can tell those are ghost manifestations. They look very real, but there's an odd sort of plasticity to them. Like they were cast in one piece, doorknobs, wood grain, the works.

But the far door, my door, looks battered and worn. Runes and sigils carved into the unpainted wood that I wouldn't want to try my luck disarming. Most I don't recognize, the rest I don't trust. Good thing I have this key then, huh? I slide the key into the doorknob and turn. There's a click and the door swings open easily. I cross the threshold and I'm in another world. Probably literally.

It's a hotel suite, all right. A living room, two bedrooms, bathroom, kitchen, and dining area. Guess gramps didn't want to depend on room service. It's done in a forties Art Deco style, all elaborate curves and straight lines. Furniture in walnut, comfortable club chairs, plenty of light from lamps scattered around the room. I tug aside a curtain covering one of the windows, and it's not what I was expecting.

Not really sure what I was expecting, actually, but it sure as fuck wasn't this. This doesn't look onto the ghost hotel's lands, or onto the new school that's taken its place.

Outside is a thick pink fog, but even with that there's enough visibility to see the giant gas planet in the sky, and a landscape teeming with lumbering creatures that look like masses of tentacles and not much else.

I close the curtains quickly. Jesus, Gramps, you couldn't have built this place in, fuck, I dunno, Detroit? Pensacola? I guess if you really want to hide something well, you put it in the middle of a Lovecraftian wet dream.

I can't even begin to guess at all the spells that went into making this place. When I cross over to the dead side I can't access any magic but my own. I'm cut off from the pool. But in this room I can feel plenty. I don't know what casting any spells in here would do, but if I had to I'd have a lot of energy to work with.

Does it draw from the horror show outside? Does it bypass the ghost lands and hook directly into the living side? And what about the electricity? The hot and cold running water? The gas stove?

There's a large console tube radio in the living room. When I power it on I can pick up some AM stations playing 1940s hits, but most of the dial is this weird piping music like vuvuzelas played by monkeys on acid. Must be a local station.

On the one table in the living room is the thing I've been ignoring since I stepped in here, a large wooden box with hinges at the top and sides allowing each side to unfold. Each unhinged side has a small latch. Best to get my bearings before I fuck around with any magical artifacts I'm not on a first name basis with. There are no markings, no sigils. It was designed to be as ignorable as possible. So I continue to ignore it.

After checking the bedrooms, bathroom, kitchen, all fully functional, the beds even made up all professional-like, there's only one thing left.

I undo the top and front latches of the box, slowly opening each panel to lie flat on the table. I look at the contents from different angles, close-up, from across the room. As near as I can tell it's a bottle.

I mean, it's a pretty bottle. It's fairly short, about the height of a fifth of Jack, but it's fat and curved. It hurts a little to look at, actually. It's not square, it's not round, and yet it is. One moment it looks about twice the width of a baseball, then no larger than a flask. But at the same time it doesn't seem to change at all.

Instead of being made from one continuous piece of glass, it's a collection of multicolored glass panels bound together by thin bands of brass. Each pane has sigils engraved in its surface. Different languages, some I recognize—Hebrew, Arabic, Phoenician—others that look like nothing I've ever seen before. Even the thick metal-and-glass stopper is covered in runes.

The ones I can read, and I'm assuming the ones I can't, all amount to the same thing. They're binding spells. This thing is designed to keep inside whatever goes inside. It is not fucking around.

Unlike the nuclear one back in the storage unit, this one isn't labeled. No THIS END TOWARD ENEMY simplicity to it. Sure, these things look simple, open the bottle and pull in whatever you're pointing it at, but spirit bottles are rarely that easy. If I'm lucky there's a manual around here somewhere.

After a minute of looking I find an unlabeled envelope slid beneath the wooden case. Newspaper clippings spill out when I open it. L.A. Times, Herald Examiner, Evening Herald. Nothing big, certainly not front-page news, but in a couple of them there's a photo of a man who, just like Miriam said, looks a whole hell of a lot like me. He's standing at the edge of a scaffolding over a pit, holding something wrapped in cloth in his arms. He doesn't look happy that someone's taking his picture.

The headlines are the kind of sensational bullshit you get from the era. INDIAN GRAVES YIELD SURPRISING FIND; ANCIENT SECRETS SHED LIGHT ON EARLY CALIFORNIA; CATALINA ISLAND EXCAVATION FINDS SPANISH TREASURE. No help there. And then I realize what I've just read and my brain seizes.

Spanish treasure, Catalina Island, an ornate spirit bottle.

Fuck me. People have been looking for this bottle for hundreds of years. This is the bottle that if opened would let loose an entity that wiped out almost all of the Aztec gods with Quetzalcoatl's help, and under Cortés's command. A bottle that only ended up here because it hitched a ride with Cabrillo in his travels along the coast, stopping at places like Catalina Island.

This is Darius's bottle. And now everything starts to make sense.

# Chapter 26

**Juan Rodríguez Cabrillo.** Cortés orders him to hit Mictlan with a bunch of soldiers, priests, Quetzalcoatl, and the Djinn, Darius, right? You know this bit. Everything goes to shit, Cabrillo escapes with Darius's bottle, nobody's happy.

Twenty-some odd years later, our boy Cabrillo has made his fortune in the slave trade, brutally oppressing the indigenous people, yada yada yada. You get the idea. Real charmer, this guy.

Anyway, around 1540 he goes on an expedition up and down the California coast, somehow missing San Francisco Bay, which people give him shit for to this day. He makes a pit stop at Santa Catalina Island, where he trips over a rock while stepping out of a boat. Shatters his shin. Can you say Vitamin C deficiency, kids? Wound goes septic, gangrene sets in, and about a week later he's dead. Huzzah.

Now a question for the class, and think carefully. Where is Darius's bottle?

Folks who know about it through legends, and then later after meeting the Djinn, dig all around the California coast looking for it. Eventually everybody settles on "somewhere in Los Angeles." Even going so far as to use an excuse of hidden tunnels beneath Los Angeles filled with lizard people and gold to dig a pit near Downtown.

Stupid, I know. The lizard people are way further down.

Then in 1947, some archaeologists on Catalina dig up a bottle along with some Spanish crap and lots of busted up Chumash and Tongva artifacts. For god knows what reason, Robert Carter, Granddad, happens to be there and gets his hands on the bottle because it just about screams magic.

He locks it up. Then he figures out what it is and realizes that if anybody gets their hands on this thing, it's game over. Because whoever has the bottle has control of Darius. And the last time that happened, an entire civilization crumbled.

I sit in one of the leather chairs staring at the bottle on the table. I found a completely stocked bar and I'm on my second whiskey. Maybe if I drink enough this will all turn out to be a really bad dream.

I get why Gramps stuck the bottle here. Best place for it. I just wish he'd never found it in the first place. Then I wouldn't be in this mess.

I think I've mostly got it figured out. I think some people knew my family had it and were hoping I'd go looking for it without figuring out what it was. Make Quetzalcoatl enough of a threat and I'd go looking for a spirit bottle to take him down with, and grab the most powerful one I could find.

Hell of a gamble to get the bottle. But what do they lose? Not much. If I grab the wrong one, as long as it's not strong enough to trap Quetzalcoatl, they can do it again. "Well, that one didn't work. Do you have another?"

But if I show up with the right bottle, all they have to do is take me down to get it. The hard part's done. It's out in the open. Easy after that, provided they know how to undo the spell that locked it up tight back in Mictlan.

Obviously Quetzalcoatl's in on it. He knows what the bottle is, what it looks like, and how powerful he could be with Darius under his control. And Sastre, though I doubt Q would have told her everything. She's hired help, or a true believer, but either way Q's not stupid enough to let an unstable lunatic in on a secret that's been buried five hundred years.

But why have her around at all? To do something he couldn't. Sow enough chaos with the blame pointed at me that I lose my balance and can be steered in the right direction. She could have killed me pretty much any time she wanted to, or at least tried. But kill some mages, start some rumors, and now I've got everybody crawling up my ass. The obvious solution is to take her off the board. But she's got Q's protection, so he's gotta go first.

But there's somebody else. Has to be. How would Q have known my grandfather found it? I can't see him or his pet assassin rooting through the stacks at the L.A. library looking through old newspaper articles.

But who? I'm pretty sure I've got it narrowed down to a couple. Now I just need to figure out what to do about it.

My phone rings in my pocket and I almost spill my whiskey. I answer it without looking at who it is. "Jesus fuck, who is this?"

"Hello to you too," Vivian says. "Catch you at a bad time?"

I look at my phone. I've got full bars. You get a signal

in a hotel room on the other side of the universe in the realm of Nyarlathotep. Who knew?

"No, just unexpected. It's almost 4 a.m. What's wrong?"

"Good news for once," she says. "Gabriela's conscious. Woke up about half an hour ago. I figured you'd want to know, and you were never much of a sleeper, so I figured now's as good a time as any. She's not crazy about the spell you cast but she gets that it saved her life. She'll yell at you a lot, but she really means thank you."

"Conscious is good. How is she otherwise?"

"Not well enough to go out and fight an Aztec god, I can tell you that much."

"Good. The fewer people stuck in the middle of this shit, the better. Too many people getting fucked up as it is. Hey, now's probably not the time but I think these might be the most words we've spoken to each other in over a year, so . . . Are you doing all right?"

Silence. I'm the one who breaks it. "You know, forget it. That wasn't cool. None of my business, it's 4 a.m. and that was an ambush. Unintentional, but still. I'm sorry."

"I need out," she says. I'm about to say something but in a rare moment of my-head-out-of-my-ass, I don't.

"I've always known our world's fucked up," she says. "But I thought things were a tolerable kind of fucked up. And then Lucy got murdered. And you came back. And Alex died. And Tabitha . . . I'm still not entirely sure what the deal was with Tabitha."

Her voice is getting shaky. She pauses. I can hear her take a drag on a cigarette. "I threw myself into the cleanup. Wrapping up Alex's business, liquidating assets, handling the will, leftovers from Lucy's death. When I gave you all that paperwork about the inheritance, that was the end of it. I was done. I was about to leave. Had a job offer at a hospital in Seattle, picked out an apartment. I was one foot out the door."

She says nothing for a long time and finally I say, "What changed?"

"I got scared. Everything I knew was here. Everything I'd loved. Everything I'd hated. I'd already shut down my practice, sold my condo. Needed to get my head together. Did some volunteer work treating some of the homeless supernaturals, the ones Gabriela's been trying to help. We got to talking. She was up front about everything. About the challenges and the bullshit and the violence. Scared me at first, but she was doing good things, and I figured if this is the world I live in then fuck it, live it all the way. I started working for her. I'd spent my life denying that this was the world I came from and once I took it on, everything was good."

"You don't seem good."

"Because you came back, you fuck," she says, voice filled with a barely controlled rage. "Everything else in my life had been squared away. I'd cut my ties, I'd started over. I stayed out of the Westside. Changed my routines. And then you had to fucking show up again and bring all your shit with you. It was like I'd finally gotten something I'd wanted and it turned out to be a trap."

I don't know what to say to that. Apologize for existing? I'm sorry she got caught in my orbit again, but I'm not fucking apologizing for who I am.

"It's not even you," she says, before I can jump in. "It's our world. The whole goddamn thing. You know the fires at Vernon are still burning. People are still dying from toxic smoke. I know you didn't do that. We did that. All of us. So, no. I'm not all right. I'm not sure I'm ever going to be all right. I can't deny my magic, just like I can't deny that I went to medical school, or that I'm white. I have an ability to help people, but why bother? When I was doing trauma at County I'd see the same guys come in every few months with new gunshot wounds. I'd patch 'em up, but they'd just go out and keep getting shot. There's no point. I don't even know why I'm trying. Magic's not power. It's a fucking curse."

I've heard it enough times to know she's crying and trying not to. I think back on what I would have said when we were together. Comforting words, everything will be all right. Something to cheer her up.

Instead I say, "Yes. It is a curse. And you're fucked. So what? We're all fucked. We're more fucked than most people because we know what's on the other side of the curtain. This is your life. And you're stuck with it."

"Great pep talk," she says.

"You want me to lie to you? I won't. You want me to tell you it'll be all right? I can't. Living's hard, Viv. Living with magic's harder. I've seen and done shit just to stay alive that I'm not proud of, and sure as shit won't talk about. I don't know what'll make you feel better. Maybe nothing. Maybe Xanax, or a bottle of wine. Hell, maybe just some sleep. I don't know. I've never known."

There's a long pause and I can hear her taking drags on her cigarette and not saying anything. Finally, she says, "Sleep. I should go to sleep. Call Gabriela later. She'll want to talk to you."

"Will do. Night, Viv."

"Good night, Eric. Oh, and I know I said I was over it, but I still hate you for what happened to Alex."

"I know. Get some sleep. It's best to hate somebody on a full eight hours."

She hangs up the phone. Well, that's some good news,

I guess. Gabriela's alive, even while Vivian is slowly killing herself. The only way I can help her is by staying
away. But that's going to be a challenge with the circles
I run in.

What was it that she'd said? She feels trapped? No.
"It was like I'd finally gotten something I'd wanted and
it turned out to be a trap."

And then I know exactly what I'm going to do.

# Chapter 27

"**Son, you got any idea** what time it is?" Jack MacFee says over a bad connection.

"Six in the morning," I say. "I think I've been up for two days. I've honestly lost count."

"You sound awful awake for not having slept for two days," he says.

"Cocaine," I say, my nose still numb from the two lines I did off the dashboard. Adderall lasts longer, like hours longer, but for the shit I'm about to pull, cocaine's the only thing that'll work. A few hours from now I'll switch back to the speed, but right now, cocaine's what's on the menu.

"Ah, that would explain it." MacFee's one of those guys we mages go to when we need the sorts of things we can't find at the local 7-11. Grave dust, hands of glory, toadstools picked under a full moon on Walpurgis Night, that sort of thing. He stands by his products, and he's never let me down.

After I got off the phone with Vivian, I left the Ambassador and stole a car on Wilshire. In the last hour I've driven to the Valley and back, hit up my motel room for a few supplies, and come up with what I hope is a plan that has reasonable odds of both working and not getting me killed.

At the moment, of course, I am convinced that it's the best plan I've ever had. Partly because I was not on cocaine when I came up with it, and partly because I'm on cocaine right now. That's the problem with coke. It makes everything sound like a great idea. If at all possible, never make plans on coke.

"What can I do for ya?"

I tell him.

"I can have that by next Tuesday."

"I need it today."

"That's gonna cost. A rush order? That strong? You know the types of folks I have to go to for that."

"Whatta ya want for it?" Whatever it is it won't be money. MacFee lives by the rule that the bigger a pain in the ass something is, the less inclined he is to do it. I have basically just told him that I will handle his biggest pain in the ass. I'm prepped for him to ask me to kill somebody. Not crazy about it, but if it'll get the job done, I'm all in.

"Goats," he says, which is about as far away from what I expected as it is possible to be.

"Excuse me?"

"I got fifty black bucks on a farm in Ojai I gotta move. A cult bought 'em for a ritual two months ago but then it turned out somebody had a problem with animal cruelty or some shit, so they did the ritual and used, fuck, I dunno, tofu or somethin'."

"Demon summoning?"

"Don't know. Didn't ask. But last I heard they were all dead, so probably."

"And you want me to take the goats off your hands?"

"Yep."

"What's wrong with them? Possessed? Fire breathing? What?"

"They're just goats. My ex-wife wants 'em off her land by end of the month."

"You have an ex-wife?"

"Three of 'em. Couple kids, too."

"The thought of you raising children has suddenly turned this into a terrifying conversation. I'll get rid of the goats if for no other reason than to make it stop."

"Fantastic. When do you need this thing by?"

"Noon enough time?"

"I can do noon."

"Cool," I say. "One problem."

"I'll get it up to ya," he says. "Just call me and tell me where ya are."

"You're a pal," I say. Traffic's so snarled with the fire in Vernon that there's no way I'll get down to him to pick up anything.

"Nah, I'm just a guy who needs to get rid of some goats," MacFee says, and hangs up.

The Santa Ana winds have picked up overnight and they're blowing hard and hot through the streets, fanning the toxic flames of the Vernon fire and spreading them west into Alameda. Smoke and grit fill the hot air, get in the eyes, the nose, the mouth. A lot of people are wearing goggles and bandanas.

Mandatory evacuations as more homes are threatened. But there aren't enough shelters, enough beds, enough air conditioning, enough water. It's almost 100 degrees out and it's only six a.m.

People are being bussed down to Long Beach and San Diego as more firefighters come up to join the fight. It's the worst fire disaster in L.A.'s history and everybody with a hard hat and a hose is helping to put out the blaze.

The 110, 710, and 5 freeways are out of commission, so heading south means surface streets outside the evacuation zone, the 605 way the fuck out to the east, or the 405, which is a clusterfuck at the best of times.

Oh, and did I mention that part of the L.A. River is on fire, now? Yeah. Part of the L.A. River is on fire. Good times.

That's that part down. I know MacFee will deliver. Hopefully I'll still be alive to collect. The rest of my morning is just going to get progressively more uncomfortable.

I expect that the route down past MacArthur Park is going to be a mess, like everywhere else today. But all the lights are green, and the cars in front of and behind me are far enough away that I might as well be in my own little bubble. It takes a few blocks for me to clue in to the fact that that's exactly where I am.

I get to the strip mall holding Santa Muerte's church in record time. No cars in the lot. Boards covering the shattered windows. And of course I'm expected. The Saint of Last Resort isn't going to let something like traffic get in the way of her consort coming to visit.

Tabitha, or whoever the fuck she is now, leans against the wall between the church and the laundromat, arms crossed. I stay in the car, engine idling.

Do I want to do this? Is it the only way, or just the most immediately convenient? After the last few hours of looking at it from multiple angles, possible outcomes, and really taking stock of what I have to work with, I can only answer the first question. Not just no, but fuck no.

But as to it being the only way—well, there is another. I could shoot myself. That'd put a wrench in the works, wouldn't it? Certainly explains why Quetzalcoatl hasn't killed me. I could end this all right now and the world would be demonstrably better off.

I'm seriously considering it.

I get out of the car and step in front of her, my expression flat to her look of smug satisfaction. "I knew you'd be back," she says.

"Don't. The only thing keeping me together right now is two lines of blow off the dashboard of a '97 Corolla, and I am not in the mood."

Her expression goes sober. "You're right. I'm sorry. I know this isn't easy."

"I assume you know why I'm here, right?"

"Yes. I think it's a stupid idea, and it could very well get you killed, with or without my help, but I'll do it. You know what I want, right?"

"Thirty days," I say. "All in one chunk or on weekends, or whatever. Like community service."

"Six months," she says.

"Fuck you. Even Persephone only got stuck with three."

She jumps on that. "Three, then," she says. "Three months of the year you take your place by my side in Mictlan as Mictlantecuhtli and help me fix it. You know how broken it is."

"I'm a handyman for the underworld," I say.

"You're Mictlantecuhtli. Which amounts to the same thing. While you're there you'll take on the responsibilities of the role and the abilities to perform them."

"And those include?"

"We'll go over that. They're pretty mundane. Opening paths between sections of Mictlan, getting some of the rowdier souls in line, the occasional blood sacrifice."

"Oh, goody. I haven't done one of those in weeks. One more condition. I don't start for six months. There's shit I need to figure out here and if I'm down there it'll be a problem."

"Counter-offer," she says. "You start in a month, but you're not stuck down there. You need to come up here, you come up here. That's fine. I'm not abducting you, Eric. This isn't what Santa Muerte had tried to get out of you. That was all just a bullshit ruse, anyway. I'm not her, but I have a responsibility, and I will see it through. And I need your help."

My skin is crawling. Am I seriously considering this? I spent over two years trying to get out of this very position, and now I'm willing to go back in?

This feels different, but is it really? Last time, Santa Muerte maneuvered me into this position and it was for a very different reason.

I'm having trouble not thinking of the woman, the goddess, in front of me as half Tabitha and half Santa Muerte. I know she isn't. But I still wonder which side this request is coming from.

"So I click my heels three times and say there's no place like home?"

"Yes," she says, smiling. I catch myself smiling back and remember that this isn't Tabitha. My face goes blank. She looks away and the silence goes on too long.

"Deal," I finally say. Fuck it. It's a three-month-a-year gig. I've had worse jobs. I put out my hand to shake and instead she whips a long, thin obsidian blade out of her sleeve and slashes my palm with expert precision. Before I can even blink she does the same to hers and clasps my hand tightly, our blood mixing together and dripping down our wrists.

"Goddammit, that hurts. Why is it always the hand?

Why do people always think the best place to draw blood from is the hand? I have to use that thing, you know."

"Don't be such a fucking baby," she says. "It's already healed." I look at my palm and though it's covered in blood, the slash is nothing but a thin white scar along the palm.

"It still hurt," I say. "Is that it? We done?"

"Yes. Think of it as renewing your vows."

"And I'd been all set for a divorce. Shit, I don't have black eyeballs again, do I?" I look at my reflection in the car windshield, but no, my eyes are still my eyes. The wedding ring is back on my finger, though. It'd been sitting in my pocket the last couple days.

"Only if you want them. You had a taste of Mictlantecuhtli's power before. This isn't quite the same, or as powerful, not up here at least, but it's yours. No turning into a rock this time. At least I think. This is kind of new for me, too."

"Fantastic," I say. "Later on, when the shit hits the fan, how do I get hold of you?"

"Just think of me," she says, except she hasn't said anything. It's all in my head. Just what I need. More disembodied voices in my skull. I had enough of that shit with her ex-husband bouncing around in there before I got rid of him.

"That easy, huh?" I think.

"Exactly that easy," she says, with her voice this time.

"Can all your relatives do this?"

She cocks an eyebrow. "You mean can Quetzalcoatl do this? After all, he's the only one left."

"Yeah."

"Of course. If he binds with someone, he can do that."

"Can he bind with more than one person?"

"He's a god, Eric, he can pretty much do what he wants."

Interesting. That gives me an idea.

"Thanks," I say. "That helps."

"Call me. I'll be there. I'll do my part." Of that I have no doubt.

Two down. One to go. If I walk away from this one with my head, it'll be a miracle.

───────

The mansion in Beverly Hills has a clear patch of sky over it, as if the winds were forcing away the yellow haze of smoke and soot around it. If the normals even notice it their brains will fill in some explanation and move on. It's just a weird weather phenomenon. Not like it's magic or anything, right?

This is how powerful mages show they're powerful. Sure, they throw their money around, but for us it's all about letting everyone know how badass we are. Keeping this spell around the whole mansion takes a lot of power, keeping it up takes a lot of control. And then there's being able to do anything else while it's happening, like sleeping.

Things took longer than I expected, and the coke's pretty much worn off. I do a bump to keep things moving along. Drugs do the same things to mages as they do to normals. We just get more side effects. Normal people doing ayahuasca puke their guts out, they think their arms are turning into snakes and that they can see the future. Mages do that and the snakes are real, a demon rises out of the puddle of your own bile, and you really do see your future. Which tends to be very short.

Adderall, for example, can keep anybody awake and focused, but for a mage it makes their magic easier, faster. You see a lot of newbies depending on it, same with pit fighters. Yeah, we have pit fights. Two mages in, one mage out. It's fucking brutal. But at one point or another we all use it. We're bending reality into pretzel shapes, after all, and anything that makes that easier is going to be a popular choice. The only people who do more Adderall than mages are med students.

Pot doesn't really do much for us unless it's for a ritual that involves complete relaxation, and Valium works better. Acid is amateur hour. You're a mage and need acid to expand your consciousness, just get out of the game.

Another popular one is ecstasy. Because A) it's awesome and B) if you're doing any kind of sex magic you get really good results. You can pull some impressive shit out of your hat on that stuff. But man, are you gonna feel it the next morning.

Now cocaine is special. Cocaine hits mages like it hits everyone else. It boosts confidence, gets you all jittery, generally feels good for a while, helps you make really bad decisions. Like doing more coke.

But the weird thing it does is fuck up truth magic.

It's ironic. People on coke are horrible liars. It's so fucking obvious they're shoveling horseshit that nobody bothers to use it to defeat a truth finding spell.

Most truth spells are more like polygraphs than actual compulsions to tell the truth. Those exist, but they're less like unlocking a door than they are taking the door down with a ten-pound sledge. The after-effects aren't pretty.

What truth spells do really well is tell if someone *believes* they're telling the truth. And right now, I need to believe like a Pentecostal snake-handler in a pit full of rattlesnakes with his dick hanging out his pants.

The trick is to get just high enough that it can fuck

with the magic without taking you so over the top that nobody needs magic to tell you're bullshitting them in the first place.

It's like any drug that way. Get just enough of a buzz and you're golden. Go too far, and you're sitting naked on your ex-girlfriend's lawn crying and screaming at her to take you back until the police come to tase you.

I drive up to the mansion's gate, roll down the window, and stick my head out until I'm sure the camera on the post has a nice, clear view.

"Hi. I'm the guy whose head you want to cut off and stuff into a bowling bag," I say. "I was thinking maybe we should talk."

# Chapter 28

**Nothing happens for a good thirty seconds,** and I'm starting to think that the offer of talking is not being received well, and men with guns and dangerous spells will be appearing from the bushes to kill me. But then the gates open up and I drive on into the compound.

Mansions in Beverly Hills never show any imagination. Oh, the people who live there might think they have imagination, that they're decorating geniuses. The houses might look a little different, but it's all the same standard bullshit. There's a pool, indoor hot tub, tennis court, movie theater, the usual. It's all the same posh shit everybody else on the block owns.

Mage houses, on the other hand, when they give no fucks about hiding who they are from other mages, *really* give no fucks. As soon as I'm across the threshold of the gate and around a bend of the private road leading to the house, everything changes. The sky goes from day to night and is ringed by a brilliant display that would put the northern lights to shame.

If I hadn't just walked through the inside of a hotel's ghost to get to a room on another planet filled with things that would make Cronenberg shit himself, I'd probably be impressed.

I slow down the car to let a unicorn herd cross the road. Seriously? Unicorns? I met a breeder one time who let me in on the secret that they've only been around since about 1920. They don't advertise that fact, obviously. It'd be like De Beers admitting that a diamond is just a pretty rock.

I park the Corolla between a Rolls-Royce Silver Ghost and a black Bentley Continental. I resist the urge to "accidentally" bump into one of them.

The steps to the front door are lit with bioluminescent plants at the edges. The colors are vibrant and shifting, making it hard from a practical standpoint to actually see the steps. Probably by design to fuck with visitors.

What I don't see are the security guards. I know they're here. I probably have three of them standing behind me right now and if they're using spells I'd never know. There's so much magic in the air they could have an invisible 747 parked in the driveway and the only way I'd figure it out is to walk into it.

I get to the door, straighten my tie, pull my cuffs and look about as presentable as I'm ever likely to be. I knock on the door.

When it opens the smug look of satisfaction on Attila Werther's face drops almost to a pout when he realizes I'm not surprised.

"I told everybody you weren't dead," I say. "Nobody ever listens to me. I mean, you're what, a hundred? Hundred and fifty? You don't live that long and not know how to get out of tight spaces."

"Two hundred and three, actually. And credit where it's due, I actually did have a harder time than expected. Had to sacrifice my driver to get back. You might as well come in. I can at least offer you a drink before killing you."

I follow him inside. The door closes on its own behind me. The inside is all stark white marble, with black accents. I feel like I've walked into the end scene of 2001. "Power, grace, and snazzy interior design. You just don't see that kind of thing anymore," I say.

"I already pay someone to suck me off once a week, Mister Carter, so unless you're applying for the position, stop trying to blow me and get to the point." He leads me into a study that's just as stark as everything else I've seen.

"Have a seat. Whiskey?" I sit in the proffered chair, a surprisingly comfortable wingback upholstered in . . . is this manticore fur? Huh. Haven't seen that in a while.

"Given you're probably gonna kill me anyway, I might as well go out with some quality hooch," I say. "That's a yes, by the way. Okay. The point. I didn't murder any of those mages. And I didn't murder your granddaughter."

He hands me my whiskey. From the scent alone I can tell it's quality. And I'm usually a whatever's-closest-to-the-counter sort of whiskey drinker.

"A woman murdered my granddaughter with a bullet to the head in full view of everyone," he says.

"Yeah. Funny, you'd think she'd be easier to find. Especially for someone with your resources."

"Explain yourself," he says. I pull the folder I got from Chu and hand it to him.

"Her name's Jacqueline Sastre. She's a sicaria for the cartels in Mexico. She's very good and can do subtle if that's the job, but she really likes the flashy shit. Particularly fire. And torture. They call her La Niña Quemada, the Burning Girl. She's been hunting mages and setting them on fire using a magic Aztec lighter that will burn anything in nothing flat."

He pulls the picture from her border crossing and examines it closely. "That's the lighter, isn't it? She let them take that picture. She wanted someone to see the lighter." He looks up from the picture to me. "She wanted you to see it, didn't she?"

"Yes. I recognized the lighter, and she knew I would because I used to have it. She's not up here on her own. She's working for the Aztec wind god Quetzalcoatl. Near as I can tell, her whole job was to sow as much chaos as possible and point it at me to keep me off balance. Quetzalcoatl wanted to push me in the direction of finding a thing they think I have, but I don't."

He looks through the remaining photos and reports before saying, "That's quite a story. I wouldn't believe it of anyone if I hadn't heard about your recent troubles in Mictlan "

"You're well informed."

"I have eyes and ears everywhere, Mister Carter. I'm sure you understand."

"You also don't have any family in Europe that gives enough of a rat's ass about you to put a bounty on my head. You did it hoping to either have someone kill me, or flush me out and do it yourself. What if somebody had taken me down and showed up with my head? Would you have paid up?"

"Oh, absolutely. I have a reputation to maintain, you know. I'd let them enjoy some of the luxuries of the upper crust and then have them quietly killed in their sleep."

"Kinda figured."

"You have a history with Quetzalcoatl."

"History. That's an interesting word for it. You know I was in Mictlan. Do you know why I was in Mictlan?"

"I've only heard rumors," he says. "Something ridiculous about you becoming some sort of king of the dead."

"I was trying to avoid it, actually. I sort of succeeded. More or less. Anyway, before I went down there I made a request of the spirit of the Santa Anas. You know how wind spirits work. They all mix and match and fuck each other and what one knows eventually they all know."

"I see. And Quetzalcoatl, being a wind god, got into the conversation and gave you what you were looking for. His price was what, exactly?"

"Burn down Mictlan with that lighter. He doesn't like the place or the people. Holds a grudge like a motherfucker. That lighter contains the last of the god Xiuhtecuhtli's fire. You light something in Mictlan, the whole place will go up. You light it out here, it's a lot more limited, but you've seen what it can do to a building and a person."

"I see," he says. "It sounds as though he has something personal against you. It sounds like if I just killed you, this whole mess would end."

"I thought that, too. And yeah, it probably would. For a while. But they'd just find some other patsy later and try again. You know Darius, right?"

"The Djinn? Yes, I've met him. Ah, they think you have his prison." He looks at me carefully and—wait for it. There we go. I feel the touch of magic coming from him. Let's hope that noseful of Bolivian flake I did earlier does its job. "Do you?"

"If I did, do you think we'd be having this conversation?"

"Fair enough. But why do they think that's what they want? Or that you have it?"

"My grandfather was part of an archaeological dig on

Catalina after the war that found some Spanish artifacts. I guess he was known as something of a collector? Anyway, Catalina Island, Spanish artifacts, Cabrillo dead on one of the islands. You know about Darius, it's not a big leap. Also, bit of trivia I picked up in Mictlan, Darius and Quetzalcoatl helped the Spanish kick the shit out of the Aztecs. If anybody knows what Darius can do, it's him."

"Interesting," he says. "So how did you figure this out?"

I mentally cross my fingers. Lying indirectly like I did when he asked if I had the bottle is one thing. Talking complete bullshit is something else entirely. It helps to pepper it with enough truth to make it plausible bullshit.

"Somebody kept pushing on me to see if I could find a spirit bottle strong enough to trap Quetzalcoatl and started talking about rumors about my grandfather. That rang alarm bells.

"You know the L.A. Library has digitized copies of every city newspaper going back to the 1840s? Didn't take long to find the stories. I'm thinking someone found them a while ago, dug into the history, drew some connections, and got Quetzalcoatl involved. Now whoever did it knows Q wants that bottle, and they want it, too. Whichever one of them gets their hands on it first can let Darius loose to kick the shit out of the other. They're not only betting I have the bottle, but they're also counting on me not knowing what the bottle is."

"That's an interesting theory. You have a suspect?"

"I do, but proving it might be a little tough." Not that I really care about proving it. I know the fucker doing this. I don't need proof. But a veritable king like Werther, here, he will.

"Would a confession work for you?" I say. "If they did do it, then not only did they start all this mayhem, but they might as well have fired the gun that killed your granddaughter."

"I'm not sure if you're lying or not," he says. Thank fuck for that.

"I'm not a very good liar," I say. "Look at it this way. If it turns out I have lied to you, you'll just kill me. Hell, you might just kill me, anyway. But if I'm telling the truth, I'm sure you wouldn't want to aim your vengeance at the wrong person. Not because I think you care much about innocents, but the real killer would get away."

"And I suppose you'd like something in return for pointing me toward the real killer?"

"Call off the bounty. That file's already circulating. People are already figuring out I didn't murder their families. But it doesn't matter a rat's ass if they still think they're gonna hit the jackpot by parading my head in front of you on a stick."

He downs his whiskey. Is it too early to be drinking? I pop amphetamines like they're Tic Tacs, so the fuck do I know? I toss mine back, and wait to see if he bought it.

"All right," he says. "What do you need from me?"

# Chapter 29

**Everything burns.** Flames crawl along the floorboards, up the walls. They dance along the ceiling, flowing and dripping like a living thing. Outside the window I can see the rest of the city. The fires have spread, the streets are aflame. Cars are engulfed, paint stripped to glowing metal underneath, asphalt bubbling as it boils. Corpses lie on the sidewalks, trapped in cars, charred black, limbs contracted, drawn in from the overwhelming heat.

This is my fault. I brought this here. I brought this down on all these people not because of something I did, but because of who I am. I'm the guy with the key to an extradimensional room in a dead hotel, the guy with a bottle holding an entity that can crack worlds, the guy with a storage unit filled with the sorts of toys you play with only in nightmares.

"Everything dies, Eric. Everything is covered in blood. Whatever you touch you destroy." Santa Muerte with Tabitha's voice walks beside me down the street, a snow of ash falling to cover us both, her wedding dress as red as the embers in the flesh of burning corpses. "This is what it means to be king of the dead."

"Open the bottle." Gabriela on my other side. The

front of her shirt soaked in blood, her eyes hungry, face
feral. "Imagine what you could do if you let Darius loose.
A Djinn that powerful, you could remake the world. Or
give it to me. I'll do it."

"And let's face it," Vivian says, leaning over my shoulder from behind, her skin blackened and split like overdone barbecue. "It's a pretty shitty world."

———

I bolt up from the dream, sweating, panting. Panic wells
up inside me. I can't tell where I am, what's real, what
isn't.

I'm in my motel room. I came back here after seeing
Werther to try to get some sleep before the festivities start.
A few things are hazy. Somewhere in there I remember
calling MacFee. He used a teleportation charm to send me
what I bought. Did I actually agree to get rid of fifty goats
for this guy? I wonder if they like goats in Mictlan.

I've gotten about four hours of sleep. That's more
than I've had in the last few days and I could sleep for
another twenty. The bruises and cuts don't feel as bad,
and my ribs don't feel like the rotting beams of a house
somebody should have torn down years ago.

Then I move and it all goes to shit. Vicodin, a hot
shower, I'll be just fine. But Jesus, the last couple days
have taken their toll. I only have a few hours, and I still
have a lot to do.

I shower, shave, get cleaned up. Fresh Band-Aids
across my road rash knuckles, on various cuts and gashes
I hadn't noticed before. Gotta look professional for the
shindig later.

Then I get to work. I pour some Morton's salt in a circle around me for protection. At the cardinal points I
place a bowl filled with dirt, another with water, a dish

with a lit candle, and a blown-up balloon. Hey, fuck you. If you can think of a better way to represent air, I'm all ears.

The spell I got from MacFee is complicated, dangerous for amateurs, and has lots of moving parts. I could never hope to do it on my own. That's why the people he got it from have put it together in convenient kit form. It's less like chanting in ancient Aramaic for fifteen hours to summon pit demons than it is like following instructions from Ikea. About half an hour later, I'm done. And I don't even have any left-over Swedish screws.

Sitting on the table is a perfect—as perfect as I can recreate from my own memories and photos on my phone—likeness of Darius's bottle. I go over it one more time. Make sure the sigils match, the colors are right, the brass is tarnished in the right places.

Satisfied that it's as close as I can possibly get, down to how I remember the feel of the glass and the acid-etched glyphs, I delete the photos from my phone and pack the fake bottle in its case.

MacFee sources some good shit, I gotta admit. He works with a group that does high-end glamours. Really high end. There are pretty young things walking the runway or starring in blockbuster films who aren't what they appear to be. Hell, they're not even human. You'd be amazed how many famous actors and actresses have been around since before talkies were even a thing.

I've got an hour to kill so I turn on some 24-hour news channel and watch a talking head tell me that the Vernon fire is contained and they expect to have it out in the next day or so. But the damage is done. Hospitals are at capacity. The county morgue doesn't have enough room for all the bodies, so they've got them stored in hospitals, funeral homes, refrigerated trucks.

On the plus side, people are opening their homes to displaced strangers, blood donations are up, people are generally being nicer to each other. There is surprisingly little looting. Nothing beats horrible, gut-wrenching tragedy to bring a city together.

I dial up Letitia. She answers right before it goes to voicemail and the first thing I hear is someone, presumably her wife, yelling, "Don't you turn your back on me!" in the background.

"Hey," Letitia says. She sounds ground down.

"Bad time?"

"These days I don't know if there's such a thing as a good time."

"Have you had The Talk?" I say.

"God, no. And I'm not talking anymore about this. What do you want?"

"I'm heading over to Chu's. He's got that fundraiser going on. I figured I'd go surprise him with a little present."

"You found a sp—You found one?"

"Yep. Thought he should get a chance to see it before I hunt down a god with it."

"Jesus, that's the first good news I've heard."

"Head over to Chu's. We'll talk more then."

"Uh . . ." I hear glass crashing in the background. "I don't know if that's a good idea."

"If you don't get out of there and let things calm down, eventually she's gonna nail you with one of those glasses she's throwing. And I don't think either one of you is going to like the result. Trust me on this one."

"Speaking from experience?"

"You have to ask?"

"I'll think about it."

"Think fast," I say. "The more she throws, the more

you're looking at stitches and sending your wife to jail for a domestic."

"Don't even fucking joke about that," she says. "Look, I'll try to get over there. But no promises."

"That'll have to do. See you then. And good luck." I hang up to the sound of another glass shattering. Though I want to, I don't entirely trust Letitia. I really don't trust Chu and his lapdog. I want her there to see how she reacts to the fireworks once I've got everybody where I want them.

The inside of the motel room is hot, and that's with air conditioning. It's nothing compared to the temperatures outside. Nobody's predicting a break from the heat for the next few days. Then it might drop a degree or two. The car, the same Corolla I stole last night, is a piece of crap, but whoever owns it really took care of the A/C. It's like stepping into a pizza oven at first, but cools down by the time I'm heading up the hill toward the Valley.

Though the greenery in the hills of southern Encino has a cooling effect, the temperatures are soaring. As I get closer to Chu's place, I start seeing more and more expensive cars parked along the side of the road. Of course. He has a lot of parking in that driveway, but he's the political hotshot right now. This fundraiser is a big deal and it attracts a lot of attention.

I get up to Chu's place and sit in line as the valet guys park the Maseratis, Ferraris, Mercedes, and BMWs in front of me. When it comes to a twenty-year-old Corolla, they stare at it a minute before one of them, a sweaty, pimply-faced Asian kid, comes up to take my keys.

He takes them but I don't let go. "This is a very valuable piece of antique machinery that's worth more than all of these cars combined," I say, face serious. "Less than a hundred of these prototypes were made. I don't want to see a goddamn scratch on this car when I come back. Do you understand me?"

"Uh, sir, there are a lot of—"

"Do. You. Understand. Me?" Tabitha told me I could do the black eyes trick whenever I wanted, so I give it a whirl. From the kid's own widening eyes and stammer, I'd say it worked. "Well?"

"I—I understand," he says, shaking. I let my eyes go back to normal. He calms a little, but just about runs once I let him have the keys.

That was mean. And he's got a shitty job. Parking cars in this weather for these assholes? But I guarantee I won't be the biggest dick at this party, and if I can get some kid to say "fuck this job" and not be here when things go bad, I'll have done my good deed for the year.

"Hey," I say and he freezes in place. I storm up to him. He's shaking so hard he almost drops my keys. I shove a wad of hundred dollar bills in his vest pocket. I lean in, voice barely a whisper. "When the shit hits the fan," I say, "you run. Got me?"

"I—what?"

"Trust me, you'll know it when it happens." I leave him staring at my back as I head to the door where an attractive young lady and an intimidatingly muscular gentleman check invites and let people inside.

The looks on their faces when I step up are dubious at best. The way I look, bandages, bruises, my messenger bag slung over one shoulder, a thick metal briefcase in my hand—I'd look at me funny, too.

The woman recovers first. "Good evening, sir," she says. "May I see your invitation?"

"Don't have one, sorry. But I am wearing a tie. And I'm kind of a dick. That's gotta put me into the same category as at least some of these people."

I can feel magic on both of them. She's got some sort of protective charms, and his feel like they might make him bulletproof. From the look of them, stance, posture, they both have some military training and combat expertise. Gotta hand it to him, Chu does know how to recruit good people.

"Then I'm afraid I'm going to have to ask you to leave," the young man says, stepping forward.

"Tell Councilman Chu—or since he's probably busy, that puppy that keeps following him around and shitting on the carpet, Peter something—that I'm here and I have the thing he asked me about."

"Sir," the woman starts.

"Tell him it's Eric Carter." They both take an involuntary step back, eyes widening a fraction. Is my reputation that scary?

"I thought you'd be bigger," the man says.

"I am," I say, giving him a wink. "Where it counts. Come on. I don't have an army of the dead in my back pocket to toss at this place. I just need someone to tell Chu that I'm here and—"

Peter comes out the front door, suit immaculate, shoes mirror-polished, nose as brown as you'd expect from the way he shoves it up Chu's ass. "Mister Carter," he says, clearly annoyed. This is a side of him I haven't seen, yet. I wonder how much worse he can get.

I give the door staff my best winning smile. "This is the carpet-shitter I was talking about."

"Please stop harassing the staff," Peter says. "They're specially trained and I would like to continue to use the services of their employers. Did I hear you right that you've found something?"

"Yep. Pretty sure it'll do the trick, too." He thinks about it, weighs his options. Leave me out here where I can do untold damage to anyone else coming up, or usher me into a side room where I won't scare the straights, but will be inside along with them. I kind of feel for him. Neither of these are great choices.

He finally comes to a decision and scowls. "All right," he says. "Come with me. I'm pretty sure he can spare a few minutes for you."

"You're kind of an annoying prick, you know that?" I say.

"Yes. That's why I've got this job. Come on. Let's not make it any easier for David's guests to see you."

Oh, we can't have that. When shit gets heavy I want these people one foot out the door already. The minute we're inside I veer off and grab a handful of chicken on little toothpicks that a waitress is passing around and a glass of wine from another and start looking for Chu.

The place is balls deep in L.A.'s elite. I recognize faces, but I don't know most of the names. Politicians, rockers, actors, financiers. This is an industry town, after all, but it's not always clear what that industry is. I recognize a couple of mages, and apparently they recognize me, throwing wary glances my way as if I'm going to call up Santa Muerte herself. I give them a big smile as I walk by.

I see Chu in deep conversation with someone who looks pretty important. I've seen his face, at least, and at this point I don't think Chu'd be talking to anybody who wasn't.

"Davey!" I yell, immediately getting everybody's attention. I nibble at one of the chicken skewers, bite into some gristle and spit it out over the shoulder of a woman standing next to me. All of the color drains out of his face.

That's right, Davey boy, I'm your worst drunk uncle

flappin' his penis at the party guests at your senior prom nightmare. Best deal with me quickly.

"Hey, are these canapes?" I say, my voice way too loud. "I've never had canapes. Am I pronouncing that right? Oh, hi, how ya doin'?" I toss the chicken skewers aside and stick my greasy hand out to shake the hand of the guy Chu's been talking to. He stares at it like I'm presenting him a live snake. "Oh, sorry." I wipe the grease on my pant leg and stick my hand back out.

"Excuse me, Senator," Chu says. "This is one of my more eccentric donors. Maybe we can pick this up again sometime next week? I'll have my assistant call your office." I feel a little magic and the Senator blinks as if in a daze.

"Oh, yes, certainly." He walks away without even acknowledging me.

"Well, that was rude," I say.

"The fuck are you doing here?" Chu says, the smile never leaving his face, but the tension in his jaw telling a different story.

"I've got the thing you were talking about. Thought you might want to see it in person."

"The bottle? You found it? I mean, you found one strong enough to hold Quetzalcoatl?"

"And then some. Let's go find a dark corner someplace and I can show you. Maybe we'll even start some rumors."

"Study. Down the hall, second door on the right. I'll meet you there in a few minutes." He looks somewhere between giddy and panicked.

"You got it, chief. Don't keep me waiting."

# Chapter 30

**He doesn't.** I've only just broken into his liquor cabinet and poured a liberal dose of some Balvenie 17-year-old DoubleWood when he comes in, Peter close at his heels, closing the door quietly behind them.

Legs on his desk, the briefcase next to them. I've stuck my messenger bag to the side.

I lift my glass in a toast. "Gentlemen, I drink to my health." I down the glass.

"Actually, you've got that wrong," Peter says. "It's 'I drink—'"

"Shut the fuck up," Chu says, snarling at him. "Nobody fucking cares, Peter." He turns back to me. "Where's the bottle?"

"Oh. I put it back in the cabinet. I didn't think you'd want any."

"The spirit bottle," Chu says, each word coming out like breaking glass. "You cannot be as fucking stupid as the rest of these people."

"Oh, right," I say. "That bottle. It's right here." I take my legs off his desk and snap open the briefcase, lifting out the glamoured fake.

"One certified, Grade A spirit bottle. Accept no

substitutes." It's weird holding it. I know what it is, what it really looks like, how heavy it really is, but it feels just like Darius's bottle. Color me impressed.

Chu almost leaps over the desk to get it, but I pull it out of his reach. "Why, Councilman Chu, you seem awfully eager to get your hands on this. Why might that be?"

"You fuck, I will take that thing off your goddamn corpse." I'm so focused on Chu that I don't notice that Peter has come around the edge of the desk until it's too late.

I get my shield spell up in time to block a bolt of energy, but there's enough power behind it that I stagger back and drop the bottle. There was something weird about that bolt. And then I realize. It was completely silent. They've got a crowd of Senators, celebrities out there. Normals. Whatever they do in here, they have to be quiet about it. I, on the other hand, do not.

This spell's more flash than substance, though it'll slow them down a bit. I open my mouth wide and let loose a Banshee's wail, the keening shattering glass and knocking Peter to the floor. Before he can get back up, I run over and kick him in the face until he's puking up blood and teeth.

The spell hit Chu, too, but he only caught the edge of it. It's shoved him into a corner, knocking him down. He pulls himself up and makes a run for the bottle. I use a pull spell and it springs out of his reach toward me. Mages don't use that one against each other often, and Chu reminds me why when he throws out one of his own.

The bottle hangs in the air between us. I consider pulling out the Browning and shooting him, but that kind of defeats the purpose here. I'm trying to figure out what to do when the door opens and Letitia rushes into the room. The distraction is all I need. Chu loses his grip on the bottle and it flies into my outstretched hand.

"The hell is going on?" Letitia says. I'm about to explain, but then I don't have to after Chu uses the same pull spell and yanks Letitia's Glock out of the holster at the small of her back, pulling her over as he does it.

He points the gun at me. "You're gonna give me that bottle or I'm gonna put a hole in you big enough to drive a car through."

"Why do you want it so bad, Councilman? It's just a bottle to catch Quetzalcoatl in. You're acting like it's the Holy Grail."

"You already know why," he says, "or you wouldn't have been acting like an asshole out there, trying to get me in here. That bottle changes everything. What are you going to do with it? Hide it away? Lock it up?"

"David, what the hell are you doing?" Letitia says, voice calm, pitched low. Her stance and movements designed to de-escalate. I don't think that's going to work in this situation.

"And you," he says. "God, you're an idiot. You don't get it at all."

"What don't I get, David?" she says.

"You were just one more piece of bait," I say. "We knew each other. He figured since my sister was murdered, the idea that your wife could be killed because of something I had done would make me want to help you."

"What?"

"Yeah," I say. "This whole thing's been a scam to get hold of this bottle, hasn't it? Stop me if I start to go off track. You found out about it through, what, newspapers? Old stories you wanted to figure out were true or not? You heard about Darius, and Cabrillo, and you run into the story of my grandfather finding something on Catalina. How long ago did you make that connection?"

"Ten years ago," he says. "Give or take."

"And then you heard the rumors about my family owning some kind of vault, right? Time goes on and you hear all those weird stories about me and Mictlan, and something about Quetzalcoatl and Darius."

"You make it sound easy," he says. "Getting hold of Quetzalcoatl was a pain in the ass, but once I did, everything fell into place. Have him and his pet assassin fuck with you, turn the mage community against you for all those murders. Show you those pictures so you know what you're up against. I just had to spoon-feed the bullshit to you and you ate it right up. Man, when Werther's family put that bounty on your head? That was just frosting on the cake."

"You wanted to push me hard enough that I'd go looking for a powerful spirit bottle, hoping I'd run into this one. You were pretty sure I had it. And that nothing else would have been anywhere near as powerful. How come?"

"Because everyone knows about that vault. It's an open secret. Everybody knows the Carters hoarded shit, even if they don't know where they put it. My grandmother helped put the thing together. Fucking bitch wouldn't tell me where it was before she died. But now it doesn't matter. Because once I take that bottle off your corpse, not a goddamn thing's gonna stop me."

"Then we can't let that happen, can we?" Attila Werther steps out of nowhere. One second he isn't, and the next he is. Chu slams against the far wall, Letitia's Glock hanging in mid-air where he had been standing a moment ago.

"I believe this is yours," Werther says, floating the gun over to Letitia, who plucks it out of the air.

"We square?" I say.

"Yes," Werther says. "I've lifted the bounty. You may still get a straggler or two, but I don't think you'll have any trouble with them. You haven't so far."

He walks over to Chu, looks him up and down like he's inspecting a bug. "You brought murder into my home. You had the very light of my life killed. What should I do with you?"

"Not that my opinion means much," I say, "but vengeance hasn't really worked out well for me."

"If you can say the same when you're over two hundred years old, I might take it under advisement. Try as you might, ours is not a world that allows such luxuries as turning the other cheek."

"You know, things are about to get kinda hairy around here," I say. "Could use your help."

Werther laughs. "You would have me stand against a god?"

"Hey, I stood against two of 'em."

"Yes, and look how that turned out for you. No, Mister Carter, I'm very sorry, but you're on your own." He and Chu disappear as quickly and silently as he appeared.

"What the fuck, Eric?" Letitia says. She's already holstered her weapon, and her stance says she's ready to face anything, but her face is ashen.

"If I'm right, Chu and Quetzalcoatl are connected, though I doubt Chu knows that. I'm betting everything that just happened here, Q knows about. He's going to want this bottle and it's going to get really ugly, really fast."

"Shit," she says. "Annie's out there. I have to get her out."

"You're fucking kidding me."

"Hey, you're the one who told me to have The Talk. So we did and she didn't believe me and then I showed her a spell and she lost her shit and then when she stopped yelling at me she told me to show her more so I was gonna introduce her to some of the mages here who aren't raging assholes like you. This was supposed to be a goddamn mayoral fundraiser, not some vengeful god's FUCKING STOMPING GROUND."

"That was impressive. I don't think you took a breath once. You done?"

"Yes," she says, pumped with adrenaline. "I'm getting people the fuck out of here. If your god shows up, his pet's not gonna be far behind."

"If you're lucky, a lot of people will have already left once they heard the noise in here."

"I don't think anybody heard anything," she says. "I didn't, and nobody was acting like they had, either. And believe me, if security had, they'd have been in here in nothing flat."

"That's just as well. Things are going to shit already. We don't need a bunch of normals knowing about us."

"Yeah, until the god shows up."

"Then get them out of here before that happens." She glares at me, but she's through the door in a blink of an eye, and I can hear her using her cop voice to get people moving.

"Oh, Sweetums," I say to the air, thinking the same very hard. I get nothing in response.

"If you call me that again I will fucking skin you alive." Santa Muerte's voice with Tabitha's cadence in my head. This is going to get some getting used to.

"Hey, you're the one who wanted me, so you might as

well get used to it. A friend of mine suggested Honey Bunny earlier. How's that strike you?"

"Like a hammer to the back of my head," she says, with the sort of tone that says she's wondering if she's made a horrible mistake. "Is he there yet?"

The orderly sounds of people being evacuated are suddenly shattered as gunfire rips through the air. Pistols, shotguns, automatic weapons.

"I'd say the show's about to start." Clever fucker. Have Sastre sow some chaos out front, bet on me caring about any of them enough to be distracted. I can already feel people dying, ghosts coming into being. I'd love to help them, but I've got priorities.

There's a tremendous tearing sound above me. It's a two-story house. I don't know what's above this room, but I kinda doubt it matters anymore.

I hunker under the desk. There's a sound like a tornado through a trailer park and the room fills with sunlight and debris. He's pulled the whole second floor off. A spear of flame tears in from above, shoots out, threads its way through the ceiling. Takes me a second to realize it's Quetzalcoatl's tail. He yanks back, peeling off the second story floor like the lid of a sardine can. Pieces of plaster and wood rain down. The flaming wind god flaps his wings and starts to descend into the room.

"You think you can hide from me?" he screams, voice filled with a burning rage.

I poke my head out from under the desk. "Hide? Dude, you're dropping a ceiling on my head. I don't even have an umbrella." I pull myself out completely, brush dust off my pants. It's a futile gesture. The heat intensifies as soon as he sees the bottle.

He descends lower into the room and I get a good

look at him. He looks awful. His flames aren't as bright as I've seen them before. Barely any form left to him. He's more a tattered blob of flame than a winged serpent.

"I knew I could count on a foolish human like you to find the bottle," he says. "Now give it to me."

"This bottle?" I say, putting my hand on the stopper. "The one with the Djinn in it? Yeah. Surprise! I figured out your plan. But then, you knew that already, because you saw it through Chu's eyes. You know he was going to take it for himself?"

"Of course, he would have tried."

"Hey, remember that spell that Mictlantecuhtli cast to seal the bottle? That was the fight where he handed you your ass. In case you forgot. Anyway, I got some help getting those seals pulled off. So what's say I pop the cork and we celebrate together? I bet Darius would love to hang out, don't you?"

"You wouldn't dare." He backs up a bit, his form tightening into something a little more recognizable.

"Let's find out." I put my hand on the stopper, really hoping this works like I think it does.

And Quetzalcoatl slams down on me with all the fury and power he can muster.

# Chapter 31

**I jump out of the way,** almost make it, but the force of Quetzalcoatl's power clips me and slams me into a wall. I drop the bottle and brace for the end. When gods go a-smiting, well, it's not a huge room is what I'm saying. All he's got to do is a little shimmy and I'm a charcoal smear on the wall. But the fiery killing blow of an angry deity doesn't land.

I twist around and see that it's because Santa Muerte, eight feet tall, in a black dress, eye sockets glowing with an intense blue fire, has her hand around Quetzalcoatl's neck.

"He is not yours," she says, the power of her voice shaking the room. Quetzalcoatl whips his tail and wraps it around her waist. They both squeeze, but neither gives. There's some exchange of power I can't see and the two are thrown apart.

I'm sorely tempted to get out of their way and let them slug it out. But if I want to end this, that's not an option. Muerte's scythe is in her hand, slashing through the air and tearing fiery chunks from Quetzalcoatl's form.

A great wind picks up inside the room and a mini twister of debris spins around him, slapping onto him, chunks of trash armor like when I saw him in Zacatecas.

Muerte's scythe tears through a piece only to have another take its place.

Quetzalcoatl's attacks are feeble. Feints and dodges, as if his entire focus is on keeping his armor.

Waiting them out is looking more and more like a better idea than my original plan. Yeah, it's a dick move, but even though she isn't Santa Muerte, Mictecacihuatl, or even Tabitha, there's a part of me that wants to see her fall. And there's a part that really doesn't.

Either way I need the bottle back. It's rolled over near Quetzalcoatl, but close enough to me that I should be able to stay out of the line of fire long enough to grab it.

I duck-walk behind a chunk of fallen ceiling the size of a refrigerator, hoping Quetzalcoatl either doesn't see me or can't get a shot off at me. A little further and I'll almost have it.

"You killed them all, you traitorous fuck," Santa Muerte yells. Her voice switches in and out from the formal tones of Santa Muerte to the enraged screaming of Tabitha. It's a weird up-and-down mixture that sounds oddly like a boy going through puberty.

"You all let our culture rot and twist away," Quetzalcoatl screams back. "Creation was dead long before Cortés came to our land. Ours were a people steeped in blood, and we needed more, not less."

"There were too many," she yells back. "We saw what would happen if our people continued at the rate they were going. Droughts, starvation, disease. We could have saved them, but we needed you."

"You all turned your back on me," he hisses. "If I wasn't going to get my due, I would take it on the backs of invaders from another land."

"God, you are such an asshole," she says.

Quetzalcoatl laughs as his junk armor loses more of

itself to Santa Muerte's scythe. "I am not the one cor-rupted," he says. "I have not died and been reborn twisted with a human's shape. She has desires and plans that you do not. How soon before you are too weak to keep her and her necromancer lover at bay? How long before they strip you of your powers?"

If this were a telenovela I'd go make some popcorn, but fascinating as it is to see these family dynamics play out, I have shit to do. I crawl within reach of the bottle, but just as I'm about to grab it, a gunshot rings out and a bullet embeds itself in the wall a couple inches above my hand. I pull back quickly behind cover.

The Burning Girl has joined the party. Yippee. I steal a quick glance and see her holding herself upright against the doorframe. She's covered in cuts, and blood that prob-ably isn't hers. Dark red blooms on her left thigh from a bullet hole. She's breathing heavily and shaking. Every step through this place was hard won. I felt at least fifteen people die. She either let the others go or only wounded them.

I pull back as she takes another shot. It goes wide and thunks into the wall. A tremendous crash gets both our attention. Santa Muerte has torn away most of Quetzal-coatl's debris armor and managed to get her scythe half-way through him. He shudders, the power holding him together fading fast.

I'd like to just have her kill him, but then I remember that gods don't die like people die. Mictlantecuhtli was dead and he caused plenty of trouble. It might take cen-turies, but eventually this fucker'd be back and even more pissed off. I reach out again and snag the bottle.

No gunshot this time. Another quick glance shows me that Sastre knows a bad bet when she sees one. She's bailed. Gonna have to do something about that.

But first things first. I jump out from behind the wreckage and strip the glamour from the bottle. The nuclear spirit trap, plastered in warning stickers and radiation symbols, appears in its place. Santa Muerte pulls her scythe free and steps back.

I point THIS END TOWARD ENEMY and thumb the red button on the side. The top of the bottle snaps open and a loud klaxon goes off, filling the room with even more noise. A bright blue light fills the room, enveloping Quetzalcoatl. He claws at anything he can get hold of, wings of fire losing cohesion with every second. The light pulls at him, ripping him into scraps as it feeds him into the bottle. The bottle snaps closed and everything is silent.

I fall against the wall, slide to the floor. I'll probably get cancer from that stunt. Who knows how much radiation I've been dosed with just by having it out of its box?

"You're bleeding," Tabitha says, crouching down to me. Gone is the terrifying 8-foot-tall skeleton who just ravaged a god.

"Yeah, I do that a lot."

She frowns. "You know this isn't over yet, right?"

"Yeah. There's still a psychopath out there with the Zippo of Doom." I hand her the bottle. "Here, go find a deep, dark hole to bury it in that it won't get out of. I don't ever want to see that motherfucker again."

"You and I both," she says. She leans forward and kisses my forehead. "Don't die on me."

"If I do, you'll probably see me a lot sooner than we planned."

"I'll be in touch," she says. "Good luck." And then she and the bottle are gone.

My messenger bag is stuck under a piece of rubble and it takes me too long to pull it out. When I check inside, everything seems to be intact except for a Hand of Glory where all the fingers have snapped off. That's why I always put those sorts of things into Zip-Loc bags. The last thing you want is having pieces of some elemental horror rattling through your luggage because you didn't lock that shit down.

I don't know what's outside the study, but with everyone who was here the streets are going to be filling with emergency vehicles pretty quickly, so I have to move fast. I have my shield spell ready to go and the Browning in my hand. If there's still security out there they might take exception to the gun, but I'll deal with that when it happens.

I head out of the study and I'm shocked at the devastation. Overturned tables, shredded chairs, bodies everywhere lying in poses the living can never twist into. It looks like Sastre focused on security and any off-duty cops, but she mowed down anyone who got in her way. There are a lot of people missing, which I hope means they got out before this nightmare started.

I don't see Letitia or Annie anywhere, but I can feel magic, a spell being maintained. I start looking under tables, moving bodies out of the way. I finally find Letitia under a thin bubble of a shield. I crouch down and look at the pile of rifle and pistol slugs flattened at its base.

Letitia is barely conscious, her entire focus on keeping the shield up. I touch the shield and it pops like a soap bubble. Her gun is up in an instant and the only thing that saves me is that I'm not standing up when she shoots.

"Whoa, hey, it's me. Eric. You already stuck holes in me in high school, we don't need a repeat performance."

"What?" she says, snapping out of the trance she'd put herself into to maintain the spell as best she could. Her eyes go wide. "Annie." She spins around and there's her wife, unconscious and the reason's obvious. She's been gut shot.

"No, no, no," she says. "I need, fuck . . . Goddammit. Eric, I—"

"Hey," I say loudly, snapping her attention to me. "LAPD detective, remember. You have a civilian casualty. You know what to do in this sort of crisis."

"She's my—"

"She is a civilian casualty."

"Right." She takes a deep breath, does a basic triage. Checks Annie's pulse, breathing, tags the wounds as best she can. "She needs a hospital. Fuck me."

"Is there one nearby?"

"Every emergency room and bed is dealing with overflow from the Vernon fire. By the time she sees a doctor it's going to be too late."

"Hang on." I pull out my phone and call Gabriela. When she answers, she immediately starts cursing me out in Spanish.

"Yes, I am a goat's ass, have a tiny dick, should be butt fucked with a thousand bees . . . though, I have to say I hadn't heard that one before."

"My grandmother said it a lot. The fuck, Eric? Why didn't you shoot her when you had the chance?"

"So not the time to get into this. Is Viv there? I'd call her but she usually ignores me. I have somebody who needs immediate help and can't go anywhere else. And we don't have much time."

Her tone changes immediately. "One second." Viv comes on the line.

"What's going on?"

"Letitia's wife has been gut shot and all the hospitals are going to be full up because of that fucking fire."

"How far away are you?"

"Encino."

"That's at least an hour, probably more with traffic snarled this much. How's she doing?"

"Badly."

"Can you do that thing? Like you did with Gabriela?"

"Already planning to."

"All right. That should give you enough time. Get her over here as soon as possible."

"She'll be there as quickly as she can. Tell Gabbie's boys and girls not to shoot if a cop car shows up."

"Got it. See you soon." She hangs up.

I pull out a Sharpie and write an address onto Letitia's hand. "You remember Vivian from high school?" She nods. "She's a doctor now. Take her here. It's a warehouse. Now I'm going to do something to Annie that will save her life. But she's going to look dead. So don't freak out. This'll buy her the time she needs. Got it?"

"Do it."

I pull the spell together and cast it at Annie, putting as much juice into it as I dare. I want her stable, but I don't want a repeat of what happened to Gabriela. Her breathing slows, then stops. Blood stops pumping out of her. As far as anyone will be able to tell, she's gone.

"Jesus. Did it—"

"Yes, it worked." I help Letitia stand. She's wobbly but not injured. I haul Annie up and Letitia and I head outside, Letitia with a heavy limp.

There are still cars in the driveway, including a blue Crown Vic that screams police. "That's yours, right? Got sirens?"

"Yeah."

"Then we might just save your wife, after all."

# Chapter 32

**We head toward the car** and my eye hangs on something sitting on the edge of the porch. "Hang on," I say, and gently lay Annie down. I pick up a small bundle of pine sticks held together by twine. The ends have been dipped in pitch. The last time I saw one of these, Sastre was making hundreds of them in a factory in Vernon. I finally realize what they are and my blood goes cold.

"What are you looking at?" Letitia says. "We have to go."

"Tlepilli," I say. There's a spell on the bundle. Sympathetic magic. This thing is connected to another somewhere else.

"What?"

"Never mind." I pick Annie back up and run her to the Crown Vic. "You need to get her out of here."

I lay her down in the backseat and we belt her in until we're sure she's as secure as she can be. Short of a major crash, she's not going anywhere.

Letitia gets behind the wheel of the car. "You gonna tell me what that bundle of sticks is?"

"Later," I say. "You don't have time. They're just really

bad. I need to find that sicaria. She can still do a lot of damage. Like *a lot* a lot."

"Okay. I'll put out a BOLO. We've got her description. And I saw what she was wearing. And she's wounded. No idea what she's driving, but if she so much as runs a red light we'll have her."

She backs the car out of the tightly packed driveway, kicking on the lights and sirens as soon as she hits the street.

I pull out my phone and call Gabriela.

"What'd you do now?" she says.

"Tlepilli," I say. She knows Nahuatl and she knows her Aztec lore. "I just found one and it's linked to another one somewhere else." I give her a second to catch up and make the connection.

"Fuck me," she says. "I'll have the warehouse and everywhere for the next few blocks looked over."

"I'd make it fast. Quetzalcoatl's taken care of, but his assassin's on the loose and she still has the lighter."

"On it." She hangs up.

A tlepilli is an Aztec pine torch made from the Mexican ocote pine tree. Ocote sap burns really well. A tlepilli is just a bundle of sticks. You could have big ones, little ones, they're still just tlepilli. People still use bundles like the one I found as fire starters.

Before the war with the Spanish, the god Xiuhtecuhtli was a fire god. Like *the* fire god. Every fifty years or so, the Aztecs would make a sacrifice to him by carving out a victim's heart and setting a burning clump of pine sticks in the cavity. Which honestly just feels like insult to injury.

Anyway, Xiuhtecuhtli got taken out by Quetzalcoatl, who got hold of his power. When I met Q in Zacatecas he'd put the fires into something a little more portable, the Zippo lighter.

One of the things with tlepilli is that they'd be used to light others. Do it right and long enough and once you have one going, you never need to make a fire again. Just keep lighting new tlepilli.

In Vernon there were hundreds, maybe thousands of them. If each is magically linked to another, half of them could be scattered across the city and the other half somewhere else, like a bunch of remote fuses.

Tlepilli aren't big. They'd be easy to hide and nobody'd think about one if they saw it. Lighting them with regular fire probably wouldn't do much. But if they're lit with the Zippo? We could have a situation that makes the Vernon fire look like a goddamn Fourth of July sparkler.

I can already hear other sirens down below. I need a ride out of here fast. I grab the keys for a blue Porsche from the valet stand, but before I can turn around to get to it I feel a stabbing pain in my back and every muscle in my body seizes up.

I hit the ground face first, and someone kicks me over. The sicaria stands over me holding a Taser, the leads going to barbs digging into my back. I try to move, which only barely works, so she hits me again.

"Oh, no," she says, her English heavily accented, and hits me with another jolt. "I don't fucking think so." She pulls a couple wadded up pieces of paper from her pocket.

Paper charms. Kind of like my Sharpie magic. You write glyphs on the paper and cast the spell into it. When you want it to work, you trigger it, throw it on the ground, light it on fire, whatever. I saw a woman kill a train car full of people with one and then later set off an earthquake along Santa Monica Boulevard.

"One of these kills you," she says. "The other one knocks you out. But I can't read this shit." She shows me one of the charms, Aztec glyphs burned into the thick paper. "I'm pretty sure this picture's death. Or maybe a rabbit? You know, fuck it. It doesn't matter." She wads up one of the papers and tosses it onto me. It bursts like flashpaper when it hits my chest and everything goes black.

———

It's so dark when I come to that it takes me a minute to realize I'm not still unconscious. Then dim, hazy lights pass overhead. I can feel the floor move beneath me. My body hasn't caught up with my brain, and when it does I realize the floor isn't moving, I am. I'm being dragged. I try looking up to see who's dragging me, but I still can't move.

I'm not sure where I am or what just happened, but something in the back of my head is telling me that this isn't just bad, it is double-plus-un-good.

I fade back into unconsciousness a couple of times, each time coming out more aware than the last. I'm pretty sure this is an office building. Acoustic tile on the ceiling but cement on the floor. The lights stopped being the kind of fluorescent tubes that suck out all your Vitamin D and possibly your soul a ways back, and now what little illumination there is comes from the occasional work light.

I've tried casting a couple of spells, but I can't concentrate well enough to do a damn thing. I fade back into unconsciousness and when I come to again I'm in some sort of workshop. I can hear an air compressor, and one of my arms has been hauled up over my head.

"Oh, you're up." Sastre stands over me, holding my hand up over a table where I can't see it. She has a surprisingly strong grip. I guess it's from all that chopping off heads. "Good. I wanted to make sure you were awake for this."

The room is a corner office suite in a skyscraper that's being renovated. Carpet pulled out, internal walls knocked down. Windows cover every foot of the exterior, giving an amazing view of nighttime Los Angeles, a blanket of jeweled streetlights, cars, homes, all the way out to the horizon.

She hauls me up until my left arm is completely on the table. Now that I can see the table better, I can tell it's an empty cable spool that's been put on its side.

"I had these made special for you," she says. What the hell is she talking about? I try to pull out of her grip but I'm still too groggy, too weak. "He wanted something that would hurt you. I planned on crucifying you and setting you alight, but he said that would kill you too fast. This way I can hurt you for days."

She picks something up and I recognize it right before she slams it down onto my hand. The nailgun pops as she drives three long nails through my hand and into the top of the table.

If I wasn't awake before I sure as fuck am now. There's nothing but pain and blood and her laughing mixing with a noise I kind of think is me screaming. I pull myself up and look down at what she's done.

I want to pull the nails out, or my hand out, or something, but I don't know where to start and every shift brings on new agony. The nails dimple the skin like buttons. Blood wells up from the wounds, pools under my hand.

The pain isn't just in my hand. It's in my bruised ribs, all the cuts and scrapes and bruises. They light up like Satan's own Christmas tree. Behind the pain, behind the whole what-the-fuckness of being nailed to a table, there's something else; I can't feel any magic.

There must be something besides blind agony in my eyes because she smiles big and proud, like I'm the slow student who just figured out his times tables. "They block magic. You can't cast any spells. Oh, and I took these, too." She shows me the Browning and the straight razor. She drops them into my messenger bag on the floor, and kicks the whole thing across the room.

"I am so gonna fuck your shit up," I say through gritted teeth. I try to reach for the magic but nothing comes. I've been cut off from my own magic before. It's a pain in the ass. Right now, it's a pain everywhere else. Some of my tats act as pain buffers, skin and bone strengtheners. Without them I couldn't take the sorts of beatings I've had, and now they don't work. After going a couple rounds with a pissed off wind god and having nails shot through my hand, I could really use them.

"I don't think so," she says, "but it's good to have goals. It'll keep you alive longer. And I have a whole long strand of nails to use. But we'll get to that. I have one last job to do. See?"

She gestures to the side and I look, already guessing what's there. The pain can't match the shock of what I'm seeing. Pallets of tlepilli laid out in rows along the floor. Each pallet about four feet square, each tlepilli maybe an inch thick with some space separating it from its neighbor. I try doing math, but I can barely think straight. I settle on two-hundred, maybe two-fifty per pallet?

I stop counting pallets when I hit about twenty and see that they cover the floor of the rest of the open office suite leading into the darkness.

She limps over to the pallets, leaving a trail of blood

behind her. That gunshot in her leg is gonna slow her down. She'll need to get it fixed up. But I get the feeling she's not too worried about getting that far.

"These took forever to build," she says. "But they'll burn very fast." She pulls out the Zippo and flips it open.

I push through the pain and haul myself and the cable-spool table toward her. I get a few feet, my hand tearing, sweat pouring off me from the pain. But she's too far away to get to in time.

She flicks her thumb along the striker. Blue flames erupt around the wick. She limps over to one of the palettes and sets one of the tlepilli on fire. The flames are like I remember seeing on Isla de La Muñecas. They consume and spread, jumping from one bundle to another, each one transferring the magic of the flames to some unknown location. The room glows in eerie blue light, reflecting back on itself in the windows. I see other blue flames erupting outside. Tiny little dots across the city. Like voracious moths eating a tapestry, the flames grow into raging infernos in seconds. Below us, Los Angeles burns.

"Isn't it beautiful?" she says, and through the haze of pain and shock I have to agree with her. It is beautiful. A beautiful horror show of flame and death.

And that's only one palette. It burns to ash quickly. I catch sight of a protection circle painted on the floor beneath the ash before the light dies down. Smart. The flames won't spread beyond any one pallet or set the building on fire.

She lights another one and her face is orgasmic. She doesn't even look out the window. She's transfixed by the burning pallets, their blue glow pulling her in.

Which means she's not paying attention to me. Not that that does me any good. I'm nailed to a table, I can't cast, my gun and straight razor are across the room, and my pocket watch—

Huh. My pocket watch is still in my pocket. I pull it out with my right hand. If these nails are blocking me from accessing magic, does that extend to something I'm holding?

She's too far away for the pocket watch to do its thing to her, and even if it could she's too close to the tlepilli. This thing has a mind of its own sometimes and I can see it just hitting the tlepilli, which might actually be worse than the flames.

So I focus on what I can do. I point the watch face toward the top of the table. I've never used it on anything that I was physically attached to before, so it might affect me as much as it does the table. And boy will that ever suck.

But I'm out of options. I spin the crown with my thumb and push down on it. The table starts to age, wood cracking, turning black, bits falling off. I'm afraid it's making too much noise, the smell of wood rot too strong. But Sastre is in too much ecstasy over the next burning palette to care about anything else.

In a minute or so, the last of the table turns to ash and sawdust and I'm free. Well, free-ish. I still have three magic-warding nails stuck in my hand. I bolt toward Sastre, hoping I can tackle her and at least get the lighter away. She turns at the sound, my only chance of catching her unawares shot.

The look on her face is confusion at first, then rage. Then she pulls a knife and runs at me.

That's right, sweetheart. Run right into the time-bending pocket watch. Except she doesn't. Stupidly I've got it held out in front of me, waiting for her to come in close, but she's faster than I thought, and before I can tap the crown she kicks it out of my hand. It skitters across the cement out of sight.

She slashes at me, just a little too far away. She cuts across my chest, but it's too shallow to do any real damage.

I get in past her arm and get an elbow into her face. There's a loud pop, and blood streams from her nose. She sweeps her leg and knocks me onto my ass. In the long run, I can tell, she's going to win. I'm at more of a disadvantage. I'm not going to last much longer in the state I'm in, and the second I miss a block it's game over.

She raises the knife over her head and leaps down on me like a wrestler. I block her arm with mine, knocking it aside. I realize too late that it's left me open on one side. But she's exposed, too. If I had a weapon . . .

Oh, wait. I do have a weapon. I slam the palm of my left hand hard against the side of her neck, the nails sticking out of my hand punching through her flesh and into her throat.

A flare of agony washes up my arm and I want to pass out and throw up at the same time. It's a toss-up which one of us it hurt more. I'm going with her. I'm just in pain. She's fountaining blood. At most I think I nicked the artery, but she's still pumping out an awful lot of blood.

"Yeah? How ya like them apples?" I yell, more than a little hysterical. What the hell does that even mean? She gurgles as blood fills her throat and runs down her neck. I push her off of me. She rolls to her feet and hops up. I figure we're going to have another go-round. If we do, I don't think I'll live through it.

Instead, hand pressed hard against her neck, she runs, lighting the Zippo and letting it pass over a few pallets as she does, all of them bursting into blue flame.

I'm in no shape to go after her. My vision's blurring and I'm trying really hard to not throw up. She got about ten pallets lit, maybe more. That's more than two thousand fires. With the heat and the wind, they're going to spread.

I get over to my messenger bag, find my cell phone, call Letitia.

"Where are you?" she says.

"I'm good, how are you?"

"I said—"

"At the top of some skyscraper in Downtown."

"There are fires breaking out all over the city," she says. "I'm getting phone calls to come in. The entire city's on tac alert. Gabriela told me what that bundle of sticks you found was. Is that what this is? Everybody's assuming it's a terror attack."

"You could call it that," I say. "Yes, it's her. Yes, she lit a bunch of 'em on fire. But the good news is that she didn't light 'em all on fire. And I stabbed her. With the nails." I don't feel so good. The pain from the nails has turned into more of a heavy throb. Like dubstep.

"How many did she—wait. Nails?"

"Yeah, she stuck me to a table with a nail gun. Anyway, she lit a bunch of 'em, Two thousand, twenty-five hundred? But there are a lot left."

"Oh, Jesus."

"I wouldn't worry too much. I think the lighter's magic gets kind of screwy when she uses the tle—things. Sorry. I'm in a lot of pain. I think I'm gonna pass out now."

"Wait. What building are you in?"

"You sound really far away," I say. Or maybe I think it? I can't tell. I'm really not doing well. I wonder if this is because my tattoos aren't working. I've been blocked off before, but the last time I was facing down a pair of demons and that kind of sharpens your focus.

"I'm gonna lie down for a bit. Hey, if you happen to find me, can you bring me a first aid kit and a claw hammer?"

I don't know if she answers me or not.

# Chapter 33

**I snap awake,** sitting up like I'm spring-loaded, eyes wide, the world in vibrant, vibrating color. My heart jackhammers in my chest. I'm still on the half-finished office floor, Letitia kneeling next to me.

My left hand is heavily bandaged. It doesn't hurt, oddly enough, but there's a burning where Letitia has jammed an atropine autoinjector into my thigh. I've never seen one before, but even in the dim light I can read the label with disturbing clarity.

"You weren't waking up," she says. "So I hit you with the injector. We carry them in our first aid kits in case of chemical attacks."

"That happen a lot?" This shit hits hard and fast and though I'm really, really awake I can tell this is going to suck even more later.

"Not so far, but occasionally somebody huffs bug poison."

"You couldn't have used smelling salts?"

"I needed to let out some aggression."

"On me?"

"You were here. You needed to wake up. I figure it was a win-win." I'm sure there's a hole in that logic somewhere but I'm not seeing it. I look at my bandaged left hand, and spot the hammer and nails on the floor. I can taste the magic again, the mix of cultures, attitudes, and religions that makes L.A.'s magic stand out from New York, San Francisco, or any other city.

"Thanks," I say. "Please don't stab me again. Twice in one lifetime is enough. How'd you find me?"

"I can do all sorts of fancy phone shit without a warrant. I was able to have it tracked."

"How long was I out?"

"About an hour. It's a fucking nightmare out there. Massive fires are kicking up all over the place. Police and Sheriff have called a tac alert and everybody's been pulled off everything but dealing with these fires."

She helps me to my feet. Not only can I not feel my left hand, I can't move it. I raise it up so she can see it flopping uselessly to the side.

"Vivian told you I probably broke something and to pump it full of Lidocaine, didn't she?" That would happen from time to time when we were together. I'd get into a fight I couldn't punch my way out of. If it wasn't for her I doubt I'd be able to hold anything.

"Xylocaine," she says. She holds me steady as I take a few tentative steps. The atropine has me a little wobbly, and there's something wrong with my leg that's got me limping. "Other than that, how are you feeling?"

"My heart's about to explode out of my chest, I don't even want to think about what my hand looks like. Now that the magic's back, my tattoos are doing their job and I don't feel like I've been run over by a train quite so much. Could still use some Vicodin."

"Has it occurred to you that you might have a problem?"

"I have several problems. Just ask Vivian. Right now

it's finding a psychotic arsonist who, unless she's dead, isn't done lighting shit on fire."

"With all the chaos out there she's going to be hard to find."

"I don't know if this'll help, but I think she might be in a blue Porsche. I was stealing one when she tased me and had the keys in my hand. Other than that, I don't know where she might be. Other than burning everything down."

I take a moment to look out the window and watch Los Angeles in flames. A thick blanket of smoke has covered the city, the fires and streetlights glowing beneath. Occasionally one flares up over the smoke.

"She left a lot of these things," Letitia says. "We can't leave these lying around. If we break them, will the ones they're connected to break?"

"Maybe," I say. "I don't know. As long as they haven't been triggered, they—" An idea pops into my head. I wonder if it would work. I search the ceiling until I find what I'm looking for, a circular metal plate a few inches wide. Every ten feet or so there's another one. I drag a ladder over from the corner of the suite underneath it and climb on top.

"What are you doing?"

"If I'm lucky, cooling things off a bit." If I understand the magic that was used to link the tlepilli together it should be a one-shot deal. At the very least this should deactivate the tlepilli.

I cast a small fire spell and a flame appears at my fingertips. I hold it under the plate until it pops off from the heat, revealing a recessed sprinkler. A moment later, the sprinkler goes off.

Realizing what I was about to do, Letitia's grabbed a piece of cardboard from the floor and put it over her head. It's not helping much, but it's keeping the worst of the water off her.

"Why aren't the others going off?" I say, yelling over the waterfall roar of the sprinkler. I'm soaked to the skin. Considering the temperature is in the upper nineties, at the very least I'm not complaining.

"They all have their own sensors." She drops the cardboard, puts her hands out toward the far end of the room over the pallets. The plates go red hot within seconds and pop off, the sprinklers kicking in a moment later.

"Fine. Be all efficient about it."

"Do you think it'll work?" I'm about to say it depends on what she means by "work," but before I can answer her, a flash in the sky outside is followed by a peal of thunder.

"It'll do something," I say. The sprinklers will only go on for about five minutes. It might help the flames from spreading a little bit, but not by much.

Raindrops begin to tap the windows. Within seconds it's a torrent, then a monsoon hammering at the glass, washing ash down in thick streaks. The tlepilli are soaked all the way through. A few minutes later, the sprinklers shut off, the rain outside dying down a few moments later.

From our vantage point there doesn't appear to be any difference, but I wouldn't expect there to be. We added water to the mix, but the winds and heat are still high and shit's still burning. A four minute power wash isn't going to stop it. I just hope it helps contain things a little bit, and even if it doesn't, we've taken the remaining tlepilli out of play.

I gather up my messenger bag and check inside. It's a little damp, but nothing's ruined and the ledger is dry as a bone. I wonder if it, like everything it's used to record, has some magic of its own. I find the pocket watch over by a window, dry it off on my sleeve, and slide it into my pocket.

We take the elevator down, clothes dripping. "Maybe you should have thought that out a little better," Letitia says, wringing out one pant leg.

"Hey, you said we couldn't leave them lying around," I say. "Besides, I only turned on the one sprinkler. You—" I double over like I've been punched in the gut. Through the elevator I can hear a distant, muffled explosion.

"You all right? What happened?"

"I'm fine. It just hurts." I wave her off. "It's a necromancer thing." A hundred and twelve people just died in one shot nearby. Eighty-seven left ghosts behind.

There are factories, warehouses, and trains just on the other side of the river. What if a propane tower went? Christ, what happens if a gas main goes up? A couple years back a natural gas pipeline under a suburban neighborhood in the Bay Area sprung a leak. It left an entire neighborhood devastated. Leveled more than 30 houses. Just completely gone. In their place was a 40-foot-deep crater. It even registered as an earthquake. Miraculously only a handful of people died.

With the inferno raging outside, it isn't a matter of if it will happen, it's a matter of when.

The elevator opens onto a brightly lit, empty lobby. Outside, thick smoke swirls through the streets, blown along by the hot, dry Santa Ana winds.

"Shouldn't there be a security guard?"

"Yes," Letitia says, drawing her pistol. We step out of the elevator, Letitia checking one side, me checking the other. I have a spell ready to snap off if anything goes south.

"Found the security guard," I say. "Sort of." I point out a wide blotch of blood and bone about head height on the outside of the glass doors. From there a thick trail goes up and finally disappears near the top. Wide drops of heavily spattered blood lead out into the street. A blue cap with the name of a local alarm company lies on the ground soaked in blood.

"Do you feel that?" Letitia says. I do. There's magic in play. It's not a spell, but it feels very familiar. I don't see any way to go except out those doors or down to a parking garage, which I'm not sure will be any better.

"Fuck it," I say, hit the doors and step out into the smoke. Inside the building, with its ventilation, the air was clear enough that it was just a faint background scent, but when I open the doors I'm assaulted with the smells of burning wood and rubber, gasoline and meat, the chemical tang of unidentifiable toxins. A thick slurry of ash mixed with the already drying rain sluices through the gutter.

Letitia comes out behind me. It's hard to see through the smoke. The halos of streetlights, a nearby skyscraper burning out of control a few blocks away. The wind isn't helping. It pushes and pulls, and somewhere inside it is that feeling of magic flowing like—

"Swindler," says a voice, breathy and whistling.

"Cheater," says a second like dry leaves blowing through a cemetery.

"King of the Dead," says a third, filled with spite and rage.

"Oh, goddammit." Like I need this right now.

"Eric, what the hell is going on?"

"Letitia, I'd like to introduce you to the spirit of the Santa Ana winds."

# Chapter 34

**"The what?"** Letitia stares around, looking for the source of the voices. A furnace-heat blast of wind shoves at us, ash gusting around and over us, coating our still-sopping clothes in gray. We both instinctively put up a shield and stand our ground.

"The fuck is happening, Eric?"

"Don't worry about it." I think for a second. "Well, don't worry about it too much. This isn't an ambush. It's a parley." If they really wanted, they could have taken me out the same way I'm assuming they did the security guard. Poor bastard. The only reason to kill him was to use his corpse as a calling card.

"You broke," says one voice.

"Our agreement," says another.

"King of the Dead," finishes the third.

I called up the winds out in Vasquez Rocks, asking for help and making an agreement that ultimately led to all this.

"First off, I am not King of the Dead. At best I'm Handyman of the Dead. Or maybe Groundskeeper, I don't fucking know. So stop calling me that. Second, I call bullshit. I didn't break an agreement with you, because I wasn't fucking talking to you. You were just a pass-through for Quetzalcoatl. Whether you went along with it willingly or not makes no difference. You misrepresented yourselves, so you can fuck right the hell off."

The wind picks up again, another gust from multiple directions hammering at our shields. Smoke and ash swirl past. It's a little hard to breathe and the winds aren't making things any easier.

"Hit a nerve, did I?" I say. "Big tough wind spirit got taken for a ride by a half-dead Aztec god. More people believe in you than believe in him, yet you're the patsies. That's gotta sting."

The wind dies down, and there's an expectant pause. "Yes," say all three voices together. "Where did you send him? We would see this forgettable god again and . . . have words."

"I—"

"Hang on," Letitia says, putting a hand on my shoulder. "You're really the Santa Ana winds?"

"We are," they say. "We are the Devil Wind, the fire-breath, the wind that gives and the wind that takes."

"Not to mention Bane of Asthmatics Everywhere," I say. "Yes, they're the spirit of the Santa Ana winds. As I was saying, I'm not going to tell you where I sent him, because that's privileged information. Any dealings we had in the past are done."

Letitia's eyes light up. She gets where I'm going. "This is a clean slate," she says. "You want that information, you'll need to pay."

Whispers through the smoke, a back and forth, unintelligible voices raised. The wind is arguing with itself.

"What is the price?" one says.

"Right now you're fanning all these fires," I say.

"It is what we do," they say. "We are the Devil Wind, the fire-breath, the—"

"Yes, I get it. Stop." The wind goes quiet.

"That's not what I meant. Well, it is what I meant, but I also meant 'stop' as in 'stop fanning the flames.' In fact, try putting some out, or at least helping. Quetzalcoatl might have started this, but you're keeping it going. He's playing you. You're still dancing to his tune."

"So help stop the fires," Letitia says. "Clear the smoke. Give the firefighters a chance. This is Los Angeles. We curse you every year, like we curse the rain's absence. We curse the fires you fan, the air you turn to dry dust. You're the closest thing we have to the Devil. Try being an angel for once. Trust me. Do this, people will notice."

"Whatta ya say? Not only do you get the location of Quetzalcoatl, you get your fickle nature as the giver and taker of flame cemented into the history books. All you have to do is what you normally do, just the other way around."

More whispered bickering. Finally: "Agreed. We will help put out the flames as best we can. We cannot put them out ourselves, but we can assist where possible, and not hinder where it is not. Now, where is the forgettable god?"

"Sitting in a bottle at the bottom of a hole in Mictlan."

Silence. Then more whispered bickering. "We were hoping it was . . . closer."

"Getting to him is your business. A deal's a deal. You have your information. Now get blowin'." I get a distinct sense of grumbling, like a frustrated child who's just lost at marbles kicking a can down the street. "Oh, it's not all bad. You still get to play with fire. It's just a different game."

A blast of wind swirls around us, blowing away smoke and ash, then everything goes still. A moment later, no longer blowing through the streets, ash begins to fall like snow.

"I'm dreaming of a gray Christmas," I say, catching a handful of ash in my hand. I'm still dripping wet, so it's sticking like lint. Letitia slaps me on the back of the head.

"The fuck was that for?"

"You're making jokes while people are dying," she says.

"Have you met me?" I say. "Cut me some slack. I made it rain and I just commanded the wind. I'm like fuckin' Moses or something. Now let's go find our arsonist and end this."

———

Letitia's car is half a block up, covered in a layer of ash an inch thick. The other cars on the street—not many at this hour in Downtown—aren't exactly pristine, but it looks like all the ash and dust that was blown off them was deposited on Letitia's Crown Vic.

"They're like a goddamn child, aren't they?" Letitia says.

"A deadly, arsonist, psychopathic child, yes. Don't forget what they did to the security guard just to get our attention." I wince, my step faltering.

"You all right?"

"Yeah."

"Necromancer thing?"

"Necromancer thing." Ever since we got down to the lobby I've been feeling more and more deaths. No big waves of them, but clusters. A handful here, a dozen there. It's like standing in a hailstorm. I still feel the small ones, but the big ones really sting.

More worrisome are the ghosts. I can feel the population really starting to stack up. That's not usually a problem, but too many into one area and things get a little dicey.

The place with the most ghosts I've ever seen was in Hong Kong, where Kowloon Walled City had stood just a year before. Originally a fort built in the ninth century, it was beefed up in the late 1800s when the British took over Hong Kong. Seems the Chinese didn't really trust the Brits. Who'da thunk?

Time goes on. Ownership of the fort goes back and forth. The fort gets torn down when the Japanese invade, but there are still enough chunks left that when the war ends a couple thousand squatters show up and camp out and the population keeps growing. Fire nearly burns the whole thing to the ground in the 50s, kills a whole fuckton of people.

Not a group of people to let wholesale death keep them down, the remaining residents start building on top of the remaining bits of the old. And build. And build. And build. Homes on top of homes. Places sealed away from the sun when somebody builds a new walkway above it. And all this time more and more people move in.

By the time it was cleared and torn down, it was an urban maze of huts and shacks stacked one atop the other and crammed side by side until it filled a six acre space 150 feet high and held 50,000 people. It survived on stolen electricity, illegal wells, and a black market economy.

A place that had been occupied almost two-thousand years that finally ends as a squatters' paradise. That's gonna leave a ghost or two. Or a couple hundred thousand. Haunts stuck wandering rat warrens that weren't there anymore. It was like getting rid of an anthill but leaving all the ants behind.

Too many ghosts and the barrier between our world and their world thins out. Some spots in Kowloon, the barriers might as well have been made of tissue paper. Ghosts passing between worlds from one step to another. Fortunately, most of them were Haunts and Echoes. They weren't going anywhere. But a couple Wanderers got out while I was there.

I did not enjoy my stay in Hong Kong.

I don't know if we'll get anything like that here. L.A.'s so spread out we're not going to get that kind of density. But before this whole mess is over, the death toll is going to be astronomical.

We get into Letitia's car, a wash of ash following us inside. Letitia swears, turns on the radio, and listens. It's like they're speaking a different language—I don't know the codes. But after a little while it starts to make sense. It helps that a lot of the calls include some form of the word "fire." Then one stands out.

"Any Central unit, 480, 487, and possible 502, exiting 110 Freeway at 6th Street. Blue Porsche, license plate 2ZUB069. Code 3. Incident 994 in RD 151."

Letitia grabs the microphone in a flash. "Control, this is One-Henry-Five. I got this. Code 3, Third and Spring Street. Over." She's already peeling the car away from the curb.

"Henry?"

"It's a call sign. Means detective. A two man patrol car is Adam, like Adam-12?"

"I have no idea what the hell you're talking about," I say. "Who the hell is Adam?"

"TV show? About police? In the 60s?"

"Jesus, Tish, I thought we were the same age. I had no idea you were an old lady watching fifty-year-old television shows. Did they drive dinosaurs?"

"Fuck you."

"Can I call you Henry now?"

She gives me the finger and hits the lights and sirens. I wonder, not for the first time, what the point of an unmarked police car is when it's so obviously an unmarked police car.

"Seems kinda coincidental that there'd be a blue Porsche just around the corner," I say. "Henry."

"Maybe she's coming back to finish the job," she says. "Asshole."

"Ah, shit."

"What?" she says. "Oh." The nearby fire we'd seen earlier turns out to be the Bradbury. Vintage building with steel art deco stairs and cage elevators in the middle and offices on the outer edges. It's an L.A. icon. And flames are pouring out of every opening.

"That's gonna piss a lot of people off," I say.

"Where are the firetrucks?" Letitia says.

"Dealing with other fires, I imagine. There are kind of a lot of them right now."

Something's bothering me. It makes sense that Sastre would want to finish what she started. Downtown is a series of one-way streets. Though traffic's light, and in some cases non-existent—I mean, would you be out during an apocalypse? Letitia's still obeying street signs.

"Turn around," I say. "I don't think Sastre was planning on getting out of this alive. If she's headed back to the office building, she's not gonna bother paying attention to one-way streets."

"Shit." Letitia pulls the car into a tight U, tires skipping along the pavement, and heads past the burning Bradbury down the street and—yep, there she is.

She pulls to the curb moments before she sees us, and peels out again, gunning the engine. She heads right at us. Letitia gets ready to turn into the Porsche to knock her off the road with a PIT maneuver, but Sastre feints, and pulls a U just as Letitia begins to swerve.

Letitia corrects, but now it's officially a chase. Letitia calls in for backup, but something tells me we're on our own.

# Chapter 35

**We head east going** the wrong way down Third toward Little Tokyo and the river, and I begin to see how bad things are. Looking down from the office building, I could see how far out the tlepilli had been placed, but I couldn't appreciate the magnitude.

We pass whole blocks in flames, some burned down to ash. People have cracked open fire hydrants to help put out the fires. Burned corpses hang half out of windows, dead before they could escape.

I look out on San Pedro Street as we speed by. Skid Row. Over five thousand homeless living in this four square mile area, not to mention all the people living in lofts or working to support the homeless.

It's nothing but a tunnel of flames, as both sides of the street as far south as I can see burn bright and high. Occasional blue flames lick up from the blaze. Xiuhtecuhtli's fire still has some life left in it.

I was probably unconscious when people started to die out here and didn't feel it, but I can feel a fuck-ton of new Haunts and Wanderers down that street now. Will it tip the balance? Will we have another Kowloon in L.A.? I hope not, but I'm not inclined to hang out down

there. Still, when all this is said and done, I'm going to
have to see how it is.

We stay on Third, the Crown Vic trying hard to keep
her in sight. We start to merge with Fourth and I figure
she's going to keep going across the bridge and hit the
101. But she makes a hard right on Central.

As Letitia cranks the wheel I can see why. The rest of
Fourth is an inferno. I can see the Fourth Street Bridge
engulfed in blue and orange flames, buckling under the
heat. As it goes out of sight I hear it collapse behind us,
a massive crash of cement, rebar, and history.

All along Central it's the same scene. Burning buildings, people desperate to put out the flames. Some
buildings untouched, but many, hell, most of them are
nothing but ash and skeletons of charred wood or steel.

"I think she's gonna hit the freeway," Letitia says.

"Isn't that gonna be gridlocked?" We've seen surprisingly little traffic so far besides the occasional emergency vehicle on a side street. Letitia's calls for backup
are too low a priority to get any sort of traction. The rest
of the police are helping to put out fires, assisting with
rescue efforts.

"Maybe," she says, "but with all this going on I think
it's a good chance that anybody still driving up there is
either trying to get home, or parked on the side watching shit happen. Folks did that during the Northridge
quake. Parked their cars and watched buildings go
down, transformers explode."

I remember that. I was driving on the 405 at the time.
Even after the shaking stopped the freeways stayed
mostly clear. People were either frozen in place panicking behind the wheel or pulled over to the side and out
of their cars.

Sure enough, Sastre pulls a hard left on 16th and hits

the onramp for the 10 Freeway. Above us, helicopters dot the skies, surveying the fire. News, police, fire. Anybody who can get a bird in the air.

"How far does the Cleanup Crew go?" I say.

Letitia looks up through the windscreen at the helicopters. "Not nearly far enough to hide all this shit. This is all going live across the country. The YouTube videos are probably going viral."

"I was thinking more about us," I say. "Everybody knows you're on this. You called it in." I'm not crazy about the idea of being on national television in any capacity.

"That actually makes it easier," she says. "A lot more control over things when it's official. We'll figure something out."

We hit the freeway and it's like Letitia had predicted. There's very little traffic, most of it parked off to the side, people out of their cars taking selfies with a burning L.A. backdrop.

I wonder what they'll call this. The Great L.A. Firestorm? Firepocalypse? I wonder how many churches are packed tonight thinking this is the actual End Times. How many mosques, how many synagogues?

And holy fuck, the cults this will create. The guys walking around with signs on Hollywood Boulevard yelling at everyone to repent for their heathen masturbatory ways or whatever are going to come out in droves. It'll get blamed on climate change, gays and lesbians, the sex industry, the movie industry, immigrants, Jews, Muslims, Mexicans.

Dammit. As soon as anyone hears about Sastre's involvement and her link to the cartels, the shit's really gonna hit the fan.

"What kind of story you think they'll spin?" I say.

"I don't know. It's not like anybody's in charge. Whoever gets on it first. Hopefully it won't be something stupid that gets more people killed. But it might."

"That's what I was afraid of."

The Porsche puts on more speed, and starts to pull away from us. Letitia guns the Crown Vic to stay close, and has to brake hard when Sastre taps her brakes and closes the distance.

Something flies out of the driver's side window, and just before it lands on the freeway in front of us we both recognize what it is. She's got some of the tlepilli in the car with her and she just chucked a lit one at us.

Letitia slams on the gas and turns, the blue flaming torch bouncing past us and lighting the concrete of the freeway on fire. I look behind us to see a massive section of the freeway go up. Concrete's not supposed to burn. But then, the Fourth Street Bridge shouldn't have collapsed.

Bystanders are caught in the blaze and I feel a bunch of them go fast, each death a little pinprick in my psyche. Goddammit. I roll down the window and draw my Browning.

"What the hell are you doing?" Letitia says.

"Get closer."

"You're not jumping on her car too, are you?"

"No, I'm gonna blow her fuckin' head off." I unbuckle my seatbelt and lean out of the car, the Browning tight in one hand.

Miriam said my grandfather left me this little piece of evil because only a necromancer could use it. So far, I've only seen it make bigger holes in things than it should. I've ignored the feel of it under my skin, the sense sometimes that it wants me to do something. Something more than just pulling the trigger.

"All right, you little bastard, let's see what you can really do."

A feeling of satisfaction, of "it's about time," floods through me. The gun taps into my magic, into something else I didn't think I'd ever feel again. Tabitha told me I'd have some of Mictlantecuhtli's power back. But now I can feel it.

I pull the trigger. The gun goes off like a cannon and my sense of time slows, my vision sharpens, and I can track the bullet. I can see exactly what's going to happen. It's going to go through the Porsche's rear window and punch through the back of Sastre's head.

And then it doesn't. The bullet hits a barrier around the car, exploding into flames in midair. I can feel the gun screaming in frustration in my head. I cut it off and holster it. It's furious. At Sastre, at me, at the whole fucking world. It was made for murder and when it finally gets to bring its power to bear it's denied.

"Jesus, will you shut up?" I say to it, closing myself off completely and shoving it into my messenger bag. If this is what shooting with its full potential is like, I may have to stick it back in the storage unit. I rub my hand across my pant leg. I can't get rid of the feeling of cockroaches crawling through my skin.

"I thought she didn't have any magic?" Letitia says.

"I don't think she does. Quetzalcoatl gave her a bunch of paper charms. She probably tossed one on the Porsche. Probably gave her something for healing, too. I tagged her pretty hard."

Behind us there's a tremendous crash and in the rearview mirror I can see the burning section of the 10 collapse behind us. Great.

"Is there anything we can do to block her off?" If we want any hope of catching her, we need to stop her moving. With her tossing tlepilli out the window like hand grenades, getting too close is a bad idea.

"You know, I think I do." She grabs her cell phone and punches in a number. It rings a few times and picks up. "Hey, Harvey," she says. "You want to help end this nightmare you're watching from up there?" Pause. "Yeah, I'm chasing the blue Porsche. No idea where anybody else—Oh, shit."

"What?"

"We're the only car in this chase. Nobody's got time for a pursuit when the world's ending. That could work in our favor." She turns back to the phone.

"We need to stop that Porsche. I don't know how you want to do it, but she's got these fucking grenades and if one hits your bird, you're fucked." She listens more. "Perfect. I'll see you in a minute." She hangs up.

"Harvey?"

"Pilot with LAPD air support. He's one of us," she says. "He's watching us from over near Culver City. He says the 10 west is on fire right after the 405, and the 405 north is blocked with a ten-car pile-up. Big rig tipped over. Santa Monica, Culver City, and LAPD are all trying to keep people off the freeway. Seems there've been a couple more collapsed sections, so they've got cars blocking the offramps. Her only option is to head south on the 405."

"How does that help us?"

"You'll see."

We keep playing chicken with Sastre all the way down the 10. She tosses grenades, we dodge them, another section of the freeway catches fire. When this is all over I wonder how much is going to be left. She drives a couple cars off the road and they carom into our path, but between Letitia's driving skills and me shoving shit out of our way with magic, we manage to get past them without much damage.

Sastre's probably listening to the radio or has one of those traffic apps on her phone, because as soon as the South 405 interchange comes up, she veers onto it with no hesitation. I don't know what her plan is, or if she even has a plan. She can't keep driving that Porsche, and now she's got the police on her ass and eyes in the sky. She has to know she's not getting out of this.

Maybe she doesn't want to.

We take the curved ramp and dump out onto the 405. Once we're on the straightaway she guns it and tosses four burning tlepilli held together with a rubber band out the window.

She must be getting desperate, because there's no way we won't dodge it. But that might not be her plan. If she already knows she's fucked, she just might want to create the maximum amount of chaos.

When they hit the freeway behind us the flames are incredible. Bright blue and a hundred feet high, each feeding into the others. One took out a section of the 10. Four might take out the whole interchange.

"Jesus. You think she's run out of those yet?" Letitia says.

"Maybe. Or she hates the 405 enough to use what she had left."

"Everybody hates the 405," Letitia says. "We're coming up to where Harvey's going to set down."

"Set down?"

"Yeah," she says. "He's gonna bounce his bird off her roof."

"That's gonna take some tight timing."

"He's an aeromancer. Believe me, he'll land where, when, and how he wants to."

Harvey makes his move as we come up on Venice Boulevard. It's not the controlled landing I was expecting. The police helicopter drops out of the sky like a stone. But instead of crashing, it slows just enough at the last second.

The left landing strut bounces off the side of the Porsche, sending it spinning. It flips a couple of times, then stops right side up. One of the tires is shredded. Black smoke is coming out of the engine.

The helicopter rocks back and forth and then lifts jerkily into the sky.

"Did he just fake a crash?"

"Yeah. He wants to keep his job. Needs to make it look like a lucky accident. He'll set down at the airport." Letitia stops the car about twenty feet away from the smoking Porsche.

"How you want to do this?" she says. I think about it.

"Stay here with the engine running. I'll go check if she's alive. If she tries anything, run her car over the edge of the freeway."

"Solid plan," she says. If sarcasm was currency, she'd be richer than Werther.

"You got a better idea?"

"You got a rocket launcher?"

"No."

"Then, no," she says. "I don't have a better plan."

I pull the Browning out of the messenger bag and mentally tell the gun to behave. It starts to protest, but I think really hard about melting it down into thumbtacks and it shuts up.

I get out of the car. Stand there a moment. Just based on the death toll from tonight, Jacqueline Sastre has got to be the deadliest person on the planet.

I start walking. One way or another, this ends now.

As I get closer, I can see into the car. But I don't see her. Maybe she's slumped over to the side. Or maybe she got out somehow. There is a lot of smoke. I slow as I get closer.

"La Niña Quemada," I say loudly enough to be heard over the distant flames, the helicopters above us stabbing the area with searchlights. "You dead yet?"

She slowly rises from the other side of the Porsche. Her skin is ashen. The left side of her face drips like raw hamburger, her eye along with it. A thick white bandage covers where I tore into her with the nails. It's soaked through with blood.

"Not yet," she says, smiling. Half her teeth are missing on the left. "But soon. You killed me, necromancer. If it wasn't for one of Quetzalcoatl's charms, I'd be dead already. It's fading. I won't be here much longer."

"Excellent. Where do you think you'll wind up?" If she says Mictlan, I'll need to get hold of Tabitha and give her a heads up.

She shakes her slowly, wincing. "I'm Catholic. I've known where I'm headed for a very long time. Maybe someday you'll go to hell, too."

"Probably," I say, "but it won't be yours."

"I followed you in Mexico, you know," she says. "Hired by three different cartels. Zetas, Sinaloa, Cartel del Golfo. I saw your handiwork. You're a very bad man."

"Never said I wasn't."

"Do you know what they called you?"

"El Gringo Sin Ojos," I say. "The Gringo With No Eyes."

"They said your eyes were like pools of midnight."

"I got 'em fixed. Why'd you do it?"

"Hunt you? Because they were paying good money for your head."

"No," I say. I wave out to the burning city, the thousands of dead. "This. Why did you do this?"

The smile she gives is wide and bright and filled with the wonder of a child. "I like to burn things," she says. "How could I pass up a chance like this?"

"Did Chu know about it?"

She shakes her head. "No. We knew he was going to betray us. I was going to kill him and burn down his house, like I had the others. This was all for you. Quetzalcoatl wanted you to know the price of betrayal. You were supposed to burn Mictlan, but you saved it. Why? Everyone there is already dead."

"They're souls," I say. "Strip away everything else and that's what you've got left. If I'd done that, it would have just been more murder. I won't commit genocide."

Sastre blinks, her eyes unfocused. "I think I'm dying now. I have to tell you something. Something very important. Come closer."

"I can hear you just fine from here, thanks."

"Oh. All right. It's simple. A last request. Can you do that for me? Something simple?"

She's playing me and I think I know how. I ready a spell in my mind in case I'm right, and tell her, "Sure, I'll bite. What is it?"

"Catch." She pulls a burning tlepilli out from behind the car and throws it at me. I let it get about halfway before triggering the spell. It stops in mid-air for a split-second, then flies right back at her with enough force to embed in her skull just above her good eye.

The flames erupt around her, the look of surprise evaporating from her face as the flesh is consumed from her bones. She falls onto the Porsche, lighting it up.

I'm in a really bad spot. The flames flow across the freeway toward me, but something wells up inside and I

stand my ground, put my hand out toward the crawling
fire, willing it to stop a few feet away.

It does.

I open my hand and something small and brass
bounces through the fires to land in my palm. It should
be red-hot, nothing more than molten brass, but it's cool
to the touch. Xiuhtecuhtli might be a dead god, but his
fires are very much alive. I slip the Zippo in my pocket
and watch the fires burn until the section of freeway col-
lapses in front of me.

If I were to look in a mirror right now I know I'd see
my eyes gone black, like pools of midnight.

# Chapter 36

**Four hours later,** L.A. is still burning. It's an impressive sight now that I'm not chasing after a psychopathic arsonist with a supernatural Zippo.

Without Xiuhtecuhtli's flames, they're all normal structure fires. I overhear a cop say that the only buildings left burning are over five stories tall. That's a lot of buildings.

We're still on the freeway. I'm sitting at the edge of the burned-off section looking down on Venice Boulevard, my feet dangling. I've got a Hi My Name Is sticker with THESE AREN'T THE DROIDS YOU'RE LOOKING FOR, MOVE ALONG written on it in Sharpie. Between that and an obfuscation spell Letitia's cast on me, nobody's paying any attention. I'm just some random guy who's supposed to be there.

We would have left, but by the time the Porsche went up, half a dozen black and whites that had been covering the freeway on and offramps we passed were pulling up to us. Getting out unseen wasn't an option.

Letitia's been spinning a story to the other cops, and then to assorted sergeants, captains, and even a guy from the mayor's office, about this nutcase throwing out weird Molotov cocktails. Too much was caught on video to deny it outright.

She used the word thermite a few times and pushed a little magic into it. By tomorrow the word will spread and the story that gets out will be about somebody chucking massive thermite bombs out the back of a van or something.

Letitia made a quick phone call in between reports to somebody else in the Cleanup Crew and they let her know the story they're going with. A series of minor earthquakes ruptured gas lines all over the city. One went off and the others followed. I don't know how they're going to back it up, but at least they're not trying to blame it on terrorists. This city has enough problems without everybody panicking over that, too.

Sastre's involvement is going to be scrubbed. When Chu said he'd gotten the file out to the masses, it was all horseshit. Only a few people know she was involved at all, and now there's not even a body.

"How you holding up?" Letitia says, wandering over to me. As she gets closer, everybody else stops paying attention to her, too. I pushed a lot of juice into this sticker.

My left hand is a throbbing mess and blood is starting to seep through the bandage. The Xylocaine wore off hours ago and it's taking a lot to push the pain away. Every conceivable surface of my body inside and out hurts. I'm bone-tired. I want to sleep. I'm not sure I want to wake up again.

"Fantastic," I say. She gives me a sidelong glance—it's obvious bullshit even if she wasn't a walking lie detector, but she doesn't question it.

"You want to get out of here?"

"The powers that be are letting you go?"

"They've got my report. It's one of the more

prominent ones—losing chunks of two freeways and an interchange kind of gets attention—but it's only one of thousands right now. Cleanup Crew will leak my name to the press and it'll be a shitshow for a while, but it'll give us more control of the situation."

"And me?"

"With that thing on your chest? Put any more magic into it and people will forget you exist."

"Not a bad idea."

"Yeah, right. Come on. I want to go see my wife. And you need to get that hand looked at."

In the car, a different Crown Vic that hasn't been through so much punishment, Letitia calls ahead to Gabriela's warehouse. We take surface streets and even with the sirens and lights it's slow going. Culver City to East L.A. is a parking lot of panicked drivers, emergency vehicles, burning cars.

And then there are the fires. Some streets are blocked off because every building on both sides is a massive block-long blaze. The fire crews have stopped trying to put them out, and instead are letting them burn. Some of the taller ones are a lost cause, and the most the crews do is keep people out of the way of falling debris.

We pull into Gabriela's lot a couple hours later, some of her crew running us inside with guns drawn. Seems in all the chaos there's a lot of gunfire in the neighborhood, some aimed, most not. Give people an excuse and they'll shoot guns in the air. One guy got a round through the head that way a couple hours ago.

We stagger in exhausted, and I hang back, letting Letitia go ahead. Vivian's waiting for her and she disappears into the infirmary to see Annie. I've kept the sticker on, and all the normals ignores me. I go sit in a corner and watch people buzzing around the warehouse, around me. Even at almost 6 a.m. things are always in motion.

"I hear you had a problem with a roofer," Gabriela says. She sits in a chair next to me, wincing. Vivian does good work, but she's not going to be at her best for a while.

I show her the bandaged hand, blood crusted over the gauze. "Could have been worse. Could have been a drywaller."

"Ya know, Vivian could—"

"Don't even finish that sentence. She's got enough shit to deal with without me taking up her time. It's not like she's the only mage doctor in town. Some of them owe me favors. Might take a few days, though."

"Gonna suck until you get it fixed," she says.

"That's why God made Oxy," I say.

"That shit's gonna catch up to you one of these days, man."

I shrug. "Oh, I know that. That's nothing new. But that's what detox spells are for. If magic can't let you do a shit-ton of drugs, then what good is it?"

Gabriela shakes her head and pulls herself out of the chair. "We're fucked up, you know that? Not just you and me, all of us. I don't even know what I'm doing anymore or why I'm doing it but I can't stop. Do you know why you do it?"

"Trying to not make things worse? Fuck knows I'm not making things better."

"Maybe try harder. Now go get some sleep. You look like shit."

"Stones and glass houses, chica. Stones and glass houses. Just gonna sit here for a bit, then I'll be on my way."

"There's a bunk around here somewhere you can crash on, ya know."

"Thanks, but I'll pass."

"Suit yourself." She heads back and meets Letitia and Vivian coming out of the infirmary, the relief on Letitia's face taking years off of her. I hope she can make it work with Annie. Maybe Gabriela and I don't know why we're doing what we're doing, but Letitia sure as hell does.

I catch snippets of conversation. Letitia tells them about what happened, about the freeways, the tlepilli, all of it. Well, most of it. She doesn't know about me and Santa Muerte, or that I have the bottle. I'd like to keep it that way a while. Gabriela will figure it out before too long. She knows enough of Darius's history to piece things together.

I catch them glancing at me every once in a while. Particularly Vivian. Like I'm some weird organism she's never seen before.

They give me space and I don't intrude. Vivian starts to come over, but Gabriela stops her with a hand on her arm. Eventually their conversation shifts away from the nightmare the city has become.

Letitia talks about the Cleanup Crew, about how she and Annie met. Letitia's good people and has a good sense of a person's character. I mean, she did stab me and all.

Vivian and Letitia recount stories of high school. Gabriela talks about her family in Mexico, stories I've never heard, how she killed an El Cucuy to save a boy on a train, how her grandmother told her to be a revolutionary before she died.

They're exhausted and wired at the same time. It's funny to watch people tighten the bonds that hold them together. By the time they finally head their own ways they'll be thick as thieves. You can see it all slowly come together and then it clicks, and you can't imagine a time when they weren't. Gabriela looks more at ease than I've seen her in months. Vivian actually laughs. I haven't heard her laugh like that since before I left L.A.

This is theirs, and I've got no place here. I wait until they're all engrossed in each other's conversation and then get up and limp out of the building. The air outside is filled with smoke and reeks of burning chemicals. It will for weeks, I'm sure. Nobody pays attention to me as I leave. I'm okay with that.

I break in to a car that hasn't caught fire or been vandalized a couple blocks away. I turn on the radio and listen, still parked, to an AM news station. It's a grim night out there, and when the sun comes up it won't be much better.

A litany of places damaged or destroyed. Staples Center, the entire row of old theaters on Broadway, Grand Central Market, Grauman's Chinese, Hollywood and Highland, the Bradbury Building, Olvera Street, most of Chinatown. Huge sections of Beverly Hills, Studio City, Encino, Tarzana, Boyle Heights, Leimert Park, Burbank, Pasadena, El Segundo, Long Beach, North Hollywood, Torrance. On and on and on. Nothing has gone untouched.

There's no final death toll yet, but they're already saying it's in the thousands. They're not even close. I've felt the deaths until they all blur together into one seamless montage of agony and fear, and even I don't know how many died.

But I do know how many new ghosts there are. I can feel them as far south as Long Beach, as far north as Pasadena. It's a general sense, like listening to static and gauging decibels.

In general I've found around 1 in 5 people who die of

trauma become a ghost, and the few other necromancers
I've spoken with about it have told me the same. Echo,
Haunt, or Wanderer, those numbers are pretty solid. I
don't know why. I'm sure a mathematician could work it
out. If they hold true here, and I really hope they don't,
this will be the worst disaster the U.S. has ever seen.

There are about 25,000 new ghosts across the whole
of the Southland. I can almost deal with that number. I
can picture 25,000 people. That's half of Dodger Sta-
dium. But that means 100 to 125,000 died tonight. I can't
fit that in my head. It's too big, too abstract. The dead at
Hiroshima numbered 150,000. Nagasaki, 75,000. They're
statistics.

In one night, over a hundred thousand dead because
I pissed off some psychotic wind god with an axe to
grind and wouldn't do his dirty work for him. He made
everyone in this city pay. All those deaths are on my
hands.

No. I push the thought aside. Plenty of time to place
the blame once everything's, well—not back to normal,
but stable? I can't think about this right now. It'll eat me
alive if I let it.

I start the car and head back to my motel, not sure if
it's still standing until I get there. A couple buildings a
few lots over have been reduced to ash, but it's just fine.
I ditch the car a block away and head into the courtyard.
I fumble for my room key in my pocket, a thin plastic
card. But when I look up, my door's not there.

Instead there's a red, leather-upholstered door with
large brass tacks set in diamond patterns from top to
bottom. I need sleep, not this crap. But it's not like I
didn't know it was coming.

Fuck it. Fine. Might as well get it over with. I push the
door open and instead of walking into my motel room,

I end up in an empty speakeasy, the inside of which I haven't seen in a while.

It's empty of customers. Chairs are overturned and stacked on tables and lights are dimmed, except for one piercing bright light by the bar. Darius, the Djinn, stands in that light polishing a couple of shot glasses. A massive black man, he has thick biceps, linebacker shoulders. He looks like he's been carved from stone.

He puts the glasses down, picks up a bottle of tequila, and pours a full measure into each. I limp up to the bar, the only sound my shoes against the wooden floor. I pull out a stool and sit. I put both hands on the bar. His eyebrows raise at the bandaged, blood-soaked hand, but he doesn't say anything.

We lift our glasses in a silent toast. To what, I don't know. To surviving? To life? To death? To one more day that there's a chance to make a difference? Or one more day that there's a chance to destroy it all?

We down our shots in single gulps. The tequila burns on the way down, a warmth in my belly far different than the temperatures I've been baking in all week.

"I understand," Darius says, refilling our glasses, "that you found yourself a bottle."

# Joe Sunday's dead...

### ...he just hasn't stopped moving yet.

Sunday's a thug, an enforcer, a leg-breaker for hire.
When his boss sends him to kill a mysterious new business partner, his target strikes back in ways Sunday
could never have imagined. Murdered, brought back to
a twisted half-life, Sunday finds himself stuck in the
middle of a race to find an ancient stone with the power
to grant immortality. With it, he might live forever.
Without it, he's just another rotting extra in a George
Romero flick.

Everyone's got a stake: a psycho Nazi wizard, a
nympho-demon bartender, a too-powerful witch who
just wants to help her homeless vampires, and the one
woman who might have all the answers — if only
Sunday can figure out what her angle is.

Before the week is out he's going to find out just what
lengths people will go to for immortality. And just how
long somebody can hold a grudge.

---

# City of the Lost
## by Stephen Blackmoore
978-0-7564-0702-5

---

DAW 209

# Tad Williams

# The Dirty Streets of Heaven

"A dark and thrilling story.... Bad-ass smart-mouth
Bobby Dollar, an Earth-bound angel advocate for
newly departed souls caught between Heaven and
Hell, is appalled when a soul goes missing on his
watch. Bobby quickly realizes this is 'an actual,
honest-to-front-office crisis,' and he sets out to fix it,
sparking a chain of hellish events.... Exhilarating
action, fascinating characters, and high stakes will
leave the reader both satisfied and eager for the next
installment."   —*Publishers Weekly* (starred review)

"Williams does a brilliant job.... Made me laugh.
Made me curious. Impressed me with its cleverness.
Made me hungry for the next book. Kept me up late
at night when I should have been sleeping."
—Patrick Rothfuss

**The Dirty Streets of Heaven: 978-0-7564-0790-2**
**Happy Hour in Hell: 978-0-7564-0948-7**
**Sleeping Late on Judgement Day: 978-0-7564-0987-6**

To Order Call: 1-800-788-6262
www.dawbooks.com

DAW 207